SECRETS AND SURRENDER

BOOK TWO OF THE GATES MANOR SERIES

JAN HEMBY

Published by Blue Ink Press, LLC

Cover design by Dee Graphic Design

www.deegraphicdesign.com

ISBN: 978-1-948449-03-8

Library of Congress Control Number: 2018965148

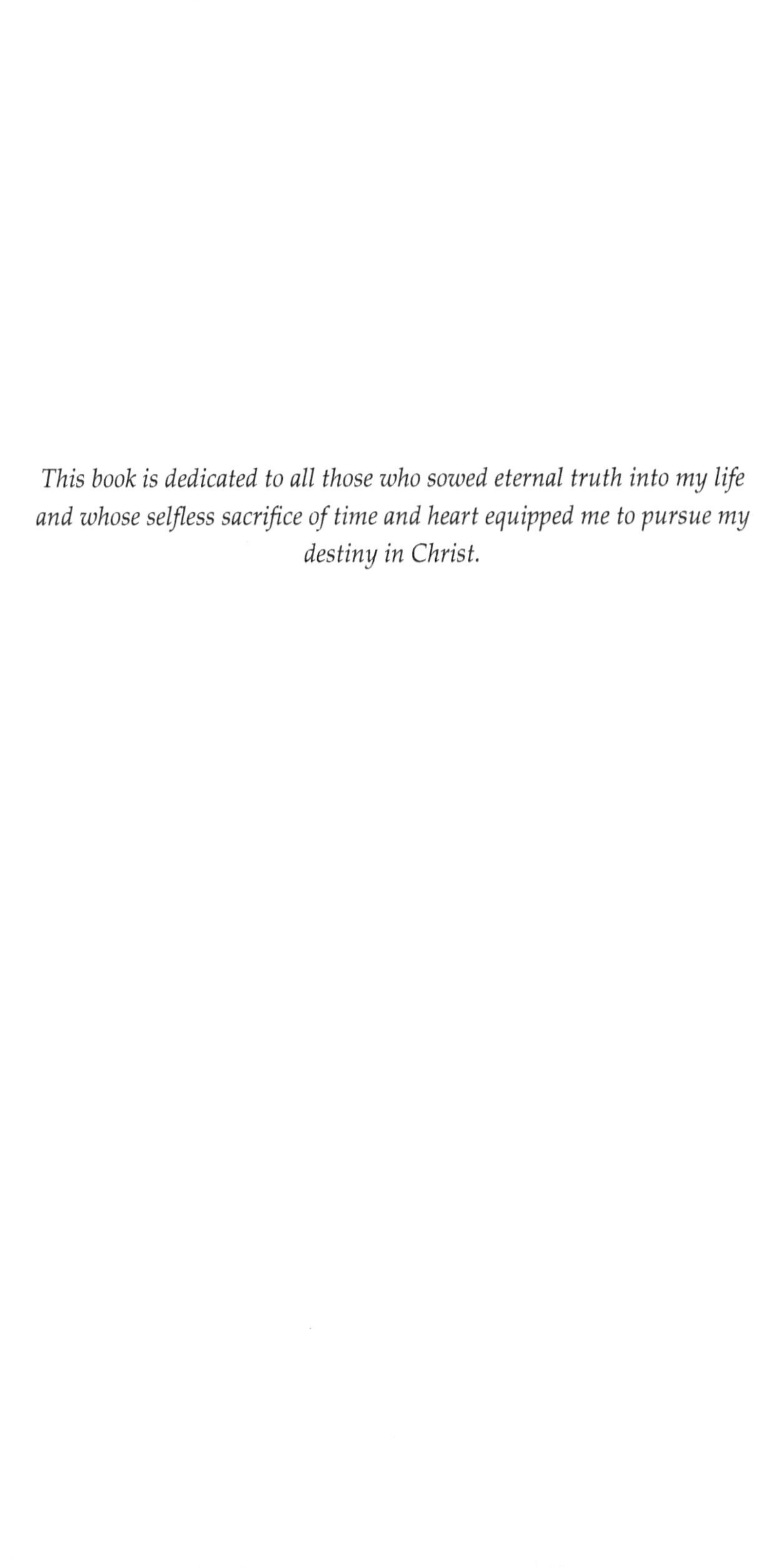

This book is dedicated to all those who sowed eternal truth into my life and whose selfless sacrifice of time and heart equipped me to pursue my destiny in Christ.

"All my sufferings, by admirable management of omnipotent Goodness, have concurred to promote my spiritual and eternal good."

– Susanna Wesley

As Margaret took the pills out of the plastic bag, the phone continued to ring. She could either answer and pretend she was okay or ignore it altogether. She chose the latter. A few sips of tap water later, she stretched out on the old, worn-out sofa. The continual chiming of her cell phone became a morbid lullaby as she pulled the crumpled blanket up over her shoulders. Suddenly the shadow of a man appeared. She knew him — all too well. She wanted to undo what she had done, but it was too late. The phone had stopped ringing.

Julia bolted upright in bed. Her heart was racing. The few seconds necessary for the sleep to clear from her head couldn't pass by quickly enough. She desperately wanted it to be a dream. The sound of her husband, Bill, snoring next to her was reassuring.

She took a deep breath and whispered to herself, "It was only a dream, Julia. There's no need to panic."

And there really wasn't. The dream couldn't have been more off-course from present reality. Julia knew that Margaret had never been happier and more successful, both personally and professionally. Helping troubled teens at the Gates Manor had been a great source of purpose and fulfillment for her, and it had brought her even further along in her own healing from drug addiction and sexual abuse. So why did the dream feel so real? More importantly, why had she dreamed it at all? Three years ago, it would have made more sense. Still, something about it made her uneasy. She looked at the clock on her nightstand. It was 12:45 a.m. Julia knew it was silly, but she did it anyway—she reached for her cell phone and texted Margaret.

Couldn't sleep. Just wondering if you're doing okay.

A couple of minutes later, Margaret wrote back.

Did you have coffee at dinner again?

Julia breathed a sigh of relief.

No, I had a bad dream. Are you ready for the concert tonight?

Julia could see that Margaret was writing a response.

Hmmm…does that question remind you of another phone call? We keep having this conversation…every thirty years or so!

Julia hadn't thought about that. She shook her head in amazement. What a coincidence.

Or was it?

Before she could text back, Margaret sent another message.

To answer your question, yes, I'm ready. I wouldn't miss it for the world.

Julia texted back: *I guess missing concerts is a thing of the past.*

Margaret responded: *I guess it is. (:*

* * *

The woodwinds and the brass harmonized as the timpani drums rolled to a dramatic finale. The last note was held until Mr. Ortega, the director, silenced it with a wave of his baton. The second he lowered his arms, the crowd jumped to their feet in applause. From where Julia and Bill Burch were sitting in the back of the auditorium that had been built at the Manor, Julia could see parents proudly taking pictures with their cell phones. Mr. Ortega bowed and then had the students stand. The crowd's applause swelled.

Margaret made her way to the front of the stage as the audience and the band students found their seats once again. Julia never tired of hearing Margaret talk about how young people's lives were being transformed at the Gates Manor. More importantly, she would never forget the miracle of Margaret's own transformation. Every time Margaret stepped up to that microphone, Julia got a lump in her throat.

"Thank you, students, parents, members of the city council, and all who came out to support our program tonight. Not only is this our spring concert, where we get to show off our awesome students." Margaret turned around and acknowledged the band once more. When the audience's applause subsided, she continued. "But it's also the time of year when we ask for your help. The initial Manor renovations and much of our operating expenses were made possible through the generosity of Joseph Bennington. Joseph is the one who had the vision for what we are accomplishing here for so many young people in our community.

"However, our goal is to be able to extend our reach *outside* of our community. We've already received a referral from out of state. We'd like to have the resources to assist with the travel expenses for this student. And, if we continue to grow, it may become necessary to add an additional wing. Either way, we need and appreciate your help. Any donation you make is tax-deductible. If you need any help sorting through all of that, I think Bill Burch is in the audience tonight." Margaret shielded her eyes from the spotlight as she looked out over the audience.

The spotlight zoomed in on Bill who stood up briefly and waved as the audience clapped. Julia lovingly patted his knee as he sat back down.

As the spotlight was shifting back to where Margaret was standing, it caught the image of a man leaving the room.

Julia noticed Margaret's expression change. She looked distracted and didn't say anything for several seconds. Julia could sense the audience growing uncomfortable with the silence. She spotted Joseph Bennington a few rows in front of her and Bill. He shifted in his seat and looked concerned.

Finally, Margaret spoke. "So, I guess nobody has any questions for Bill!"

The audience laughed. Julia breathed a sigh of relief. She whispered to Bill, "What was that all about?"

Bill shrugged his shoulders.

Margaret made a few closing announcements, and then invited everyone to enjoy the refreshments that would be served in the lobby. Julia wasted no time excusing herself through the crowd so she could speak with her.

"Hey, what happened up there?"

Margaret leaned in toward her so she could be heard over the conversations going on in the room. "You're never going to guess who I saw leave the building."

Julia could see Margaret was shaken. She put her hand on her shoulder.

"He looks so much like his dad that, at first, I thought it *was* his dad. That's what freaked me out!"

"Who are you talking about?" Julia asked.

"Wyatt Bennington. Wyatt was here tonight."

GINA MERINO REACHED INSIDE HER STARCHED UNIFORM SHIRT AND quickly found the small key at the end of her necklace chain. Her hands were shaking as she unlocked the wooden box she'd retrieved from her closet. Years ago, she'd discovered a couple of loose planks in the floor which provided the perfect hiding place. She wanted to make sure the small vial was still there. She didn't touch it, as she wasn't wearing the white gloves that were also a part of her uniform. It was important that the fingerprints on the bottle remained perfectly intact and undisturbed.

She locked the box once again before carefully placing it back underneath the floorboards. Stepping over to her dressing table, she sat down on the stool. She stretched her legs out in front of her. Per usual these days, her feet were swollen. The heels on her work shoes weren't all that high, but the design was a dressy one to have to wear eight to ten hours every day. In order to slip them off with the least amount of discomfort, she reached for the shoe horn on her dressing table. As she did, she caught her reflection in the mirror and tilted her head to one side. She almost didn't recognize the person looking back at her anymore.

She lifted the wrinkles on her forehead with her fingertips to erase the years for just a moment. She studied her hands. Once youthful and smooth, they now were scarred and aged from decades of heavy housework.

She unwound the bun she was required to wear, her hair more gray than black now. She missed the silky, smooth hair she'd had as a child. It had been wavy for years now, a change that had occurred when she was a teen. Her thoughts went back to a time prior to that, to when she was growing up in Santa Maria. She had been both a stellar student and a talented singer. Her parents were well aware of her potential and wanted her to have opportunities that only existed beyond their poor village. So, they'd arranged for her to come to the United States, where they hoped she would experience the American Dream.

For a moment, she did something she rarely allowed herself to do; she considered what life would have been like if she had stayed in Santa Maria. Her almond-shaped brown eyes welled with wistful tears.

The thunder from an early June storm startled her back to the task at hand. She hung her uniform in the closet and shook her head at how Wyatt—*Mr. Bennington*—insisted that all the staff start wearing uniforms and call him Mr. Bennington. It was particularly insulting to her, as she had been with him from the time he was born.

She remembered when Wyatt's father first announced that Mrs. Bennington was expecting the family's first child. For someone who had grown up into a man who thought he knew it all, there was so much Wyatt didn't know. The box under the floorboards contained a few of those secrets, but most were hidden in the recesses of Gina's heart. She'd prayed that one day those secrets would come out into the open, not knowing when—or how—God would answer that prayer.

She picked up the worn, leather Bible on her nightstand and clutched it as she slipped under the covers. The light from her bedside lamp was quickly replaced by flashes of lighting filtering through the window blinds. She could hear the steady tapping of the rain against the roof.

This downpour will wash the pollen off the terraces, she thought. *It will save the groundskeepers from having to do it. They will have their work cut out for them tomorrow clearing debris and picking up snapped tree branches though.*

She smiled in awe as she considered how only God could create such an event that reflects His work in our lives: storms that bring both a cleansing and a removal of faulty support structures.

Then she thought about Wyatt. A storm was about to come into his life, unlike anything he'd ever experienced. She'd prayed for it. It wasn't that she wanted Wyatt to suffer. On the contrary, she loved him in a way no one else could. But she did want him to change. After his father's deathbed conversion, she now had faith that it could happen.

As the rhythm of the rain lulled her to sleep, she reflected on how her prayers for Wyatt were finally being answered. God certainly did move in mysterious ways. He was working through the one person she never thought He would use.

And one day soon, she planned to thank Margaret Gates.

CHAPTER THREE

About forty minutes away, in the neighboring town of Raleigh, Holly Sparrow awoke with a start. It wasn't the evening thunderstorm that had pulled her out of her sleep, but the crinkle of Olivia's Pull-Up pants as she tried to quietly slip into bed with her parents.

"Olivia," Holly whispered, "are you scared of the storm?"

As Olivia wedged herself between Holly and Steven, she responded in her endearing way of pronouncing her Ls like Ws. "I don't wike storms, Mommy."

Holly turned over to face her daughter and gently swept the cascading blonde curls away from her eyes. She loved looking at those eyes: green like her own, but round and deep-set like Steven's. She had resolved never to complain whenever being a mom required small sacrifices on her part, such as having her sleep interrupted. Holly was well aware that Olivia, and motherhood in general, was a gift.

After suffering from a serious eating disorder in high school, Holly had been concerned that she had done permanent damage to her body and would have trouble conceiving. When she and Steven didn't get pregnant after trying for several months, she feared that she wouldn't be able to at all. It turns out she didn't have a health issue; it was just a timing issue. And God's timing is always perfect. Olivia arrived on May 11, the same month and day Holly's mom had received the mysterious phone call that had changed all their lives. Both were examples of how even through the difficult, and often the unexplainable, God is weaving His plan.

"It's okay, sweetheart," Holly whispered. "Storms don't last forever. It'll be over soon."

Olivia closed her eyes. Holly watched as her two-year-old slowly drifted off to sleep, then she quietly reached for her cell phone on the nightstand. She keyed in the prompts to display her personal calendar. A meeting with her dad, Bill Burch, was scheduled for nine o'clock the following morning.

She turned back over and stared at the ceiling. A tear slipped out of the corner of her eye. *Storms don't last forever, Holly. It'll be over soon.*

CHAPTER FOUR

WYATT BENNINGTON SET THE CRYSTAL CARAFE BACK IN ITS PLACE ON
the silver serving tray. He noticed the elegantly placed monogram
embossed onto the surface of the tray. It had been there for years,
but tonight it caught his attention, perhaps for the first time. He
paused and traced the letters with his finger. They were his
father's initials, HWB, the same as his own. With his other hand,
he gingerly swirled a single ice cube in the glass of scotch he'd just
poured himself. He was having trouble sleeping, but it wasn't
because of the frequent thunder or drubbing rain. A more turbu-
lent storm was brewing that was consuming Wyatt, and it paled in
comparison to anything Mother Nature could dish out tonight.

He briefly glanced outside before taking a seat in the wingback
chair by the window. The heavy drapes and walnut paneling of the
study surrounded him with a sense of comfort. It was in this room
that his father, Horace Bennington, had conducted most of his
business deals with James Gates.

Wyatt scoffed and took a sip of his drink as he thought about
how his goody-two-shoes brother, Joseph, had once again caved to
an outdated set of morals. This time it had resulted in him giving
away a third of their parents' estate. So their father had had a fling

with a teenage girl. Nobody's perfect. Who knows? Maybe young Margaret Gates had seduced *him*. She'd been quite the slut in high school and college from what he remembered. Perhaps Horace had gotten tired of Margaret and had simply wanted to spice things up a bit when he ended up getting her mother pregnant. Regardless of Preston Gate's paternity, there were usually ways around wills and legal documents; his father had taught Wyatt that. Money can buy you all kinds of, as his father used to say, *wiggle room.*

Wyatt never had any delusions of Horace being a saint. In his estimation, that was what had made him so successful, and he didn't have a problem with that. However, what festered like a boil in his soul was thinking about the one person he held responsible for his current state-of-affairs; and that person was Margaret Gates.

As he saw it, Margaret was ultimately to blame for him being forced to forfeit the money that was rightfully his. If she hadn't blown the whistle on Horace, then nobody would have ever known that Preston Gates was Horace's son. It was impossible for Wyatt to get that money back now; he'd already explored every possible loophole with his attorney.

Not that he necessarily *needed* the money. With or without that one-third of the inheritance, Wyatt still had more in his checking account than the average person would see in a lifetime. What angered him was the fact that the money was being used for a cause that made Margaret Gates look like a hero. Her picture was regularly featured on the front page of the local paper accompanied by another glowing review of her work at the Manor. Wyatt remembered back when Margaret's name used to show up in the newspaper, but in the public records section where her latest DUI or drug possession arrest was reported. Now she had a great job, a nice house, and a bright future—all financed by Horace's hard-earned money.

Wyatt had been indoctrinated by his father to believe that Margaret was nothing more than the Gates family black sheep, someone who had brought James Gates great shame and humiliation. The fact that Margaret's own father had all but disowned her spoke volumes to Wyatt. Now this…this *loser*, who had caused her family such heartache, was practically a celebrity. It was more than he could stomach.

True, there was nothing he could do to get that inheritance money back. If he was honest with himself, it wasn't really about the money anymore anyway, though.

Now, it was about revenge.

It had been almost three years since Horace had passed. During that time, Wyatt had endured numerous sleepless nights like tonight. But they weren't without purpose. They had provided him with the silence and the solitude he'd needed to devise a plan. He hadn't been interested in rushing the process, as he had to make sure that the plan was ironclad and, well, perfect. He smirked as he considered how he may have been shortchanged part of the inheritance money, but he had received one hundred percent of his father's mind for business.

And to Wyatt, this was just business.

He was well acquainted with Margaret's past. Since the estate settlement, he hadn't responded in anger or vengeance. In fact, he'd been quite amiable about the whole thing. As he poured himself another scotch, he thought about how brilliant his plan really was.

Margaret had "found religion" shortly before Horace passed away. But she'd spent a good majority of her former life as a drug user and a drunk. Anybody could do *that* math: she had many more years under her belt as an addict than as a Christian. Wyatt was about to prove how all that religious mumbo-jumbo was just that. He wouldn't stop until he had made a complete mockery of her, just as she had made of him. Then he would get rid of her altogether. The best part was that the world would simply think that Margaret Gates had finally self-destructed, and no one would even think to suspect him.

Wyatt was going to make it look like a suicide.

Tonight, he was not only satisfied with this plan but also ready to execute it. He put his empty glass back on the tray and turned off the study lamps. He paused and looked around, the lightning flashes providing brief interruptions to the darkness in the room. He wondered if Horace Wyatt Bennington, Sr. had ever devised such a brilliant plan within these paneled walls. As he savored this moment of self-proclaimed victory, the storm outside intensified. The thunderclaps occurred in quicker succession. One in particular shook the entire house. When it did, Wyatt thought he heard the sound of an object hitting the floor. He turned one of the lamps back on but didn't see anything out of place.

Well, as long as nothing landed on the roof, he thought as he ascended the stairs. *I'll get Bivens to check the house tomorrow to make sure nothing was damaged.*

He entered his bedroom, where his covers had already turned down by one of the maids. Opening the bottom drawer of his nightstand, he shifted a few items aside to reveal a hand-held recorder hidden underneath. He'd started listening to the old enclosed tape numerous times but had never had a chance to hear it in its entirety. There was a sister recording device hidden at Julia's parents' old house where he knew Margaret would be spending a lot of time helping her friend with the clean-out and renovations. He'd placed it in a cabinet there during the initial renovations, when workers had been in and out of the house all day, and he could enter and exit unnoticed. He'd been listening in ever since. He was relieved that no one had found it yet.

As he scanned through the recording, he could hear various conversations, most which didn't interest him. Every now and then he would pick up on something useful. It was important that he become familiar with the details of Margaret's present life, just as he was with those of her past. He paused the tape and jotted down a quick note.

Takes cream and sugar with her coffee.

CHAPTER FIVE

Julia Burch slowly drove up the street to her parents' house. She was preparing herself for what she anticipated would be a tearful last visit. As she pulled into the driveway, the first thing she noticed was that the FOR SALE sign in the yard was leaning to the side. Evidently, last night's storm had tried to uproot it but had only succeeded in bending the metal posts. She made a mental note to fix it before she headed over to Minnie Morgan's house. The Gates Manor administrative staff was gathering there for a meeting, something they hadn't done in weeks.

Her visit here would be brief. She would do a final walk-through and then leave her key on the kitchen counter for the real estate agent. It had taken several months, but the repairs and updates were finally completed, and the house was ready to go on the market. Even though she'd been there numerous times since her father's passing, it never got any easier. She still expected to hear his greeting or see him asleep on the couch – sitting up, of course. He'd lived for two years following her mom's death from Alzheimer's; two years longer than Julia had expected for a man so heartbroken over losing the love of his life. But, then again, her dad was a fighter. A World War II veteran, he'd never given up on her mom getting better, even when it became evident that she wouldn't. He'd faithfully stood by her for the duration of her ten-year battle with Alzheimer's. After her mother's passing, her dad's own health had eventually begun to deteriorate. Surviving one heart attack, he'd succumbed to a second. He was ninety when he joined his bride in Heaven.

The day was shaping up to be a scorcher. The rain from the storm hadn't cooled things off but had added even more humidity to an already sticky start to the summer. Just walking from her car to the front door caused Julia to break a sweat. She wiped her brow with the back of her hand and then jiggled her key into the lock.

Typically resisting on the first attempt, she had to shove it open and was keenly aware of the empty sound that followed. All her parents' belongings—furniture, drapes, dishes, clothing, keepsakes—had been either given away, thrown away, or divided between Julia and her two siblings, Scott and Caroline. Wearing casual clothes, she neglected to remove her tennis shoes at the door, and the rubber soles squeaked against the hardwood floors as she moved from room to room.

For the past several months, it had been necessary for her and her siblings to approach the renovation project as academically as possible. While they couldn't suppress their memories, they'd had to keep their emotions in check. Otherwise, it would've been too painful. Now that the FOR SALE sign was in the yard, they'd each taken turns going through the house and doing what they couldn't do before: say goodbye.

Julia had invited Margaret to accompany her on this final walk-through since she had also devoted many hours to the project. In addition to having served as the official coffee and fast food supplier, she'd also proven to be very handy with a paintbrush. Margaret expressed her appreciation, but had declined the invitation as she felt this was something Julia should do alone. Instead, she'd promised to save her a seat at Minnie's and, more importantly, to save her a portion of whatever Minnie was serving for refreshments.

Julia took her time going through every room, savoring the memories each contained. As she walked back to her parents' bedroom, she remembered the day she'd received the mysterious phone call just after her mom's passing. She shook her head in disbelief as she considered how much her life had changed for the better since then.

In the bedroom she and her sister had shared, she could picture two twin beds, one containing her six-year-old self who spent the majority of her sleeping hours running from bees and spiders. Julia's older sister, Caroline, was always faithful to check on her whenever she'd had a bad dream, even if it meant receiving a swat meant for an imaginary bug.

She wandered down the hallway to the bathroom. She turned the light on over the old porcelain sink and marveled at how a family of five had ever functioned with only one bathroom, especially compared to today's standards. As she made her way into the living room, she fought back the tears. This room was always the most difficult for her when confronting her memories. In the corner by the sliding glass door, which looked out onto the back deck, she could still envision the hospital bed that hospice had provided, first for her mom, and then for her dad. Two and a half years apart, they had both passed away in that corner of the room.

As she moved through to the kitchen and dining area, her mind went back to all the family dinners they'd enjoyed here. When she was growing up, the evening meal hadn't involved napkins in the lap or pinkies extended when picking up a glass. The only rule, besides not eating until after the blessing, had been not talking with your mouth full. Other than that, the main course had always been stories from the day served up with extra helpings of laughter.

When her gaze fell on the old, outdated stove, she felt the lump return in her throat. There was nothing her mom had enjoyed more than cooking for the family, especially around the holidays. In the early stages of her mother's Alzheimer's, preparing a meal had involved a certain amount of risk for injury. Often, she would have forgotten she'd been chopping carrots, or some other vegetable, and ended up carrying a knife around. And once she nearly set the house on fire when she forgot about a casserole heating in the oven. As the disease progressed, cooking became something she forgot how to do altogether. After that, Thanksgiving and Christmas dinners became a collaboration of the three children, evidenced by a table laden with an assortment of Pyrex dishes covered in tin foil.

After a few more minutes of walking around and looking at nothing in particular, Julia reluctantly placed her key on the kitchen counter. Before she turned to leave, she noticed that the cabinet door to the upper right side of the sink wasn't completely closed. She couldn't imagine why, as the contents had been cleaned out weeks ago. Out of curiosity, she carefully opened it further just to make sure there wasn't a mouse or some other unwelcomed guest inside. She was about to close it, properly this time, when her eye caught something in the far-right corner underneath the bottom shelf.

She climbed onto the counter to get a better look. She wasn't sure what she had found, but it looked like a small electronic gadget of some sort. She heard the front door open and assumed it was her brother, Scott. He and his wife, Wendy, lived only five minutes away, and he had mentioned stopping by to say hello. His timing couldn't have been better.

As Julia backed off the counter, she called out, "Hey Scott, will you take a look at this? And do you have a pair of pliers in your truck? The sign out front—"

She stopped mid-sentence and gasped. It wasn't Scott standing in the kitchen, but an older, lovely-looking woman in a dark-colored dress and low heels. Her hair was arranged in a tight knot at the back of her head. She offered a friendly smile and raised her hands, as if reassuring Julia that she was harmless. She motioned toward the front door. Julia was shaken, but quickly reasoned that if she were going to talk with this total stranger, she would feel safer doing it outside. So, she followed her to the front porch.

Once they were both outside, Julia was temporarily distracted as a passing breeze tossed a few stray hairs that appeared to have fallen out of the woman's bun. Moreover, she was taken aback by the fact that this woman—whoever she was—was strikingly beautiful.

"Mrs. Burch, I apologize for just walking in like that," the woman said with a warm smile that put Julia a little more at ease. "I really didn't mean to scare you, but we need to talk."

Even though she seemed friendly enough, Julia could sense the woman was afraid of something—or someone. She kept nervously looking over her shoulder and her hands were trembling. When she spoke, it was barely above a whisper. However, Julia needed more information before having a conversation with a stranger who had just showed up in the kitchen of her parents' house.

"Who are you? How do you know my name?"

The woman looked around, almost as if she hadn't heard Julia's questions. "I'd rather not talk here. It may not be safe. Meet me at Riverside Park in ten minutes."

The woman turned around and hurried toward the taxi waiting for her in the driveway. Julia hadn't even noticed it sitting there during their very brief exchange. She didn't want to be rude, but she had to be cautious, so she called out matter-of-factly, "Since I don't know you, I may call for a police escort."

This caused the woman to pause. She turned and slowly came back to where Julia stood on the steps. "Please don't call the police," she pleaded in a whisper. "They won't be able to help." She looked down and then looked back up at Julia as if collecting her courage. "I am the only one who can help you now." She turned and hurried back to the idling cab.

Julia watched the cab until it reached the end of the street and then disappeared in the direction of the park.

She whispered under her breath, "What was that all about?"

C H A P T E R   S I X

MINNIE MORGAN NERVOUSLY CHECKED HER WATCH AGAIN. IT WAS already noon and Julia still hadn't arrived for the meeting. She was beginning to feel uneasy. She discreetly hit redial on her cell phone in another attempt to reach her. No answer.

She struggled to focus on what Joseph Bennington was saying. The Gates Manor administrative team hadn't met in a while, and she didn't want to miss any of the details. They'd waited on Julia as long as they could before starting. It wasn't like her to not show up without a phone call to let them know.

Margaret must have picked up on Minnie's concern. She leaned over and whispered, "I'm sure she's just running late."

Minnie nodded in agreement, but she knew her face displayed her worry.

She'd wait a few more minutes and then interrupt the meeting.

* * *

Julia hadn't been to Riverside Park since her dad passed away. Prior to that, she'd attended numerous family reunions there over the years. She parked her car as close to the exit as possible. As she proceeded down the gravel driveway, she quickly assessed her surroundings. There was a young mom with two preschool-age children playing at the toddler swings. A city employee was spearing trash over by the narrow creek that ran behind the baseball field. The taxicab that had been in her driveway was now idling in the parking lot near the picnic shelter.

After looking around, Julia spotted the lady sitting at one of the tables under the shelter. If nothing else, she took comfort in the first thing she noticed—the woman's head was bowed, and she appeared to be praying.

Julia had already started across the grassy area when she realized she didn't have her cell phone.

She chided herself as she headed back toward her car. *None of your precautions are going to do you any good if you don't have a way to call for help!*

Sure enough, she had left it on the front passenger's seat. After typing in her password, she discovered she had several missed calls from Minnie. *The meeting!* She had let the time slip away from her.

She quickly sent Minnie a text message.

I'll be late and may not make it at all. Something unexpected came up. Please pray. Details later.

Minnie jumped as her phone vibrated in her hand. She breathed a sigh of relief when she saw it was Julia. But her relief was short-lived. Again, it wasn't like Julia to not give more information.

Minnie raised her hand. "Joseph, I apologize for interrupting, but I'm worried about Julia. I think we need to stop and pray."

* * *

The woman looked up as Julia approached the table where she was sitting. "Please, sit down," she said.

Julia was still nervous and wanted to know one thing from the outset. "Were you praying just now?"

The woman nodded and then looked away. Julia cautiously sat down beside her. When she turned to face Julia again, there were tears in her eyes.

"Have you ever prayed for something and then, when it finally came to pass, you wondered if you should have prayed for it?"

Julia squinted and shook her head. "I'm not sure I follow you."

"We are talking right here, right now, because of something I prayed about for many years."

Julia's voice was gentle. "And what was that?" she asked.

"Have you ever been in prison, Mrs. Burch?"

Before Julia could answer, the woman continued as she gazed over toward the children playing on the swings. "You know, there are many types of prisons. Bitterness and unforgiveness imprison us. Hatred imprisons us."

Julia nodded. "That's true. I felt trapped a few years ago before I completely surrendered my heart to Christ."

The woman quickly turned to look at Julia. "There is someone who will be going to prison soon. I didn't know God would answer my prayers in this way. Now I believe it's the only way he will be set free. He is a powerful man, but God's power is greater."

Julia got a sick feeling in the pit of her stomach. "What does this have to do with me?"

The woman's eyes darted back and forth. "In recent weeks, I've overheard phone conversations he's had with his attorney, noticed last-minute changes on his calendar, and witnessed him making unusual purchases. He's devising a plan, and it is this plan that will send him to prison. I've intercepted evidence that proves what I'm saying is true. And, as crazy as this may sound, it's important that we let him think his plan is succeeding."

Julia put her hands up in frustration, trying to process every-thing this woman was saying. "Okay, you seem like a nice lady. But I don't know who—or what—you're talking about. I don't even know your name. If you're really here to help me in some way, please give me a little more information."

"My name is Gina Maria Merino. I work for Wyatt Bennington."

Gina took a deep breath before continuing. "Wyatt Bennington is planning to kill Margaret Gates."

CHAPTER SEVEN

It felt strange to be sitting in her dad's office waiting area, but Holly had decided that an official appointment with him was the best way to handle this. His assistant, Louise, offered her something to drink. She politely declined and continued to fidget until Bill Burch emerged from his office. When he spotted her sitting in the lobby, he smiled. Holly knew that smile.

"So, Walter," he said to the client who was with him, "have you met my lovely daughter, Holly?"

Holly stood and forced a happy demeanor.

"Well, she certainly *is* lovely!" the balding gentleman in a polo shirt and Bermuda shorts said as he stepped forward and extended his hand to Holly. "Obviously took after her mother!" he bellowed, laughing loudly. "Nice to meet you, Holly."

"The pleasure is all mine," Holly responded as she shook his hand. Under different circumstances, she relished these moments. They allowed her to be her daddy's little girl again.

After escorting the client out and instructing Louise to hold all his calls, her dad led Holly into his office.

He closed the door behind them and gestured for her to have a seat on the couch across from his desk. Holly was grateful that he had cleared his schedule for the next hour so she could have his undivided attention.

"Who's watching Olivia?" he asked as he closed the window blinds. Holly reasoned he was trying to block out some of the intense morning sun that, despite the air conditioning, was warming up his office.

"Our sitter should have her by now. Steven didn't have to go into work until nine this morning. He offered to drop her off after they had a little daughter-daddy time."

Bill opened the mini refrigerator near his desk and pulled out a bottle of water. "Can I get you something to drink?"

Holly answered 'no' with a slight wave of her hand.

As she watched Bill settle into his office chair, she wondered what the protocol was for telling your father that your husband had completely gone through your savings to fund his gambling habit. How much small talk was necessary? Should she ease into it? How disappointed was he going to be? He was a financial planner, after all. Would he consider her partly to blame for their predicament?

Bill looked at her from across his desk. "So, what did you want to talk to me about?"

As usual, his eyes displayed a tender strength. It was something she'd always loved about him. And now, more than ever, it was something she desperately needed. Her eyes filled with tears.

"Daddy," she said as her voice cracked, "we're broke! Steven has a gambling problem."

Bill immediately left his seat and joined her on the sofa. She broke down and sobbed, "I don't know what to do!" He pulled her into a hug, and she buried her head in his chest. It was so comforting to have the support of someone she knew she could count on. He reached over and grabbed a tissue from a box sitting on the lamp table. Holly thanked him as she wiped her eyes and blew her nose.

"Honey," Bill spoke softly, "what happened? When did all of this start?"

Holly faced him. "Do you remember that vacation we took about a year ago?"

He nodded. "Of course, it was the first time you and Steven were able to get away after Olivia was born. Your mother and I kept her the four days you were gone."

"Well," she continued, "one evening we decided to check out the casino at the resort. Neither of us had ever played the slot machines or anything like that before. It seemed harmless enough. We thought it would be fun."

She began to cry again. He put his hand on her shoulder. "It's okay, Holly. Go on."

"We were only going to stop in for a few minutes, but we ended up staying for several hours. Steven kept winning. He netted over a thousand dollars that night."

Bill shifted in his seat. "Wow, that's a big win."

"I know! We were so excited. At the time, I saw it as something fun we could say we'd done. That was it. I really didn't think that much of it."

Evidently, the pieces were falling into place in Bill's mind. "But Steven was hooked."

"It started out so innocently! When we got back home, he found this online gambling site. That's when I began to notice money evaporating from our bank account. It was like this dark, ugly monster had sunk its talons into my husband."

"Did you confront him?"

Holly lowered her voice to a whisper to control her emotions. "Over and over and over again. Each time he promised me that he wouldn't do it again."

Bill sighed. "Then he would do it again."

Holly nodded as the tears raced down her face once more.

Bill pulled her back into a hug. "Look, you're not alone in this anymore. You did the right thing by coming to me. As a financial planner, I've helped people recover from much worse, including a stock market crash. I can show you and Steven how to get back on your feet financially. I know it's overwhelming, but we'll take it one step at a time." He kissed her on top of her head. "Everything's going to be okay."

Holly caught her breath and looked up at him. Once again, his blue eyes were kind and reassuring. She managed a smile. "I hope so, Daddy." She rested her head back on his chest. "I really hope so."

* * *

As Holly rang the doorbell at the sitter's house, she checked her reflection, which was somewhat visible in the window beside the front door. She had touched up her makeup since leaving her dad's office, but even the best cosmetics couldn't cover a broken heart, which in her case, meant puffy eyes and a red, blotchy face.

When Vicky, Olivia's caregiver, opened the door, she was holding Olivia's hand. Holly gasped. It was clear to her that Olivia had also been crying. Not only that, but her blonde curls were stuck to her forehead as if she'd been sweating profusely.

Holly immediately grabbed her. She couldn't believe how warm her body felt. Vicky reached in between them to give Olivia her sippy cup, from which the little girl eagerly drank.

Holly panicked. "What's wrong with her? What happened?"

Vicky hurried into the kitchen where she held up a nearly empty bottle of Pedialyte. "This is how much she's guzzled since she got here a few minutes ago."

Holly's heart dropped. "Wait—she just got here? Steven was supposed to drop her off this morning on his way to work!"

Vicky stood at the sink and squeezed the excess water out of a washcloth. "Seriously? No, he left a few minutes before you arrived. You told me last night you weren't sure exactly when she'd be getting here, which was fine. When she didn't show up at all, I figured your schedule had changed and you'd forgotten to call me."

Holly began to feel sick to her stomach. "Did he offer any explanation?"

Vicky wiped Olivia's face and then stepped back to the sink to rewet the washcloth. She looked over her shoulder toward Holly. "That's what was really weird. He only apologized for being late. Said he had to get to work or he'd get fired."

Holly all but collapsed onto one of the barstools as she held Olivia. "How could he have been so irresponsible?"

Vicky wiped Olivia's back with the cool washcloth. "I mean, I think she's okay. But I'm really concerned about *how* she got this hot."

Holly narrowed her eyes. "What do you mean?"

Vicky set the washcloth aside and gently stroked Olivia's hair. "Tell Mommy what happened."

Holly turned Olivia in her lap so she could see her face. "Honey, can you tell me what happened today? How did you get so hot?"

Olivia's lip began to quiver. "Daddy weft me."

Holly fought to keep her composure. "Where did Daddy go?"

"The shiny place."

Holly gave Vicky a questioning look. "Do you have any idea what she's talking about?"

Vicky sighed. "Unfortunately, I think I do. There's a casino about twenty miles on the other side of the county line. It's new and is supposed to be really"—she paused to use her fingers as quotation marks—"state of the art, high-end kind of stuff." She scoffed, "I've heard they've got this one super addictive game you would only want to play if you're *trying* to destroy your finances."

"Why do you think that's where Steven was?" Holly asked, feeling the heat rise to her cheeks that Vicky seemed even slightly aware of Steven's private struggles.

Vicky put her hand on her hip. "Holly, I may not have a fancy college education, but I'm pretty smart when it comes to reading people. Steven has been acting different lately. I didn't know what it might be, except that he wasn't himself. Then he asked me to hold one of my paychecks until the end of the month. Not that I minded, but you and Steven have always paid me on time. Then I ran across several casino receipts when I was watching Olivia at your house and straightening up…I put two and two together."

"I'm so sorry, Vicky. But what does that have to do with the *shiny place*?"

Vicky shook her head as if embarrassed she'd gotten off track. "Okay, so even though this place is supposed to be for 'cool' gamblers, the building is really tacky. It has this gold, shiny exterior. I don't know for sure, but that's where I'd guess Steven was today. That's where some of the receipts I found were from."

Holly's eyes began to well with tears. "Where do you think Olivia was?"

Vicky reached for a tissue from the counter and handed it to Holly. "Look, my dad was a gambler. They can go into these places and lose track of time. It happens a lot. My guess is he left her in the car, thinking he would only be in there for a few minutes."

Holly didn't want to get too upset in front of Olivia. "So, Steven thought he was going to be in there for a couple minutes and it ends up being—"

Vicky interrupted, "Maybe twenty minutes with Olivia trapped in her car seat?"

Holly's mind went back to their vacation. "Oh, my gosh! This happened on our trip, too. We went to a casino just for fun, you know, to say we'd done it. I was ready to leave, but Steven was on a winning streak. But it wasn't just that he was enjoying himself, it was as if he'd lost all sense of time."

Vicky sighed. "I hate to break it to you, Holly, but it's probably happened since then. More times than you'd like to know."

CHAPTER EIGHT

As Julia headed over to Minnie's house, she struggled to focus on her driving. She had to will her hands not to shake as she attempted to process all that had transpired in the past hour and a half.

She'd heard how nasty Wyatt could be, but was he capable of murder? He struck her as a bottom-line kind of a guy. What would he stand to gain? Or was his soul really so dark and warped that he would do it out of sheer hatred for Margaret?

She was so desperate to get inside and talk with Minnie that she forgot to put her car in park. She couldn't figure out why the key wouldn't come out of the ignition.

"Okay, Julia," she said to herself, once she'd realized her mistake and had managed to get the car properly parked, "you've got to calm down." At least everyone else appeared to have left already as there were no other cars out front.

Minnie must have been watching for her to arrive because she met her on the front porch.

"Are you alright?" Minnie asked nervously.

"Minnie, you're not going to believe what I have to tell you!"

* * *

From her seat on the den sofa, Julia could hear the hissing of the teakettle and the clanging of spoons and cups coming from the kitchen. Minnie brought in a tray and placed it on the coffee table. Julia stared blankly across the room as Minnie put the teacup into her hand. Julia blew at the steam before taking a sip.

Since Minnie had opened a small bakery a couple of years ago, her phone often rang with orders she needed to fill. Today, she was letting all those calls go to voice mail. She took a sip of her own tea and then set the cup back on the tray.

"First of all, I'm glad you're okay. I was worried about you earlier. To be honest, I'm still worried! What happened today?" Minnie asked.

Julia didn't make eye contact at first but continued to look toward the window on the other side of the room. "I was at my parents' house, leaving the key for the realtor. I noticed an electronic gadget of some sort under the cabinet shelf. As I was climbing up to get a better look, I heard someone come through the front door. I assumed it was Scott, but it was this older woman. She acted really nervous and said we needed to talk. She said it might not be safe to talk at my parents' house, which I thought was odd. I met her at the park and found out she works for Wyatt Bennington."

When Julia mentioned Wyatt's name, Minnie squeezed her eyes shut as if she was bracing herself for whatever Julia was going to say next.

Julia's voice began to shake, and she absentmindedly rotated her wedding band as she talked. "Her name is Gina Merino. She's a Christian, and she's apparently been praying for Wyatt for years. She said that we needed to let his plan play out. But then she also said that if his plan does come to fruition, he'll most likely go to prison."

Minnie's brow furrowed. "What plan?"

Julia realized she wasn't making sense. She was still trying to wrap her own mind around the situation. Plus, there was a part of her that didn't want to upset Minnie.

She collected her thoughts. "Gina has reason to believe that Wyatt's nice demeanor since Horace's death has been an act; he's actually been seething for three years."

Minnie reached for her teacup on the tray. "That doesn't surprise me. So, this must be about Preston getting part of Wyatt's inheritance money."

"Of course." Julia rolled her eyes. "With Wyatt, it's always about money. For some reason, he's blaming it all on Margaret."

Minnie shook her head and took a sip of her tea. "No love lost there."

"It's more serious than that, Minnie—much more serious." Julia looked down. "Gina believes that Wyatt is planning to kill Margaret."

The porcelain teacup shattered on the floor before either of them could catch it.

Julia leapt up and began collecting the pieces. "I'm sorry, Minnie. I shouldn't have unloaded all of that on you. I'll help you clean this up."

Minnie took Julia's hand and pulled her back toward the sofa. "Don't you worry about that teacup! We've obviously got bigger problems on our hands. How certain is this Gina person about all of this?"

"Certain enough that she risked her own safety to tell me about it," Julia said as she sat back down. "Evidently, Wyatt is planning to reach out to Margaret under the guise of helping the ministry at the Manor. He's been talking with his lawyers about tax deductions and charitable giving. On the outside, it looks like he's being a generous philanthropist."

"How does she know he's not?"

"Other than the fact that it would be a first for Wyatt? She's also noticed him making odd purchases lately. One that caught her attention was a box of Darjeeling and some dainty teacups. Nothing Wyatt would use himself."

"Maybe they're for Delores," Minnie reasoned.

"Oh, speaking of Delores," Julia began collecting the pieces of the teacup despite Minnie's objections. "Last week, he flew her to Europe for a shopping spree. She'll be gone for a month."

Minnie reached for a small, wicker wastebasket located beside the sofa and handed it to Julia. "So maybe that's why Gina is telling you all of this now. With Delores gone, it would be the perfect opportunity for Wyatt to spend time with Margaret without raising suspicion."

"That's what she thinks. She believes Wyatt will initially try to get Margaret drunk to discredit her."

Minnie scoffed. "Margaret wouldn't do that."

Julia shot her a worried look. "Not willingly. But what if he sneaks something into her coffee or tea?"

"You have a point. However, doing something like that is wrong and unethical, but it's a big leap from wanting to discredit her to planning her murder. Why does she think Wyatt's end game is murder?"

"You'd better buckle your seat belt for that one. Not only is she convinced that killing Margaret is his plan, but she's also concluded that his method in doing so will be by poisoning her."

Minnie looked skeptical. "Julia, is this woman for real? That seems a bit far-fetched. How does she even know any of this beyond finding tea and teacups?"

Julia adjusted the couch pillow behind her back. "If I hadn't been there with her, I would think the same thing. Evidently, she's intercepted evidence that supports her theory. She didn't want to go into detail. She seemed nervous to the point of being a little paranoid. Even in the park, she kept looking around while we talked. I think she was afraid we could've been followed, or that someone could've been listening to our conversation."

Minnie jumped to her feet. "Julia, what did you say you saw under your parents' kitchen cabinet?"

Julia was startled. "It was, uh, this little electronic gadget. Why? What's wrong?"

Minnie hurried into the kitchen. Her laptop was on the table. They sat down as she typed in several commands.

After a few moments, she leaned forward and turned the screen toward Julia.

"Is this what the gadget looked like?"

Julia nodded. "That's exactly what it looked like."

Minnie took off her glasses and sat back in her chair.

"Your parents' house is bugged!"

"What? Talk about far-fetched! Why would my parents' house be bugged?"

Minnie chewed on the arm of her glasses while she thought. "Perhaps Wyatt is trying to get as much information as possible in order to deceive Margaret."

A smile tugged at the corners of Julia's mouth. "You know, I think you missed your calling as a detective. Explain."

Minnie stood and began pacing. "Do you remember when you started the remodeling project at your parent's place, and the local newspaper did a cover story on it?"

"Of course," Julia replied. "A couple staying married and living in the same house for sixty-two years? In this day and age? That was definitely front-page news!"

"Wyatt would have seen Margaret in the pictures with you and your siblings. Knowing she was there helping with the renovations, he probably figured he could listen in on conversations and that it could help him become better acquainted with her. He'd be able to converse with her more easily and make her feel more comfortable."

Julia nodded. She was beginning to understand. "And eventually gain her trust."

Minnie pointed in Julia's direction. "Exactly!"

"But why plant the bug at my parents' house? Why not at the Manor?"

"Well, let's think about that." Minnie resumed her pacing. "Your parents' house is vacant and on the market. That makes it an easy target. Wyatt has no ties to your parents. Even if the bug was discovered, it would be hard to prove Wyatt put it there. A defense attorney fresh out of law school could handle that one. Putting it in your parents' house is close enough to Margaret's world, but not too close."

Julia raised her eyebrows. "This man is smart."

"And powerful," Minnie said as she sat back down at the table and took Julia's hand into hers. "But we have something *more* powerful, don't we?"

"It's time to pray, isn't it?" Julia asked.

Minnie smiled. "It's time to pray."

CHAPTER NINE

As Joseph turned onto the road leading to the Gates Manor, Margaret began to check out of their conversation. She was more interested in—and focused on—the busy afternoon that lay ahead. First, she had a meeting scheduled with the band director, George Ortega. She was excited they would be welcoming two new students to the Manor. After that, she had a mountain of paperwork she needed to catch up on before dinner with Preston and Annie. She would've preferred to go straight home after work, but for some reason, her brother wouldn't take no for an answer. She'd be so happy when she could finally get back home and change into her pajamas, provided she didn't fall asleep during dinner.

Margaret was baffled as to why she'd been having trouble sleeping in recent weeks. It was as if an invisible alarm went off around two o'clock in the morning. The first few times it happened, she'd tossed and turned which, of course, had made her even *more* awake. Now she had a solution; a cup of herbal tea and her prayer journal. She'd go down her list of family, friends, and the students at the Manor, and pray for each one until she fell back asleep.

Last night she'd felt like she needed to add a new name to

that list.

Spending time working with Joseph, she'd learned more about his brother, Wyatt. Not surprisingly, most of it was information she'd rather *not* know. Last night, she felt like the Holy Spirit had shown her that if she could forgive Horace, who had sexually abused her, she could at least *pray* for Wyatt.

She understood that, despite the type of person Wyatt was, God still loved him. She knew firsthand what it was like to feel undeserving of that love. Grace and mercy had been extended to her when she was a drug addict on the verge of suicide. Scripture is clear that God doesn't show partiality. What He'd done for her, He could do for Wyatt.

"So, I think I'll dye my hair bright purple. It should be a good look for me. What do you think?" Margaret heard Joseph ask her. He must have picked up on the fact that she wasn't listening.

Margaret laughed. "Okay, I'm sorry. I haven't been completely tuned in. I have a lot on my mind, that's all. You were saying?"

"So, do you like the purple, or should I go with green?"

Margaret leaned her head toward Joseph and pretended to give his hair a thorough inspection. "Purple. I'd definitely go with purple."

Joseph pulled up to the front of the Manor to drop her off. "Hey, I have to run by the hospital for a little while. Do you want to grab dinner later?"

Margaret was constantly amazed at how Joseph managed two careers. While working late hours at the Manor—which he founded and also served as executive director—he still maintained his position as head administrator at the county hospital. What would cause burnout for most people seemed to energize Joseph. She attributed his success to the fact that he had a passion for helping people. His heart was in both jobs.

"I wish I could," Margaret said as she picked up her purse and laptop.

She turned to look at him before shutting the car door. "Rain check?"

Joseph gave her a thumbs-up and smiled.

His smile lingered in Margaret's mind as she went through the rest of her day. Something was different about Joseph lately. She couldn't put her finger on it, but it had her curiosity stirred.

It was too bad she already had plans for tonight.

As the afternoon progressed, Margaret realized that falling asleep during dinner wasn't going to be the problem. She was already struggling to stay awake, and it was only a few minutes past three o'clock. She yawned several times during her meeting with Mr. Ortega and the new students. When her eyes started to feel heavy, she knew it was time for a coffee break.

"Mr. Ortega, why don't you show the students the band room? I'll meet you there in a couple of minutes."

She left the room and stepped down the hall. As she opened the door to the kitchen, her phone vibrated. When she checked it, she saw a number she didn't recognize.

"Hello?" she answered tentatively.

A robust voice responded on the other end. "Well, hello yourself! How are you, Margaret?"

Margaret cradled the phone between her shoulder and her chin as she poured herself a cup of coffee. "I'm sorry, who is this?"

The voice replied, "It's Wyatt. Wyatt Bennington."

Margaret was completely caught off guard. Why would Wyatt call her? How did he even get her number?

"Wyatt, what can I do for you? Are you trying to reach Joseph? If so, he's at the hospital."

Wyatt laughed. "No, no, I want to speak with you! I've been very impressed with your work at the Gates Manor. I always try to support causes I believe in, so I've decided I'd like to make a dona-tion—a *generous* donation—to help with the Manor's operating expenses. I don't want Joseph to know about it until it's all said and done. Kind of a surprise for my little brother."

Margaret wanted to believe Wyatt was being sincere. If he truly was trying to leave the "dark side," his business connections would be invaluable, especially with the team's ongoing effort to spread the word about the Manor beyond Enoburg. And they certainly could use the funds. But this was out of character for Wyatt. She'd need to hear more.

"So, what part of our program interests you the most?" she asked as she added cream and sugar to her coffee.

Wyatt didn't hesitate. "When I heard the Gates Manor Band had performed for Julia Burch's father shortly before his death, I was touched. I still regret not being with my own father when he passed away. Knowing these students can bring comfort and hope to the elderly is an issue close to my heart."

Wyatt sounds genuine. Maybe I need to give him a chance.

Her thoughts were interrupted as George Ortega stuck his head into the kitchen. "Margaret, Jennifer's mother is here and wants to speak with you. She's on a tight schedule. Can you come now?"

Margaret nodded to him. "I'll be right there." She returned her attention back to the call. "Wyatt, I apologize, but I'm late for a meeting. Can I call you back?"

Wyatt was more than accommodating. "No problem. It doesn't even have to be today—just whenever you get time. I'm looking forward to speaking with you more about this."

Margaret grabbed her coffee and made her way to the band room. She was glad she'd planned to call Julia later tonight. She couldn't wait to hear her take on this.

Wyatt Bennington calling Margaret Gates.

She never thought she'd live to see this day.

* * *

Wyatt placed the cell phone beside a stack of folders. He kicked off his shoes and propped his feet up on his desk. Leaning back in his office chair, he smiled.

"Good job, Wyatt, old boy," he said to himself with a broad smile. "This is going to be easier than you thought."

CHAPTER TEN

IT WAS AROUND DUSK WHEN HOLLY ARRIVED BACK HOME FROM Vicky's house. They'd spent the afternoon discussing the morning's events: Steven leaving Olivia in the car, Holly learning that he hadn't been paying Vicky on time, and the painful reality that someone else—other than herself—had noticed changes in his behavior.

Holly turned off her car and sat for a moment before going inside. She'd never been so angry. She couldn't believe Steven would risk their daughter's life so he could gamble away money they didn't even have.

She prayed quietly, *Lord, I know it's okay to be angry. Just help me to handle this in the right way. I do love Steven, and this may be a time for that love to be tough.*

Being a typical two-year-old, Olivia had forgotten about the morning's incident and giggled when her Dad greeted them at the front door. Seeing Steven interact with Olivia as if nothing had happened made Holly's blood boil.

"Olivia," she said, forcing herself to be calm, "why don't you go to your room and play with your new Elmo doll?"

"Okay, Mommy!" Olivia smiled and bounded up the stairs.

"So, how was your day?" Steven asked, leaning in to kiss her.

Holly pushed him away and stomped into the kitchen. She opened a cabinet door to get out a glass and then slammed it shut.

"Is this about me dropping off Olivia late at Vicky's? I'm sorry. I got stuck in traffic."

Holly's face flushed and her jaw tightened. Her mind went back to when she'd feared, after months and months of not being able to get pregnant, that she never would. She remembered how her heart had ached when she'd see other moms with their babies, wondering if she'd ever have a child of her own. She understood what a precious gift Olivia was to them—a gift Steven had treated with total disregard through his careless behavior.

Something inside of her snapped. In a moment of fury, she spun around and slapped Steven in the face.

As soon as she heard the sound—and felt the impact beneath her hand—she knew their marriage would never be the same. She knew, for Steven, the pain would penetrate beyond skin-deep. It was certain to travel to his heart and break it into a million pieces.

But Steven wasn't her main concern right now.

"You could have *killed* our daughter today! Do you even understand that? You get your things, and you get out. When you're ready to admit you have a problem and are willing to get help, you can come back. You crossed the line today, Steven. This is serious."

Steven's jaw dropped and his eyes widened. He put his hand to his cheek. "I can't believe you did that! You know I would never intentionally hurt Olivia!"

Holly lowered her voice. "You've got one hour."

Steven raised his hands. "Okay, I understand why you're upset, but we can work this out. Where am I supposed to go? I can't afford a hotel. You know our situation!"

Holly slammed her hand down on the counter and screamed, "You *created* our situation!"

The color drained from his face. "Holly, I'm so sorry."

Holly believed him, but sorry wasn't good enough right now.

"I don't have anywhere to go!" he protested.

She shrugged her shoulders. "That's not my problem."

As she turned to leave the kitchen, she called back to him, "One hour, Steven. You've got one hour."

CHAPTER ELEVEN

MARGARET GOT A SECOND WIND AT PRESTON AND ANNIE'S. SHE wasn't sure if it was Annie's home cooking, or the fact that she was enjoying their company so much. Perhaps it was both. It had only been a couple of weeks since they'd last shared a meal, so she was surprised at all the catching up they needed to do.

Even though Preston and Annie were approaching their second wedding anniversary, they continued to behave like newlyweds. Annie was as kind as she was beautiful. She had shoulder-length dark hair and brown eyes fringed with long lashes. She still blushed whenever Preston teased her. Preston, with his blonde hair and cornflower-blue eyes, was strikingly handsome and looked younger than a man who was approaching his late thirties. Margaret could tell that Annie's love still held him spellbound. All in all, she'd have to say she'd never seen them happier.

There was something she'd wanted to ask them, but she didn't want to seem nosey. Knowing her brother, if he thought she was, he wouldn't hesitate to tell her. She decided to go for it.

"If you don't mind my asking," Margaret said as she reached across the table for a slice of cheesecake, "am I going to be an aunt any time soon?"

Preston didn't say anything. Margaret found it odd that he reached for his cell phone and looked over at Annie.

"Well?" Margaret managed through a mouthful of cheesecake.

Annie spoke up. "How does January sound to you?"

Margaret's eyes grew wide as she looked at Preston who was laughing and recording her reaction with his phone.

After washing down the cheesecake with a few gulps of water, Margaret squealed and all but jumped over the table to hug them both.

For the remainder of the evening, the conversation revolved around one word.

Baby.

They talked about baby names, baby strollers, the baby's nursery, and whether the baby was a boy or a girl. Margaret was still beaming about becoming an aunt when she returned to her house next door a couple of hours later. She couldn't wait to tell Julia. She dialed her number as soon as she walked in the door, but after several rings, it went to her voicemail.

She felt like she'd burst if she didn't tell someone. Who else could she call? Then she remembered she'd told Wyatt she would get back with him. She checked the time. It wasn't too late. Even if she just left a message on his voicemail, at least he would know she'd tried.

She dialed his number. After two rings, he picked up.

"Well, Margaret Gates! I didn't think I'd hear back from you this soon."

Margaret was cautiously optimistic. Wyatt sounded friendly enough. And people can change; *she* certainly had. Still, she wasn't ready to completely trust him yet.

"I was, uh, just catching up on a few other calls. Is this a good time?"

"This is a perfect time!" Wyatt replied. "In fact, how would you like to come over to the estate for a bit so we can talk about this in person? I really don't like discussing matters involving large amounts of money over the phone. Gina made a chocolate torte that will melt in your mouth. I'll have her start a fresh pot of coffee."

Margaret didn't know what to say. "You mean come over right now?"

Wyatt laughed. "No time like the present, they say!"

Margaret thought for a moment. She was too wound up about the baby to even think about going to sleep just yet. At least if she spoke with Wyatt tonight, she could check it off her list.

"I certainly don't want to put your staff to any trouble."

Wyatt chuckled. "It's no trouble at all."

"Okay. I'll see you in about ten minutes."

* * *

Gina was singing softly as she finished putting away the dishes. This was her favorite time of the day. Wyatt and Delores were usually settled in upstairs, and she could sing while she finished her chores. If the weather was nice outside, she and Bivens, the butler, would share a cup of tea on the terrace and talk about the day's activities. She was startled when Wyatt abruptly came back into the kitchen.

"Gina, put on a fresh pot of coffee. I have a guest arriving in a few minutes. We'll be meeting in the study. Oh, and there's plenty of that chocolate torte left, right?"

"Yes, Mr. Bennington," Gina replied. "Right away, sir."

Who could be visiting Wyatt at this hour? she wondered.

Wyatt and Delores rarely had guests to drop by. Wyatt was very protective of his time and normally had every minute of his day scheduled.

Gina had just set up the coffee and dessert tray when the doorbell rang. Bivens had already retired for the evening, so she answered the door herself. Her mouth dropped open when she saw Margaret standing on the porch.

This wasn't supposed to happen!

Wyatt walked up behind her. In a loud voice, he announced, "Well, don't be rude, Gina. Invite Miss Gates inside!"

Gina quietly apologized and stepped aside. Wyatt showed Margaret into the study where he offered her a seat in the wing-back chair across from his.

Gina didn't know what Wyatt had planned for tonight, but she knew it couldn't be good. She would stand outside the study where she could see and hear everything that was going on. If Wyatt offered Margaret anything other than the dessert and coffee she had prepared, it could contain alcohol and she would have to intercept it somehow. She had to be careful to not make him upset with her. If she got on his bad side, she wouldn't be any help to Margaret at all. She needed to stay in his good graces to know his next move.

After a few minutes of small talk, Wyatt put his palm to his forehead. "My goodness, I'm a terrible host. Would you like some coffee and dessert? Gina makes an amazing chocolate torte!"

Gina entered the room hoping he would ask her to serve. But Margaret declined Wyatt's offer.

"No thanks," Margaret said, patting her stomach. "I had a big piece of cheesecake earlier tonight."

Wyatt seemed unmoved. "I understand. I've never met a piece of cheesecake I didn't like. Still, you must try one of these truffles. They were imported from Spain and taste like heaven."

Gina had to pick her battles. She couldn't just rush in and grab the truffles. She didn't want Wyatt to think she was there for any other reason than to serve him and Margaret. Fortunately, Margaret declined once again.

The next ten minutes or so seemed to drag on forever as Wyatt puffed out his chest and regaled Margaret with how he was a devoted brother, son, and an enthusiastic supporter of local community projects. Gina checked the time. It was getting late. Wyatt wouldn't be able to get into the details of contributing to the

Manor tonight. Margaret would have to come back. Perhaps that was his plan all along.

As if on cue, Wyatt looked down at his watch. "Wow! I certainly did lose track of the hour. I guess time really does fly when you're with good company. Can we finish this up later? I'm sure you have an early day tomorrow. How about a follow-up meeting, say, tomorrow evening?"

Margaret yawned and pulled out her phone to check her calendar. "That works for me. How about eight o'clock?"

Wyatt beamed. "Eight o'clock will work fine. Don't forget—mums the word with Joseph. I want this to be a surprise."

"Yes, of course. I won't say anything."

Margaret stood up to leave. As she reached out to shake Wyatt's hand, he made one last attempt. "Oh, and I didn't want you to get sleepy on your drive home. Wait here for a second."

Gina watched curiously as Wyatt left the room and then returned with a travel cup in his hand.

"I personally fixed you a cup of coffee to go," he said, handing the cup to Margaret. "I had to guess how you take yours. You strike me as a one cream, one sugar type of gal."

Margaret's eyes lit up. "Actually, that's exactly how I take my coffee! How did you know?" She smiled as she accepted the cup. "Thank you!"

Gina panicked. She didn't know if Wyatt had put anything other than cream and sugar in the coffee. She had to think fast.

She spoke up. "Miss Gates, let me take this to the car for you while you gather your things."

After Wyatt waved goodbye and closed the front door, Gina pretended to stumble. The coffee spilled out onto the driveway. She apologized and offered to get Margaret another cup. Margaret told her not to bother, as she didn't need the caffeine this late at night anyway.

Gina breathed a sigh of relief as she watched Margaret drive off the property.

"That was a close one!" she muttered to herself.

CHAPTER TWELVE

JOSEPH MARKED HIS PLACE IN THE BOOK HE WAS READING AND TOSSED it toward the foot of his bed. He couldn't concentrate. He adjusted the pillows behind him and reached for the television remote. After scanning past a couple of late-night talk shows, he clicked the power button and returned the remote to his nightstand.

He felt so foolish. What a predictable situation he'd found himself in—falling for a work associate. And yet, he couldn't have predicted it at all. Until recently, his and Margaret's relationship had been strictly professional. Then something had begun to shift —for him, at least. He couldn't wait to see her each day at the Manor. He admired and respected her. In fact, he'd never met anybody like her. She had a passion for the students that would often keep her talking with them long after her workday had ended. Her humility was the most beautiful thing he'd ever seen. And speaking of beauty, had she always been as pretty as she looked lately? With that thought, Joseph hopped out of bed and stood in front of his dresser mirror.

"Okay Joseph," he murmured out loud to himself. "Let's take inventory."

He ran his fingers through his salt-and-pepper hair. "Still have that going for me. If I do say so, it's twice as thick as my brother's." In a singsong type of way, he chanted under his breath, "Na-na-na-na-na, Wyatt!"

He examined his smile. "Wearing that retainer paid off. Those pearly whites are still straight as an arrow."

He turned sideways to check out his profile. "Going to the gym hasn't done you any harm either, old boy. Need to lay off the desserts, but other than that, I don't think you would completely disgust her if she saw you without your shirt."

He took off his glasses. "Well, if I could see my eyes, I think they're still a striking shade of blue. Besides the fact that I'm simply better looking, that's one thing that distinguishes me from my brown-eyed brother. Hmmm…maybe I should get contacts?"

The foolish feeling settled back over him and he sat down on the side of the bed.

"Who am I kidding? After what my father did to her, how could she ever even *entertain* the notion of us being anything other than friends? Plus, her brother is my half-brother. Could it get any weirder? I guess it's a miracle I'm in her life at all."

He set his glasses on the nightstand and turned off the lamp. "Heavenly Father," he prayed, "if my feelings for Margaret are not from you, then take them away." He turned over and closed his eyes. "Please take them away."

* * *

As Margaret drove home, she reflected on her time at the Bennington estate. Typical Wyatt, the conversation revolved completely around him. If that's what it took to get the Manor a donation and some much-needed publicity, she could easily deal with his inflated ego.

But how did he know that I take cream and sugar in my coffee?

She drove past Preston and Annie's house before turning into her own driveway, and the excitement washed over her again. She prayed for God to bless them and their baby. She unlocked her front door, set her keys down on the table in the foyer, and checked her phone to see if Julia had tried to call her. Frustrated, she sent her a text:

Where are you?? I have exciting news. And you'll never guess who I met with tonight—Wyatt Bennington! Truth is stranger than fiction. LOL. Call me!

If nothing else, the mention of Wyatt would certainly get Julia's attention. Maybe then she would call, and Margaret could tell her about the baby.

She checked the time on her phone. It was a few minutes before eleven. Was there anybody else who wouldn't be upset with her calling this late? *Joseph*! He wouldn't mind. If anything, he would be ticked off if he found out she'd thought about calling him and didn't.

What was the worst that could happen? He would either not answer or threaten to dye his hair purple again if she interrupted his sleep. He could be so silly at times! She dialed his number.

* * *

Joseph had just drifted off to sleep when he heard his cell phone ring. He sprung up and grabbed his glasses. Phone calls at this hour typically didn't deliver good news. He hoped there wasn't a situation with one of the students at the Manor. He quickly put on his glasses and saw Margaret's number. At first, his heart leapt. Then he realized she most likely needed him to get in touch with one of the physicians on call.

"Hi Margaret, is everything okay?"

"Hey, did I wake you? I hope I'm not calling too late."

Joseph sat up and regrouped. Evidently, this was not a business call. "Uh, no. It's fine. I was doing a little reading." He shook his head and rolled his eyes. It wasn't totally dishonest; he'd *tried* to read earlier. He didn't want her to think she was bothering him.

"Oh, good!" Margaret responded cheerfully. "I have some exciting news, and I had to tell someone!"

Joseph's heart warmed. "Well, I'm glad I could be that some-one. What's the news?"

"I'm going to be an aunt!" she squealed. "Preston and Annie are expecting in January!"

"That's great news! So, should I start calling you Aunt Margaret now so you can get used to your new title?"

"Maybe," Margaret replied, "if you stay away from the purple dye. I wouldn't want people to think I have this really old nephew with weird hair."

Joseph laughed and then decided to take a chance. "Okay, deal. Now, you should let me take you out to dinner to celebrate. How about tomorrow night?"

Margaret paused. "I'm sorry, Joseph. I wish I could, but I've already got plans."

Joseph's smile faded. "Okay, well some other time then."

"I'll see you tomorrow at work. Good night, Joseph."

Joseph ended the call and then looked up. "Was that supposed to make me feel better or worse?"

* * *

As Margaret got ready for bed, she thought about how kind Joseph had been. She regretted that she couldn't have dinner with him. She would much rather celebrate with him than sit through another boring meeting with Wyatt. She hoped he hadn't thought she was blowing him off, but she'd promised Wyatt she wouldn't say anything about the donation until everything was official.

She couldn't wait to see Joseph's face when he learned what his older brother had been up to.

CHAPTER THIRTEEN

"THANK YOU FOR HELPING ME SORT THROUGH EVERYTHING TODAY,"
Julia said as she and Minnie walked out onto Minnie's front porch.
"I'll call you as soon as I have any updates."

"You know I always enjoy catching up with you." Minnie
winked. "Call me even if you don't have any updates!"

"I can do better than that! How about Margaret and I come
over soon for some of your legendary baked chicken?"

Minnie broke into a big smile. "Now, that I would *really* enjoy!"

Julia reached over to give her a hug. Was it her imagination, or
did Minnie feel thinner?

"Minnie, have you lost—"

"You don't need to worry about me. You get on home before
that husband of yours starts to think I've kidnapped you!"

Julia waved to Minnie as she backed out of her driveway. As
she started down the road, she dialed Bill's number.

"There's my long-lost wife!" Bill answered.

"I'm so sorry, honey. I see where I have three missed calls from
you. You won't believe the day I've had!"

Bill sounded more serious when he spoke this time. "Yeah, me
too." There was a pause. "Have you talked to Holly?"

Julia could hear the concern in his voice. "I have a missed call from her, but I haven't had a chance to speak with her yet. Is everything okay? Is Olivia sick?"

Bill sighed. "Olivia's fine. But Holly and Steven are having problems—big ones."

Julia's stomach knotted. "What's going on?"

Bill hesitated. "Are you sure you want to talk about this over the phone while you're driving?"

"I've got a feeling I'm not going to want to talk about it at all. But, yes, go ahead."

"Steven has a serious gambling problem. Holly met with me today to talk about their finances. She's really upset."

Julia's breath caught in her throat.

"Are you still there?" Bill asked.

"Yes, I'm here," Julia said. "I'm in shock. That doesn't sound like Steven at all. How did this happen?"

"They visited a casino on their vacation last year. Steven won a lot of money, and after that, he was hooked. It happens more often than people realize. In my line of work, I've seen the devastation it can cause. The sooner he can get help, the sooner they can recover. And I'm not just talking about recovering financially."

Julia's heart sank. "I know exactly what you're talking about. I'm sure this has taken a toll on their marriage."

The phone beeped, and she glanced away from the road and down at her caller ID. "Bill, Holly is trying to call me. I'll get back with you in a few minutes."

Julia pressed a button and answered. "Holly, are you okay?"

Holly's voice was shaking. "Mom, I have something to tell you—"

Julia interrupted, "I already know, honey. Dad told me everything."

"Not everything," Holly replied.

"What do you mean?"

"I kicked Steven out." She began to cry. "Mom, I need you. Can you come over now? Please?"

"Of course," Julia replied. "I'm on my way!"

Julia did a quick U-turn. As she drove, she prayed. She asked God to return the real Steven to them. She prayed for strength for Holly and for God to send her people who could support her and not be judgmental. As soon as she ended the prayer, she knew exactly who to call.

She quickly dialed her younger daughter, Claire's, number. Claire had just finished her sophomore year of college—as well as the first session of summer school—and was driving home from the western part of the state. After Julia explained the situation, she was more than willing to cancel any plans she had made in order to stop by Holly's house on her way into town.

Claire had grown up considerably in the past three years. Transitioning from her identity as Holly's cute little sister, she had matured into a stunning young woman with a passion for hiking, camping, and any activity that took her outside to enjoy the beauty of the North Carolina mountains. One thing that hadn't changed was her tender heart and her ability—more than anyone else in the family—to cheer up her sister. A visit from Claire was just what the doctor ordered.

Julia was about to ring Holly's doorbell when Holly opened the door and crumpled into her arms.

"Mom, I can't believe this is happening!"

Julia managed to get inside and held her daughter close. After Holly had calmed down a bit, they sat on the couch and she explained all that had happened. When she finished, Julia studied Holly's face.

"You've been through a lot today. Why don't you get a shower while I see what needs to be done around the house?

"Thanks, Mom." Holly sniffed. "I think I'll take you up on that."

While Holly was upstairs, Julia picked up Olivia's toys and started a load of laundry. After tidying up the kitchen, she located her phone in her purse and sat down at the table to call Bill and let him know where she was. She saw where she had a text message and a missed call from Margaret. After speaking with Bill, she opened the text message.

Where are you?? I have exciting news. And you'll never guess who I met with tonight—Wyatt Bennington! Truth is stranger than fiction. LOL. Call me!

Julia gasped. She put the phone down and sat back in her chair. What else could possibly happen tonight? At least she knew from the text that Margaret was okay. She'd need to catch her first thing in the morning to warn her about Wyatt, though.

"Is everything okay, Mom?" Holly had quietly entered the kitchen.

Julia forced a smile. "Nothing you need to worry about."

Holly unwrapped a towel from her head. She ran her fingers through her damp hair and pulled it back into a ponytail. Julia noticed that her eyes were still red and swollen.

"How are you holding up?" she asked as she pulled out a kitchen chair for her.

Holly shrugged as she sat down. "Okay, I guess." She picked up a paper napkin on the table and began folding it. "The hardest thing is that I keep asking myself what I could have done differently. Should I have pushed harder for Steven to get help? Should I have talked to you and Dad sooner? Maybe I didn't want to go through the upheaval and," she paused, "the embarrassment. That's selfish, right?"

Julia shook her head. "You can't blame yourself for this. Steven is a grown man who knows right from wrong. You weren't trying to sweep it under the rug. You talked to him—numerous times. He's your husband and a good guy, not to mention a strong Christian. When he said he was going to quit, you wanted to trust him. More importantly, you thought you could."

"At one time, I *knew* I could. I kept hoping things would go back to the way they were. It caught me off guard, Mom. I didn't think Christians could get sucked into something like this. When it only affected Steven and me, it was bad enough. But when it compromised Olivia's safety and well-being, that's where I had to draw the line."

She put her elbows on the table and rested her head in her hands. "I think I'm mostly upset that an addiction came into my home and forced me to choose between my husband and my daughter."

Julia spoke gently. "Holly, you didn't have a choice. You had to protect Olivia."

"I know. I still can't believe he left her in the car. If a police officer had seen it, Steven would have been arrested." She flung the folded napkin across the table. "Maybe that's what should've happened."

Julia suddenly remembered her conversation with Gina about Wyatt. "One prison for another..." Julia muttered out loud. "One enslaves, one sets free..."

Holly scrunched up her nose. "Mom, what are you talking about?"

Before Julia could answer, they both heard a faint knock.

Holly glanced over her shoulder toward the front door. "Who on earth could that be?" She turned back and anxiously looked at Julia. "What if it's Steven?"

"Steven has a key. It's still his house. He wouldn't knock," Julia assured her.

Holly quickly nodded her head. "You're right. I'll go check it out."

Julia smiled as she heard Holly open the door. "Oh-my-gosh, oh-my-gosh! It's Claire!"

From her bed in the guest room, Julia could hear Claire and Holly talking into the early hours of the morning. Claire had a way of manifesting the tender heart of the Father. The atmosphere in Holly's home had already changed since her arrival. There was a fresh peace and a renewed sense that God was in control.

Julia marveled at how music continued to be the theme of her life. Claire's sweet spirit reminded her of a lullaby. She'd arrived at bedtime like a lilting melody that soothed and quieted their spirits.

As Julia sat up to fluff her pillow, she saw a family picture of Steven, Holly, and Olivia on the nightstand. She turned on the lamp and picked it up. Taken a few weeks earlier at Easter, it showcased what a handsome and happy family they were.

Julia threw her head back onto her pillow in frustration. *What a waste!* If only Steven could see what he had forfeited in exchange for a temporary high; a high that, ironically, was taking him to new depths of misery and pain.

If only he could see, Julia thought as she was drifting off to sleep. *Lord Jesus, help him to see.*

CHAPTER FOURTEEN

Not long after Julia had left her house, Minnie Morgan opened the screen door again and stepped out onto her front porch. She loosely tied the belt on her bathrobe as she breathed in the bouquet of the summer evening. The gardenias around her front porch were blooming and filled the air with their perfume. An Easter lily perched on the wicker table between the two rocking chairs delivered notes of spice and musk.

She sat down in one of the chairs and reached over to gently set the other one in motion. Her mind went back to all the times Caleb had sat there on evenings like this one. She could still hear his voice, see his smile. It had been almost three years since he'd passed. She missed him more than words could express.

One of the things she missed most about him was his wisdom. While Minnie tended to get bogged down in the details, Caleb had had a gift for seeing the big picture. There had to be something in the big picture with Gina Merino that Minnie was missing. So much was still unclear. The one thing that *was* clear was that the situation needed to be handled delicately. She felt certain there was more Gina hadn't told Julia yet.

"Gina Merino, Gina Merino..." Minnie kept repeating the

name. Why did it sound so familiar? Maybe she was overthinking the whole thing. She closed her eyes, allowing her senses to take in the fresh night air for a few more minutes. The fragrance swelled as a breeze swept across the front porch. A strange peace washed over her. She thought she heard the faint whisper of her name. She opened her eyes but didn't see anyone. Perhaps she had fallen asleep and was dreaming. That being the case, it was her cue that it was way past her bedtime.

When she stood up to go inside the house, she felt a little disoriented. Then a pain shot through her right midsection. She leaned against the side of the house to steady herself. In a few seconds, the pain subsided.

"*Okay, Minnie,*" she thought to herself, "*you're getting too old to play detective. It's time to give this to Jesus and go to bed.*" She closed the front door and turned off the light.

Out on the front porch, another breeze brought with it what appeared to be a page from a newspaper. It gently landed in front of Minnie's rocking chair.

CHAPTER FIFTEEN

JAKE DUNLOP AWOKE TO THE SOUND OF SOMEONE KNOCKING ON HIS front door. He rolled over and picked up his watch from his nightstand. It was just past midnight.

He sat on the side of the bed and rubbed his eyes. The knocking resumed. He quickly pulled on the pair of jeans that had been draped across the foot of his bed, then unlocked his nightstand drawer and took out a 9mm Glock. After clicking in a full magazine, he tucked the gun in the back of his jeans.

Still groggy, he lumbered down the stairs and looked through the peephole in his front door.

"You've got to be kidding me," he mumbled under his breath.

He quickly darted from room to room picking up any memorabilia or photographs that he didn't want his visitor to see. In a panic, he stuffed everything in the bottom drawer of his desk. After taking a few deep breaths, he opened the front door and calmly swatted at a mosquito that flew past him. He then addressed the man standing on his stoop with a duffle bag.

"Steven Sparrow. I've been waiting for this."

* * *

Steven winced as he sipped the cup of coffee Jake had prepared for him. It was bitter, much like everything else in his life right now.

Jake lit a cigarette. "So, when did Holly kick you out?" He flicked a match head toward Steven. "You know, I warned you this was going to happen."

"Yeah, well you aren't exactly a priest, Jake. It's not like I hang on your every word."

Jake sneered and blew smoke in Steven's direction. Neither are you, pretty boy, or you wouldn't be in this predicament. Besides, why wouldn't you trust me? I'm the mechanic who fixed your car, remember? You weren't too happy over the prospect of having to call Holly to pick you up that night. Come to think of it, I've saved your hide more than once so your lovely bride wouldn't find out about your expensive little habit."

Steven looked down at his coffee cup. "I let it get out of hand, that's all. I should have quit months ago."

Jake raised his eyebrows. "I disagree."

Steven was confused. "What are you talking about? You just said you warned me that this was going to happen if I didn't quit gambling."

Jake shook his head. "All I said was I warned you this was going to happen. I didn't say you needed to quit."

"But that's what got me into this mess, right?"

Jake took a draw from his cigarette. "What got you into this mess was *losing*." He turned his head to blow the smoke away. "I've got a card game this Saturday night that's a sure thing."

"How do you know it's a sure thing?"

Jake leaned in toward Steven. "Because it's a trick deck, dummy. If you don't leave that game with less than fifty grand, I'll give it to you myself. That's about how much you're in the hole for, right?"

Steven cast him a sideways glance. "How did you know?"

Jake smirked. "Lucky guess. And you could use some luck, couldn't you, buddy?"

Steven looked away and took a sip of his coffee. "It's going to take more than luck to get me out of this."

"You've got a point there, Stevie. It's going to take a few heavy hitters like those thugs you've been hanging out with. We need to deal them in to raise the stakes. All you have to do is tell them to show up at the Gold Rush Saturday night at nine. I'll take it from there."

Steven's stomach churned, and he raised his hands in objection. "Time out. I won't participate in anything illegal. Let's get that straight right now."

Jake's eyes bored into him. "You think I don't already know that? You think those guys you've been hanging with don't know that?" He raised his voice. "You walk and talk—hell, you even smell like a Christian. You stick out at the Gold Rush like a sore thumb. They know you're not hardcore! That's why they've been taking advantage of you. Trust me, I've been watching."

Steven cocked his head to one side. "What's in it for you?"

Jake put out his cigarette in Steven's coffee cup. "Justice."

* * *

Jake showed Steven to the guest room.

"It's not much, but it's all yours."

"I can't thank you enough for this, man," Steven said.

"Just remember! No snoring! I've got an early shift tomorrow," Jake responded.

"Seriously, thanks, Jake." Steven stretched out his hand.

Jake shook his hand, but then pointed at him. "Don't thank me until after Saturday night!"

"Right," Steven replied as he dropped his duffle bag onto the guest room floor and closed the door.

Jake waited a few seconds to make sure Steven was truly settled in for the night, then he hurried across the hall. Closing his bedroom door behind him, he bolted for the bathroom where he turned on the exhaust fan and the faucet to drown out the sound of his vomiting. When he felt like the nausea from the cigarettes was under control, he showered and changed his clothes. He threw his jeans into the hamper and placed the gun back in his night-stand drawer—right next to the brass police shield with his name engraved on it.

He knelt beside his bed. "Dear God, thank you for bringing Steven here. Please protect him Saturday night, and reunite him with his family soon. Amen."

CHAPTER SIXTEEN

Steven Sparrow woke up in a cold sweat.

He gasped for air and looked around the room. *Where am I? Where's Holly?*

It took him several seconds to get his bearings. When he realized where he was, and why, the realization settled over him like a cold, dense fog.

He sat up and checked his cell phone. It was a few minutes before six. It had only been one night, but he already missed his family like crazy. Every morning he looked forward to seeing Olivia when she first woke up. Her hair was always in her face, as if she was playing hide-and-seek with her eyes. She'd recently graduated from her crib to a toddler bed. They called it her "big girl bed." Would she ask Holly where Daddy was this morning? What would Holly tell her?

Then, as if someone had punched him in the stomach, he remembered leaving Olivia in the car. He leaned forward and put his face in his hands. What had he been thinking? He hadn't planned to gamble yesterday. He'd needed to make a payment to the casino and had decided to drop off the check before taking Olivia to the sitter. No one under twenty-one was allowed inside.

The car doors had been locked, and he'd assumed the air conditioning left in the car would keep it cool enough. He'd thought he would only be gone for a couple of minutes.

Once inside, he'd heard the beeping and jingling of the slot machines. For some, the casino room noise would have been just that—noise. For Steven, it was an intoxicating melody that caused him to lose all judgment and sense of time. Before he'd realized it, ten, then twenty minutes had passed. He'd been so ashamed, all he'd been able to think about was getting Olivia to Vicky's house where he knew she would receive the care she needed and deserved. The most important job he had, besides being Holly's husband, was to protect Olivia. The gravity of his error hit him between the eyes.

He'd failed as a father.

He sat on the side of the bed and picked up his duffle bag. He unzipped the front pocket and pulled out his Bible. As he opened it, he said out loud, "If I'd been spending more time with you, I probably wouldn't be in this mess."

* * *

Jake Dunlop waited nervously in the leather chair across from Police Commissioner Raymond Mathis's desk. He watched intently as his captain, John Hartley, and the commissioner looked through the report he had submitted. Except for the occasional rustle of paper as the commissioner flipped the pages, the ticking of the wall clock was the only sound in the room.

After studying photos of the suspects, Commissioner Mathis spoke, almost as if to himself, saying, "All these guys have priors. How did our squeaky-clean Steven Sparrow get mixed up with this crowd?" He leaned back in his chair and then addressed Jake. "So, you're certain he can get them to show up at the Gold Rush Saturday night?"

Jake sat up straight. "Yes, sir, Commissioner."

The commissioner turned to Captain John Hartley, who was

looking over his shoulder. "See that Officer Dunlap has all of the backup he needs. I want to make sure this goes off without a hitch."

Captain Hartley replied, "Yes, sir. We're very proud of Jake."

The commissioner smiled. "This is detective-level undercover work, Jake. It could mean a promotion for you." He paused as his smiled faded. "But I have a feeling that's not why you're doing it."

"No, sir," Jake responded. "I'm sure you know the real reason."

The commissioner nodded. "Your father was one of the best cops I've ever had on my force. Then the gambling scene seduced him. Of course, the names and faces have changed over the years, but it's the same organization that's operating the Gold Rush right now. It must have been hard watching it destroy not just his career, but your family as well."

Jake's throat tightened. "And eventually take his life, Sir."

The commissioner hung his head. "There's a dark side to gambling that most people never see. The high rollers are usually the ones who get sucked into that vortex and can't get out. The people who can buy the occasional scratch-off or lottery ticket and stop there may not ever win much money. But, at the end of the day, *they* are the lucky ones."

"No argument there, sir."

The commissioner closed the folder and reached across his desk to hand it back to Jake.

"Let's get these guys."

CHAPTER SEVENTEEN

Margaret was getting ready for work when her cell phone rang. Her caller ID showed it was Julia.

"Hey! I've been trying to reach you!" Margaret exclaimed.

"I apologize for calling you so early," Julia said. "I'm about to drive over to your house."

"Where have you been?" Margaret asked. Holding her phone in one hand, she used the other to slip the strap of her shoe over her ankle. "Is everything okay?"

"Not really. I'll explain when I get there. And, Margaret?"

"Yes?"

"Put on a pot of coffee. *Strong* coffee."

* * *

There was a part of Julia that felt guilty for leaving Holly after all that had happened yesterday. But, with Claire's arrival last night, she knew Holly was in good hands. Plus, she planned to be back by lunchtime.

Before she pulled out of the driveway, she scrolled through her contacts. She tapped on Gina's name to text her.

We need to talk. Meet me at Oakwood Park at 10:00 a.m.

Julia was buckling her seatbelt and adjusting her mirror when her phone chirped.

I will be at the merry-go-round. Delete this message after reading it.

"Okay, Gina Merino," Julia said to herself, "I hope you don't mind if I bring company."

Julia arrived at Margaret's house in record time. Margaret greeted her at the door with a steaming cup of coffee.

"One sugar, just like you like it. You sounded desperate!"

Julia thanked her and made her way inside.

"What time do you have to be at work?" she asked as she sat her purse down on Margaret's kitchen counter.

Evidently Margaret wasn't interested in small talk. "Are you going to tell me what's going on?"

Julia took a sip of her coffee as they both sat down at the kitchen table. She hesitated for a moment and then said, "When we reconnected a few years ago, I had the best news in the world for you. I had the privilege—and the joy—of telling you God loved you, and that He had awesome plans for you."

Margaret looked wistful. "Yeah, that was one of the best days of my life."

Julia glanced down. "Now I have the *worst* news for you. I have to tell you that someone is planning to destroy you; not just mar your reputation or cause you to lose your job, but destroy you."

"Is that a nice way of saying somebody has threatened to kill me?" Margaret asked, half joking.

"Yes. But it's not some random, stalker-person."

Margaret gripped the arm of her chair and swallowed hard as she realized Julia was actually serious. Then she replayed what Julia had just said in her head. "Wait, you're saying it's somebody I know?"

Julia winced. "It gets worse. You were at his house last night."

Margaret recoiled. "Wyatt?"

"I'm afraid so," Julia said.

Margaret's cheeks flushed. "I can't believe this!"

Julia put her hand on Margaret's. "Why don't you go sit on the couch, and I'll bring you a cup of coffee. Maybe you should call in sick today."

Margaret nodded, picked up her phone, and walked zombie-like into the living room. After she brought Margaret a cup of coffee, Julia began filling her in on the details.

Margaret stared at the steam rising from the cup as she listened. Then she looked up as if something had clicked in her mind.

"You know, I think Wyatt's hatred for me started years ago, way before the estate settlement. When we had that unfriendly little exchange at the hospital right after his dad died, he told me how his family used to make fun of me when they read about my drug arrests. I can't believe I actually thought he'd changed."

Julia leaned forward in her chair. "You thought he'd changed because you know change is possible."

Margaret set her coffee cup on the end table beside the sofa. "You're right. I wanted to give him a chance. I was hoping he was ready to bury the hatchet. Little did I know, he was sharpening it." She raised her eyebrows. "Literally." She shook her head. "I still can't believe I went out to his estate last night! I walked right into that one. And he bugged your parents' house? This is scary, Julia. Are you sure we shouldn't contact the police?"

"The police will get involved eventually. All we have right now are Gina's suspicions and something she said she'd intercepted. And, of course, the fact that Wyatt is being uncharacteristically nice to you. It would be his word against Gina's. We both know how that would go."

Margaret groaned. "So, let me get this straight. The first part of Wyatt's scheme is to make it look like I've gone back to my old life-style. Then, he plans to poison me and make it look like a suicide?"

"It's hard to believe, but that's what Gina said."

"Here's the million-dollar question. How do we let him think he's killed me without him *really* killing me? How far do we let this go?"

"That's exactly what I'm going to ask Gina. She was really scared the last time we met. I hope she'll open up a little more today. Just think, if God hadn't put her at the Bennington estate, Wyatt's plan probably would have worked."

Margaret shuddered. "I can't believe I have another Bennington out to destroy me. It's like Horace passed the torch to Wyatt."

"The good news is that Horace changed. The better news is that God hasn't. What he did for Horace—and all of us—He can do for Wyatt. It may take something different for Wyatt to get to that point."

Margaret reached for her coffee cup. "What do you mean?"

"When Christ rescued you, you were morally and spiritually bankrupt. You were depressed, in poor health, and your finances were a disaster. Wyatt, on the other hand—"

"Is healthy, financially secure, and thinks he has the world by the tail."

"Which means he doesn't see his need for a savior. Sometimes God has to evict those things occupying the space in our hearts that was designed only for Him."

Margaret nodded. "In other words, he may need to hit rock bottom."

"Which, for Wyatt, may take something drastic, like going to jail."

"Well, we have to make this work. Nothing is going to take me away from spoiling my new little niece or nephew when he or she arrives."

Julia sipped her coffee and then coughed. Her eyes began to water. "Are you serious? Annie's pregnant?"

Margaret laughed. "She's due in January."

Julia moved over to sit on the sofa. She put her arm around Margaret. "I'm so happy for you!"

Margaret rested her head on Julia's shoulder. "It's going to take a lot more than Wyatt Bennington to get me off track. I've never had so much to live for."

Julia looked off into the distance. "I agree. If you don't mind a little musical humor, you're just getting warmed up!"

Margaret chuckled, "And I am not going to miss another concert!"

Julia smiled and then looked down at her watch. "I thought Minnie might want to come with us to meet Gina. If you don't think it's too early, I'll give her a call. We need all the help we can get today!"

CHAPTER EIGHTEEN

Joseph tapped his pencil on a chair in the band room as he waited for George Ortega to arrive. He always enjoyed their meetings. George could have retired several years ago, but he was still going full steam ahead serving as the middle school band director as well as the band director for the Gates Manor. Most days, he could run circles around Joseph. Joseph smiled as George bustled into the room, carrying a thick music folder under his arm.

He marveled at how young George looked for his age. He attributed most of it to the fact that he exercised regularly and maintained a healthy lifestyle. His olive complexion displayed minimal wrinkles for a man approaching his mid-sixties.

"Hola, Joseph," George greeted him. "Sorry I am running behind. Fernando took forever on his walk this morning, if you know what I mean."

"It's no problem. We all have those mornings." Joseph grinned, picturing the boisterous golden retriever that he'd met with George on one occasion. "Tell Fernando to try adding a little more fiber to his diet."

George laughed as he sat down and began organizing his papers on the music stand in front of his chair.

"So, what is this great idea you have for the band program?"

"I'm glad you asked," George said. "Do you remember Margaret's speech a couple of months ago at the spring concert?"

"Yes, I do. It was the one where she seemed to lose her place toward the end."

George stopped what he was doing and looked at Joseph. "So, that wasn't my imagination?"

"No, it wasn't. It was like something spooked her." Joseph turned the pages in his notebook until he had a clean page on which to take notes.

He looked up to find George smiling and shaking his head. Apparently he was amused at Joseph's outdated note-taking method. True to George being, well, *George,* Joseph knew he would make a comment.

As if on cue, George chuckled and said, "Is your horse and buggy waiting to take you home after our meeting?"

Joseph rolled his eyes. "I hate lugging my laptop everywhere. I still like doing a few things the old-fashioned way."

George stepped back and folded his arms. "Is that so?"

Joseph looked up from his notebook. "Yes, George. Why are you glaring at me like that?"

"Because, Amigo, if you are so old-fashioned, then why haven't you asked Margaret Gates out on a date yet? You know, a *real* date, with the flowers, the candy—the whole enchilada."

Joseph didn't see that one coming. He could feel his face turning red. "What? Wait. We're not...it's not like that. I could never..." he stuttered.

George laughed. "So, you *do* like her! Look man, you're not getting any younger. And ladies—regardless of their age—like to be courted. What are you waiting for?"

"Hold on a minute." Joseph held up his hand. "What does a confirmed bachelor like you know about courting?"

"Ah, more than you might think. You forget that I was married many years ago. My wife was only thirty-two when she died. I have asked God to send me another wife, but it hasn't happened yet. But, when she comes along, I will be ready. None of this *beating-around-the-bush-Joseph-Bennington-style* kind of stuff. I will sweep her off her feet!" George picked up one of the music stands and pretended to be dancing with it.

Joseph laughed. "I'll make a deal with you. You keep this Margaret thing to yourself, and I won't tell anyone you were dancing with a music stand."

George set the stand back in its place. "No, here is the deal. You ask Margaret out on a date, or I will personally tell her how you feel about her." He winked. "That was not my first dance with a music stand."

Joseph closed his notebook and placed it on the chair beside him. "It's not that simple. You know Margaret's story. It was my father who abused her. It's a miracle she even speaks to me. *And* her brother is my half-brother. I can't imagine things being more complicated."

"Do you want to know what I think?"

Joseph sighed. "What?"

George knelt down in front of Joseph's chair and looked him in the eye. "Margaret is a powerful example of how there is nothing impossible for God. Her life is one big example of 'God can do anything.' Sometimes life is just messy. We wish that it could always be served up in a neat little package, but that's not reality. God would not give you those feelings to torture you. That is my job."

Joseph smiled. "You're right."

"So, you'll talk to her?"

"No, I mean you're right that it's your job to torture me."

George's brows snapped together. "I will hold your little notebook hostage until you ask her out."

Joseph laughed and put his hands up in mock surrender. "Okay! I'll ask her out."

"Good! I don't have all morning to fight with you about this. I have to be back at the school for class at nine."

George sat down and opened his folder. "Now, we were talking about the spring concert. Do you remember when Margaret asked for more community involvement? I think I may have found a way for the community to get more involved. I've been writing a solo singing part for one of the songs the students will be performing at the Christmas concert. I think we should hold an audition and open it up to the public."

Joseph shook his head. "It amazes me how you can be such a goofball one minute and a genius the next. That's a brilliant idea!"

George scratched his head. "I think that was a compliment?"

Joseph smiled. "It was. Let's hear the song."

CHAPTER NINETEEN

The sun was inching over Minnie's house and brushing a stroke of yellow across the rooflines and treetops along her street. Minnie's back was stiff as she leaned over to get the newspaper. Out of the corner of her eye, she caught the movement of a stray newspaper page in front of one of the rocking chairs on the front porch. A gentle morning breeze lifted it up at the corners, causing it to ripple. *Probably blew out of someone's recycling bin*, she reasoned. She picked it up, intending to put it back into the recycling, but something on the front of it grabbed her attention. It was a picture of Wyatt Bennington posing with a group of high school students. The caption read, "Bennington's Benevolence Fund Assists Foreign Exchange Students." Why didn't she notice this article before? As much as she and Julia had been talking about Wyatt, she would have remembered seeing it. Then she looked at the date on the newspaper.

It was today's date.

She stepped over to the porch railing and peered up and down the street. Folded newspapers, still in their plastic sleeves, dotted stoops and sidewalks. Her own newspaper was still on the front steps.

"Now that's odd," she said out loud.

She examined the page more closely. Except for his eye color, Wyatt looked just like his dad. She remembered all the years when Horace's picture had frequently appeared in the local paper. While there had always been talk regarding his questionable business ethics, only his philanthropy had made it into print. His picture often accompanied a headline touting his having made yet another generous contribution to some local charity. His pet projects had been programs at the middle and high schools. He'd started donating to these when his sons reached that age.

There were members of the community who'd suspected Horace wasn't as interested in donations as much as tax deductions. But the majority had never seen past the large checks and smiling recipients. The notoriety hadn't done him any harm, and he'd always seemed to land on his feet in terms of overall public opinion.

Minnie read the names of the students in the picture: Annette Francois, George Haut, Chen Hu, and Rolando Merino. *Merino. There was that name again.* It was the same as Gina's. Of course, Merino was a common Spanish last name. But something about this picture looked familiar. Then she remembered. She hurried inside and dialed Julia's number.

* * *

Julia and Margaret both heard Julia's phone ringing in her purse. Julia checked the caller ID.

"Well, it must not be too early to call Minnie. She's calling me!" She answered the call and put the phone to her ear. "Good morning, Minnie! Margaret and I were just talking about you."

Minnie sounded winded as she said, "Julia, I may have found a clue to the Gina Merino mystery."

"Are you okay? You sound out of breath."

"I'm fine, dear. I probably stood up too quickly. Listen, do you think we could contact Gina about getting together?"

"Margaret and I are meeting her at the park at ten. Would you like to join us?"

"That time works for me. I'll see you both at ten o'clock."

* * *

George Ortega paused the song that was playing on his tablet. "Joseph, who are you texting? You are supposed to be listening to the song."

"I *was* listening. Margaret just let me know she isn't feeling well. She won't be coming in to work today."

George rubbed his chin. "Hmm. If she is very sick, that is not a good thing. But if she is a little sick, that is a good thing."

Joseph removed his glasses to clean a smudge. He held them up to the light while he talked. "Okay, you left genius status in a cloud of dust and have returned to being a goofball. What could possibly be good about Margaret being sick?"

George grinned. "Nothing if she is *very* sick."

"We've established that!" Joseph said as he put his glasses back on. "But what if she is," he paused to quote George with a mock-Spanish accent, *"a little sick?"*

"Then we don't have to worry about her well-being. Either way, it is an opportunity for you to reach out to her and be attentive. Send her some flowers or write her a card and leave it by her front door. Man, do I have to hold your hand through this whole process?"

"You touch my hand and I will belt you across this band room."

"Do not worry, Amigo. You are not my type. Plus, you do a lousy Spanish accent."

Joseph stared down at the floor. "Look, I know you're right. I'm scared of, well, scaring her off. She's such an amazing friend. I don't want to mess that up. What if she doesn't feel the same way? It could make our business relationship really awkward."

George patted Joseph on his shoulder. "That is why you start with little things. I have a feeling that she does like you, but it's in seed form. Seeds have to be watered."

Joseph looked up. "So, if I do little things to show I care about her—"

"It will bring to life any feelings she may have for you that haven't surfaced yet."

"Okay, I take it back."

George dramatically put his hand over his heart. "You mean I do get to hold your hand?"

Joseph raised an eyebrow. "Don't push it, Ortega." Then his expression softened. "Seriously, you are a genius and, more importantly, a good friend. Thank you."

"Now you are the one getting all mushy," George said. "Can we get back to listening to my song?"

"From what I have heard so far, I think the vocalist should be a female."

George smiled. "Perhaps you are the one who is the genius!"

CHAPTER TWENTY

Julia suspected Gina was uncomfortable with her bringing Margaret along. For starters, as soon as she and Margaret arrived, Gina excused herself to go to the bathroom. When she returned, she made little eye contact. A shadow of shame settled over her face as Julia introduced Margaret to her. It was almost as if Gina held herself partly responsible for Wyatt's actions. Perhaps that was the reason she had opted to meet with Julia instead of Margaret in the first place. But why would she blame herself for something Wyatt had done? Julia felt like the whole situation continued to churn up more questions than answers.

The three of them made their way over to a nearby set of benches arranged in a square. Julia looked over toward the entrance. There was still no sign of Minnie. Rather than spring any additional surprises on Gina, Julia told her that there would be one more friend joining them. Finally, Minnie drove into the parking lot. Julia excused herself and met her halfway.

"I left the house in plenty of time," Minnie explained, looking a little flustered. "But there was road construction on the Enoburg side of Interstate 40, and it took longer than usual to get here. How are you, dear?"

"I'm okay, but I don't think Gina is. Seeing Margaret seemed to unnerve her."

Minnie took Julia's hand and pulled her close. She spoke in low tones. Julia had to lean in to hear what she was saying.

"There may be a reason—one we don't understand yet—why you saw that response in Gina. Something strange happened this morning. The wind blew a newspaper page onto my front porch. There was a picture of Wyatt with a group of foreign exchange students. He looked so much like his dad that it reminded me of a newspaper article I saw many years ago. Let's just say Margaret may not be the only one whose life has been in danger."

"What do you mean?"

Minnie's eyes narrowed. "This situation might be more complicated than we realized. We seriously need answers."

Julia nodded. "There is only one person who can provide them."

Minnie looked over to where Margaret and Gina were sitting. "Let's just pray that she does."

* * *

The trees shading the park benches provided a barrier against the summer sun that darted in and out behind the clouds drifting across the morning sky.

As Julia introduced Minnie to Gina, Minnie held her breath. Her hunch was right. It had been decades, but Minnie Morgan never forgot a face. She also thought she saw a flash of recognition on Gina's part as well.

Even though she was a guest invited by Julia, Minnie settled in at the helm and sat down beside Gina.

"Gina, I know you and I just met, but I've been praying for you ever since Julia told me about her meeting with you. I can't imagine how difficult this is for you. But I have a feeling you're a strong woman of faith."

Gina was wearing a white cotton shirt and a pair of black dress pants—most likely one of her more casual uniforms. A tear slipped down her cheek and fell onto her blouse. Minnie looked over at Julia and Margaret. They nodded as if to encourage Minnie to continue, but Gina spoke next.

"It has been my faith that has sustained me through everything that's happened."

Now we're getting somewhere, Minnie thought.

"Faith does that," Minnie responded. "You've obeyed God and demonstrated the love of Christ by praying for Wyatt all these years. That hasn't gone unnoticed by your Heavenly Father."

"Yes, I can see those prayers are finally being answered. Not in the way I had hoped, but perhaps in the way that will best help Wyatt."

Minnie marveled at Gina's selflessness. It went above and beyond what would be expected from an employee, even one who had worked with the Bennington family for as many years as Gina had. There was still a piece of the puzzle missing—a big one. This process could take time, something they didn't have a lot of.

Julia passed a tissue, which she'd apparently dug from her purse, over to Gina. "Do you remember when you asked me if I'd ever been in prison?" she asked her.

Gina nodded as she wiped her eyes with the tissue.

"Perhaps you asked me that because, well, you've been in a prison. We talked about how there are different types of prisons, not just the kind with iron bars. Secrets can imprison us."

Minnie put her hand on Gina's shoulder. "God didn't just send you to us so you could help Wyatt, or even Margaret. He wants *us* to help *you*. You have carried this burden—whatever it is—by yourself for too long. Let us help you carry it."

The tears raced down Gina's face in earnest now. She seemed to be struggling to speak. After several attempts, she finally forced the words out.

"Mrs. Morgan, you would be surprised to learn just what I have carried!"

CHAPTER TWENTY-ONE

WYATT POURED HIMSELF A CUP OF COFFEE AND LOOKED OUT THE window over the kitchen sink. Gina had run out for groceries and wouldn't be back for an hour or so. With her and Delores both gone, he felt a little lonely this morning.

There was a conflict of sorts going on inside of him. Gina was kind and loyal. Her presence had always seemed to bring him a strange sense of comfort. But she was Hispanic and beyond that— an employee. His upbringing had been one of tolerating people outside his own social and economic class but never considering them as equals. It hadn't been communicated to him in those exact words, but his parents had modeled it. As Horace used to say, some things are *taught* and some things are *caught*. This was one of the things Wyatt had *caught* growing up.

There was a part of him that wanted to tell Gina how much he appreciated her dedication and hard work. But didn't her paycheck take care of that? Maybe he should give her a raise. Once his plan to destroy Margaret had been executed, perhaps that would be one way he could celebrate. In fact, he might just give the whole staff a raise.

Delores would be returning from Europe in three weeks. He

hoped to have everything neatly tied up by then. Margaret was scheduled to come back to the estate tonight. Ironically, everything he'd offered her to eat or drink last night had been safe. He had to earn her trust. Even the cup of coffee he'd sent her home with was just that, a cup of coffee.

Tonight would be different.

Wyatt looked at his watch again. He was impatient for Gina to get home. He could wait for her, but he was restless and wanted to get preparations underway for Margaret's visit. He whistled his way into the den and attended to details that really didn't matter, but made him feel productive nonetheless. First, he slid the pair of wingback chairs a few inches in one direction, and then back in the other, until they were positioned exactly across from each other. Next, he arranged two porcelain teacups on the serving tray, examining each to make sure they were spotless. Then he remembered he hadn't prepared the "tea" yet.

He slid his hand down the back of the liquor cabinet, expecting to find the key hanging from a hook he had installed. Wyatt was guarded about all his possessions, not the least of which was his liquor. He kept this cabinet locked as it contained several bottles of expensive scotch. He didn't want any of it to be disturbed.

"Hmmm," he said to himself out loud. "Where is that key?"

He'd used it recently, he was sure of it. Then he remembered: he'd poured himself a glass of scotch the other night during that intense thunderstorm. Perhaps he'd inadvertently stashed the key in his pants pocket. He trotted upstairs and checked through several pairs of trousers. No key.

Knowing he had no one to blame but himself, he stayed calm.

Okay, Wyatt. You've lost keys before. It will turn up eventually.

Besides, Gina had a spare. She was often required to serve drinks when he and Delores had guests. He dialed her number on his cell, but after one ring, he ended the call. Even though she would never outwardly question him, he didn't want her wondering why he was requesting the liquor cabinet key so early in the day.

The spare is probably somewhere in her room, he reasoned.

He seldom went into Gina's room, as there was rarely any reason to do so. He felt a little uncomfortable as he cracked open the door. He decided to conduct his search as quickly as possible and then leave. The last thing he wanted was for Gina to return home and find him rummaging through her personal items.

He was impressed with how tidy her room was. Her bed was made, and the toiletries displayed on her dressing table were neat and organized. He didn't see any key, though, so he proceeded to her closet.

He separated the louvered doors, which slid apart exposing a modest wardrobe consisting mostly of uniform pieces. He quickly searched through each. *Bingo!* He felt a piece of metal in the pocket of one of her aprons. Sure enough, it was the liquor cabinet key. As he reached to close the doors, the key slipped out of his hand and disappeared into an unusually large crack in the floorboards near the back of the closet.

Damn! What were the chances?

He knelt to see if he could fish it out and discovered that a couple of the boards were loose. He lifted them up and saw that the key had landed on top of a box of some sort. After making sure the key was securely in his pocket, he slowly lifted the box from its hiding place.

Wyatt was never one to give in to superstition, and he definitely wasn't religious. But for some reason he couldn't explain, picking up this box gave him a strange feeling in the pit of his stomach. He didn't know why, but he had to find out.

He tried to open it, but it was locked.

"Don't tell me I have to look for another key," he grumbled.

He sighed and shook his head. *No, not now. I can't risk getting caught.*

It would be hard enough if he had to explain being in Gina's room, looking through her clothes. He certainly wouldn't want to have to explain why he was trying to break into something she had obviously taken great pains to conceal. He carefully put the box back into its hiding place and replaced the loose boards.

He went back downstairs and tried to focus on the task at hand. In the back of his mind, he couldn't stop thinking about that box. It wasn't any of his business, and he certainly had more important things to worry about. In fact, it was silly to even think about it at all.

But what could Gina be hiding?

CHAPTER TWENTY-TWO

Margaret had been watching Gina as Julia and Minnie talked
with her. There was something odd about Gina's body language.
For starters, she didn't carry herself like someone who worked for
such an affluent family. She walked with her head down and regularly avoided eye contact. And she had a way of dissuading any
conversation from focusing entirely on her.

She reminds me of myself a few years ago. Margaret thought. *I
wonder if—*

Her breath caught in her throat when she realized that, while
these subtle nuances could indicate many things, they were typical
of someone who'd been sexually abused.

She prayed a silent prayer. *Dear God, please don't let it be so.*

If her suspicion was correct, then Margaret understood firsthand the pain Gina was hiding—and why.

Margaret had spent the better part of a lifetime keeping her
own heartache a secret. It wasn't just because of the nightmarish
memories, but the shame that had accompanied them. Like a slow-
burning fire, shame had produced a dark and dusty soot that
covered her soul. Margaret remembered what it had felt like to
finally come out of the shadows and receive cleansing and healing.

Her life now bore little resemblance to her life before. Only the power of God's love could create such beauty from the ashes.

The only way to find out if Gina had been abused was to ask her point-blank. Under normal circumstances, she wouldn't ask someone such a personal question after having just met them. But these circumstances were anything but normal.

She knelt down in front of Gina and gently reached for her hand. There was no easy way to do this. She swallowed hard. "Gina, when did...how old were you the first time Horace raped you?"

Gina's expression dulled. She barely spoke above a whisper, as if it required every ounce of her strength to say the words. "I came here from Santa Maria. My village was very poor. Everyone there was looking for a better life. As a child, I made good grades in school, and I could sing." Her eyes went from looking lifeless to displaying the slightest hint of a twinkle. She smiled meekly and said, "I was also quite pretty. I had long, silky black hair. My parents saw all of this as my ticket out of Santa Maria.

"I was young when I came here, only fourteen. Horace Bennington was providing scholarship money for foreign students to study in Enoburg. I was accepted into the program. A few families offered for me to live with them, but Horace insisted I stay at the estate. I had never seen a house like that. I thought I was finally living the American Dream..."

Her words trailed off as if she was reliving those days, but then she seemed to regroup. "Horace paid for everything; my plane ticket, my school supplies, even my new clothes." She stared off into the distance. "After that, he said I owed him. He told me if I did not do what he wanted, he would send me back home and tell everyone I had stolen from him and his family. I did not want to go home in shame. No one would believe me against someone who was so powerful." Her eyes welled with tears and her shoulders shook. She whispered, "So, I did what he wanted."

Margaret hung her head. Even though this was exactly what

she had suspected, hearing Gina say it made it real. Julia and Minnie both had tears in their eyes.

She got up and sat down beside Gina. Julia and Minnie slid in closer on the other side. They surrounded her with an embrace while she wept.

Margaret knew that, for now, there was nothing anyone could say to ease Gina's pain. She simply needed to be able to cry and know that she was no longer alone in her suffering. Minnie was the first to break the silence.

"You know, there is no plan Satan can devise against us where God isn't always one step ahead. He's still God, no matter what happens. We may not see it for a long time, but His timing is always perfect. That's why we can't ever give up!"

Gina nodded and wiped her nose with a fresh tissue Julia had given her. "As I said earlier, it has been my faith that has given me strength."

"Gina, my family went through a very dark season about the same time you arrived in Enoburg," Minnie said. "Our son, Kenneth, had been diagnosed with leukemia, and we were spending a lot of time at the hospital in the pediatric ward. We didn't take many pictures, especially as his disease progressed. But we did take a few. Margaret and Julia can tell you I'm much better with names than faces. With you, I remembered both."

Gina squinted. "What do you mean?"

"Today of all days, there is a picture in the newspaper of Wyatt with a group of foreign exchange students. The last name of one of the students is Merino."

Gina shrugged her shoulders. "That is a very common last name in Mexico."

Minnie smiled and replied, "But we aren't in Mexico, are we? I remembered a young girl from the hospital with that last name, but she had long, shiny black hair. The chemo caused you to lose your hair, didn't it? Often the hair that grows back after treatment is different in texture. Is that why your hair is curly now?"

Gina's response was direct. "Mrs. Morgan, you are right. But you are also very, *very* wrong."

Margaret rarely witnessed Minnie Morgan being caught off guard. But Gina's last comment seemed to leave her bewildered. Nevertheless, Minnie pulled out a picture from her purse. Her smile held a mix of nostalgia and heartache as she studied it.

"It's an old, old photo," she began. "Kenneth was so fond of the other children on the ward that, one day, we gathered them all together for a picture." She looked up briefly as if to take advantage of a teachable moment. "Back then, you didn't have to get permission to take a picture of someone else's child."

Her expression changed as she looked back down at the photo. She sadly shook her head. "Most of these children never made it out of the hospital. We wrote down their names and crossed them off when their obituaries showed up in the paper."

She looked up at Gina. "There was one teenage girl. She was older than the other patients. By the time we took this picture, your hair had fallen out from the chemo. This is you in the photo, isn't it?"

Margaret watched Gina as she took the photo. She briefly glanced at it and then handed it back to Minnie. Margaret could see it in her eyes; a volcano of emotion was about to erupt.

Gina nodded and answered flatly, "Yes, that was me. But I never had chemo because I never had cancer."

It was evident that, once again, Minnie was taken aback. Julia looked confused as well.

"I remember hearing you get sick during your treatments," Minnie persisted. "I was in the ladies' room when I heard you throwing up."

Margaret took that as her cue to speak. She had a feeling she knew what Gina was about to disclose. If her hunch was correct, then the horror that Gina went through—both psychologically and physically—was much worse than anything she'd endured.

Margaret turned in her seat on the bench so she could look

squarely at Gina. "Look, I know what's going on inside your head right now. I've been there. It's that moment all sexual abuse victims arrive at eventually where the big question has to be addressed: do you tell the whole story, or just the parts you think people can handle?

"I know the kind of monster Horace was, and what he was capable of. And I'm pretty sure I know what happened to you. You need to be able to talk about this without worrying about, or feeling responsible for, people's reactions. Yes, they will be shocked and appalled. Let God handle all of that. You've been protecting the Benningtons, and now you're trying to protect us. It's time for you to do something you never do, and that is to do something for *you*. It's your turn to be free."

Gina paused and then, after what appeared to be a mustering of all the strength she had left, she looked over at Minnie. "Mrs. Morgan, you were right about me being in the hospital. And yes, that was me in that picture. But you were also wrong. I never had cancer."

Minnie spoke softly as she said, "Gina, I don't understand."

Gina began to sob. She spoke louder and louder as if she was releasing years of suppressed anger. It was clear she no longer cared who heard the truth or what happened as a result.

"It was made to *look* like I had cancer," she shouted angrily. "They shaved my head and then...took pictures for the paper! They even said Horace was paying for my treatments. Can you believe that? At the same time, Mrs. Bennington flew to Switzerland where she stayed for several months. They told everyone the pregnancy was making her very sick, and she was getting special spa treatments. When back in Enoburg, I was the one throwing up in a hospital toilet!"

Minnie grabbed Julia's hand for support. "You mean—"

"I was throwing up, Mrs. Morgan, because I was pregnant. I was pregnant with Wyatt!"

CHAPTER TWENTY-THREE

J OSEPH PULLED INTO M ARGARET'S DRIVEWAY. A LL HE HAD TO DO WAS get out of the car, walk up to her front porch, and stick the greeting card in the door. He could do it.

So why wasn't he moving?

Okay, Joseph. It's just a card. Friends do this. She won't jump to conclusions. Remember what George said. "Water the seeds."

He made his way up to her front door. He inserted the card into the space between the door and the casing. *Wait, what if it falls out?*

It was a little windy. *Should I put it under the mat?*

He shook his head. *No, stupid, it's not a key. She'll never look under there.*

Then he realized how ridiculous he was being. He left the card in the door and turned to walk back to his car. As he did, he heard someone shout his name from next door.

"Hey, Joseph! She's probably already gone to the Manor."

It was Preston. He was in his SUV and dressed in a suit as though he was leaving for work.

Joseph panicked but tried not to show it. "Hey Preston, how are you doing?" He crossed over the yard between their houses.

Preston put his SUV in park and reached his hand out the

window to shake Joseph's. "I'm doing well. I hope you are." He nodded over toward Margaret's house. "Is, uh, everything okay?"

"Sh-sure," Joseph stammered. "Yes, it is. It's fine. Everything is okay."

Preston's expression confirmed to Joseph that he'd just sounded like a complete idiot. He quickly changed the subject. "Hey, Margaret told me the good news! Congratulations on becoming a dad!"

Preston's expression melted into a proud smile. "Thank you! Yeah, we're excited. So…is there anything I can do? Do you want me to let Margaret know you were here?"

Joseph responded much more quickly, and with a bit more energy than he had intended. "NO! I mean, no. I received a text message earlier that she wasn't feeling well today. I thought I would check in on her."

"So, this wasn't something you could have done, maybe, over the phone?" Preston appeared to be suppressing a smile.

Joseph knew it was wrong, but he lied anyway. "I tried, I but couldn't reach her. Look, I don't want to keep you. It looks like you're on your way to work, and I need to get back to the hospital. It was great to see you!"

"You too, Joseph. Take care."

* * *

Preston put his car in reverse and watched Joseph through his rearview mirror. He spoke the command to his phone, "Call Annie."

When she answered, he said, "Honey, I just had the weirdest conversation with Joseph Bennington. If I didn't know better, I'd say he has a crush on my sister!"

CHAPTER TWENTY-FOUR

Having helped Margaret heal from sexual abuse, Julia was well acquainted with the ugliness of the issue. But Gina's experience took it to a whole new level. Julia searched her heart for something—anything—she could say to help soothe her pain.

"I know I speak for all of us when I say we believe you," Julia said. "It's important that you know that. If we could have protected you, we would have. We didn't get that opportunity. All we have is right now and going forward. You're not alone anymore."

"You are the first people I have ever told." Gina said. "I desperately wanted to share it with someone for years, but I had to wait until the right time. Now you understand why I have prayed for Wyatt and have not given up. As crazy as this may sound, Wyatt gave me a reason to keep going. I knew he was mine, even if no one else did. I couldn't abandon him."

Margaret leaned forward in her seat. "After Wyatt was born, did the sexual abuse continue?"

Gina glanced heavenward. "Thank God, no. I had hoped it was because somewhere deep inside of Horace there was a sense of right and wrong, even though he did not answer to it most of the time. More than likely, it was because I was no longer inno-cent, not to mention a mother, and I didn't appeal to him anymore."

"What about Mrs. Bennington?" Minnie asked. "How did she deal with all of this?"

"Mrs. Bennington was a compassionate woman. I don't know how she ended up with Horace. Like me, she didn't have a lot of choices in that household. Horace ruled with an iron fist. If she dared to disagree with him, he threatened to cut her off financially. When it came to having children, she had hoped to have several, but he only wanted one. Horace approached everything like a business deal. Starting a family was no exception. I overheard him saying that with more than one heir, there was a greater chance his hard-earned money would get squandered. I think Mrs. Bennington's pregnancy with Joseph was so she could have a child that wasn't just Horace's, but hers as well."

"Did she ever mistreat you? I mean, besides the obvious?" Margaret asked.

"Besides the obvious, no. She was otherwise very kind to me. A few weeks after Wyatt was born, she arranged for a tutor to come to the estate so I could finish high school. After that, I was offered a job to stay on as an employee. I think they wanted me there to help with Wyatt. When he was a baby, he did so much better with me than with either of them." She paused as a faint smile crossed her lips. "He knew who his real mother was."

Julia couldn't imagine how any child who had spent time with Gina could have turned out like Wyatt. That, along with several other questions, raced through her mind. One was at the forefront, but Minnie asked it first.

"Gina," Minnie began and then hesitated as if dreading the answer. "Do you know if there were others?"

Gina stared down at the ground. "Let's just say the work you are doing at the Manor is very important. There are more abuse victims out there than you realize." She stopped for a moment and looked out over the park. "Have you heard the expression *money talks?* Well, when it came to the Bennington's money, it said *be quiet.*"

Gina jumped as she heard her phone ring. She took it out of her purse and exclaimed, "Oh my goodness, it has been an hour! I still have to go to the market. And Wyatt tried to call me."

Julia checked her watch. She couldn't believe how quickly the time had passed.

Margaret spoke up. "We definitely don't want Wyatt asking why your grocery trip took so long. However, we still need to discuss a plan for my visit tonight."

Julia wiped the sweat off her forehead. The shade afforded earlier by the trees was offering little relief as the sun rose higher in the sky. She was glad they were wrapping up this meeting.

She picked up where Margaret left off. "We understand it's important to let Wyatt think his plan is succeeding. What we *don't* understand is how we accomplish that without Margaret being harmed. How will we know when he is attempting to serve her something that is spiked, or worse, poisoned?"

Gina thought for a moment. "Margaret, Joseph has access to the hospital lab, right?"

Margaret nodded. "Yes, of course."

"With his position of authority, can he order something to be processed quickly?"

"I would think so."

"How about this? After I return to the estate, I will suggest Wyatt set up the food and beverages ahead of time. I will spin it like I am proud of him for his hospitality toward Margaret." She rolled her eyes. "Unfortunately, if I make it all about him, he will take the bait. As soon as I know what he will be serving, I will take samples and leave them in the mailbox. Margaret, you come by, get the samples, and deliver them to Joseph for immediate testing at the lab."

Minnie looked concerned. "What if Margaret is seen by Wyatt or one of the staff? She isn't scheduled to arrive until later this evening."

Gina pensively bit her lip and then responded, "If someone sees you, perhaps you can explain that you had written down the wrong time for the meeting and didn't realize it until after you had arrived on the property."

Minnie added, "You could also leave him a note in the mailbox saying you will return at the correct time. That would cover your tracks if Wyatt or anyone else sees you at the mailbox."

Gina nodded. "Good idea, Mrs. Morgan."

Margaret put up her hand. "Wait, even if this works, we have another problem. Joseph has no idea what Wyatt has been plotting. Should we tell him, or would it be better if we didn't?"

"We have to tell him," Julia replied. "We need his help."

Minnie cocked her head to one side. "Not necessarily. Does Joseph really need to know where the samples came from? Couldn't Margaret tell him something like...we were conducting an experiment to detect controlled substances in food?"

"Minnie Morgan, are you suggesting that we *lie*?" Julia pretended to be shocked.

Putting on a pious façade, Minnie replied, "We're not *lying*; we're just withholding non-essential information."

They all laughed and agreed that Joseph should receive only *essential* information, and on an as-needed basis.

The plan settled upon, Gina hurried over to the taxi that was waiting for her. Minnie, Margaret, and Julia watched until the car was out of sight and their view consisted only of the heat rising from the parking lot pavement.

Minnie seemed deep in thought. She frowned and shook her head.

"How many others do you think there were?"

CHAPTER TWENTY-FIVE

Holly awoke to the sound of Claire and Olivia playing in the nursery. Despite everything that had happened in the past twenty-four hours, she had to smile. Claire had helped her to take her eyes off the ugliness of the situation and place them on what only could be seen through the eyes of faith. Having been submerged in a situation that made her feel so completely out of control, it was great to be reminded that her Heavenly Father was *always* in control.

Her heart ached as she turned over and put her hand on the side of the bed where Steven usually slept. She wanted to go back to sleep and wake up to find it was all a bad dream. *How could this be happening?*

She sat up in bed and took her Bible out of her nightstand drawer. When was the last time she and Steven had studied the Bible together? She regularly had her own personal devotions, but why hadn't they studied the Scriptures as a couple? Had they become too busy with work and raising a daughter? She didn't know how they had ended up in this dark place. What she did know was where she could find the way out. She opened to her last study, which was from the book of John, and began to read.

* * *

Even though Steven had a problem with gambling, he had an even bigger problem with *gamblers.*

Jake was right about him sticking out at the Gold Rush like a sore thumb. Most of the regulars were shady and made Steven uncomfortable. That's why he dreaded contacting Rusty, Tyrone, and Pete about the game Saturday night. He definitely didn't want to call them too early, so he waited until he got to the office.

Pete and Tyrone both said yes, but Rusty was the one with the deep pockets. Getting him to show up was Steven's one opportunity, perhaps his only opportunity, to get back the money he had lost.

Getting his family back would be a different matter altogether.

Steven dialed Rusty's number. It rang four times and then went to voicemail. He steadied his nerves and made his pitch.

"Rusty? It's Steven. There's a high stakes game at the Gold Rush this Saturday night. Jake says it should be a big payout. Let me know if you're in."

His heart was pounding as he slid the phone into his back pocket.

He'd just gotten his focus back on his work when his cell phone vibrated. It was a text from Rusty. He held his breath.

Deal me in. See you Saturday night.

He immediately dialed Jake's number.

"Jake, it's all set for tomorrow night."

Jake sounded unimpressed. "Are you sure about that? I can't have these guys not showing up. My neck is on the line with this one. For that matter, so is yours."

Jake's words stung and were a sober reminder of what a dangerous situation he had gotten himself into.

"I'm as sure as I can be. Rusty just confirmed."

"Well, then we shouldn't have anything to worry about. Your troubles will be over soon, pretty boy."

Steven wanted to believe Jake was right. His addiction had cost him so much more than fifty thousand dollars. Even if he won all of that back tomorrow night, what would it take to win back Holly's trust and respect? Gambling had been a game of chance, but he wasn't willing to take any more chances, especially when it came to his family. He thought for a moment. There was one more phone call he had to make.

He closed his office door.

CHAPTER TWENTY-SIX

GINA RETURNED, TO THE BENNINGTON ESTATE TO FIND THE STUDY already set up for Wyatt's meeting with Margaret. She winced at the thought of how premeditating Margaret's murder had energized Wyatt and turned him into the perfect host. Her mission would continue to be keeping Margaret safe. She couldn't allow herself to dwell on the fact that she herself shared a home with a potential killer. However, every now and then, the reality of it sent a chill down her spine.

She'd just begun putting away the groceries when Wyatt burst into the kitchen. He immediately started rummaging through the bags. He reminded her of a child searching for a surprise his parents might have picked up for him at the store. Gina assumed a professional posture and politely asked him if he had decided on a dessert for tonight's meeting. She also made it a point to compliment him on how nice the study looked.

"Actually, I do have a dessert selected. I picked up some pastries from the bakery."

"What about a beverage? Shall I prepare coffee?"

"That won't be necessary," Wyatt answered, loudly crunching on an apple he'd just polished on his shirtsleeve. "We're having an old-fashioned tea party tonight. I already have a pot of water prepared. We'll be serving Darjeeling in the study."

"Very well," Gina responded as she stowed the remainder of the apples in the refrigerator and closed the door. "I will be happy to serve the refreshments. What time do we expect Miss Gates?"

"Eight o'clock. Last night turned out to be more of a time for introductions and getting acquainted. Tonight, I plan to get right down to business. Please make sure we're not interrupted."

"Yes, Mr. Bennington. In fact, since this is such an important meeting for you, why don't I have Bivens cut some fresh flowers from one of the gardens? I'll arrange them in a vase. If you show me where the pastries are, I'll make sure they are displayed on the appropriate tray."

Wyatt grinned. It sickened her to think that he could derive such pleasure from a plan to destroy someone else's life. It had both consumed him and deceived him into believing he was the exception to the rule, and that consequences didn't apply to him.

"The flowers would be a perfect touch," he responded in a day-dreamy kind of way. "The pastries are already on a tray in the study. I've got everything under control."

That's where you're wrong, Gina thought.

She waited until Wyatt left the room before she casually made her way into the study, acting as if she was checking on the tea and pastries. The pastries were large cinnamon buns. There were only two. She had no idea which one, if either, was tainted.

Dear God, she silently prayed, *please show me what to do.*

As soon as she finished her prayer, she had an idea. She searched through the rooms downstairs until she found Wyatt. He was in his office and had just putted a golf ball down a narrow strip of artificial turf. She knocked frantically, pretending to be distraught.

"Mr. Bennington, I apologize for disturbing you."

Wyatt waited until the ball slipped down into the hole before he looked up. "What is it? Is something wrong?"

"I was dusting in the study and accidently knocked over the

pastry tray. Neither of the pastries hit the floor, but it did disturb the icing and they may not look as nice as they did before. Should I replace them with fresh ones?"

Wyatt looked unconcerned. "Fresh ones won't be necessary. I'm sure those are fine."

Wyatt was a perfectionist, and ordinarily, he would have insisted she replace the pastries.

"Also, are you sure two pastries are enough? I know how much you like cinnamon buns."

Wyatt retrieved the golf ball and focused on perfecting his next shot.

"I won't be indulging tonight, Gina. I'm cutting back on my desserts between now and when Delores gets back from Europe."

He stood up straight and watched as the ball rolled into the hole once again. He looked over his shoulder at her. "I can't have her coming home to a fat husband, now can I?"

Gina forced a smile. "Of course not. Thank you, Mr. Bennington."

She prayed a silent prayer of thanks as she made her way back into the den. Without realizing it, Wyatt had just told her that both pastries were either spiked or poisoned.

She took the plastic baggie out of her apron pocket and pinched off a sample from each pastry. With Wyatt thinking they had been dropped, he wouldn't question what appeared to be a couple of blemishes. She also took out an empty pill bottle and filled it with a sample of the water and a few of the tealeaves. She placed the items in a paper lunch bag and carried the bag out to the mailbox.

She texted Margaret.

The check is in the mail!

CHAPTER TWENTY-SEVEN

Margaret had just unlocked her front door when she received Gina's text. She would call Joseph on her way to the Bennington estate.

First, though, she needed to find out who was so thoughtful as to leave a card for her while she was out. She opened the envelope and quickly read the verse on the front of the card so she could get to the signature inside.

Fondly, Joseph.

She read the card again, slower this time. Typical of Joseph, it was lighthearted and made her laugh. She assumed he had dropped it off thinking she wasn't feeling well. Little did he know how much she needed to be cheered up, considering what was really going on. The kindness of his gesture touched her at a depth disproportionate to receiving a simple drug store greeting card. She'd never had a man do something for her without expecting something in return. Potential romantic relationships had rarely advanced beyond hook-ups and one-night stands. Since drugs and alcohol had usually been involved, she had no recollection of many of them.

Not that this was necessarily problematic. Back then, remembering was something she preferred not to do. Her life had been one big effort to forget. For the first time, she had something she wanted to hang on to, even if it was just a greeting card. Before leaving the house, she grabbed a magnet and attached the card to the front of her refrigerator.

As she pulled out of her driveway, she marveled at how Joseph's timing was perfect and horrible at the same time. The Joseph she would thank for the get-well card would be the same one she would have to lie to about the samples she needed tested.

And if Margaret was out of practice at anything, it was lying.

She used to be quite proficient at it. In the past, when people would ask her how she was doing, her first inclination had been to pretend everything was fine. Then there were the times when she'd put on a tough exterior. In those cases, she'd simply pretended she didn't care that people were concerned about her. Receiving love would have required her to open her heart. Opening up made her vulnerable to getting hurt, and she had been hurt enough. It had been easier to keep her heart off-limits to everyone. Preston was the only person she had ever allowed to get close. Even though he was her brother, she'd still felt unworthy and undeserving of his love. It was a miserable way to live.

In this situation, she was going to be lying, *sort of*, to protect not only her heart, but also her very life. She hoped Joseph would buy the story Minnie had come up with.

She dialed his number.

He answered after only one ring. "Hello, Margaret! How are you?"

Margaret responded, "I'm fine!" Then she remembered. *Wait, I called in sick!*

She quickly added, "I'm actually feeling better. I think part of it has to do with a card I found in my door this morning. It made me laugh. Maybe laughter is the best medicine!"

Joseph seemed pleased. "Well, I'm glad to be of service! Are you on your way back to work?"

"Not yet. I need a favor. I have a couple of food samples that need to be tested at the hospital lab. We're checking for harmful substances. With the work we do, it could be helpful to see how quickly we can get lab results back. If I dropped them off, say, in an hour, when could they be ready? You know, like if it was a real emergency?"

There was a quiet pause, which made Margaret a little nervous. Then Joseph responded.

"So, what are you looking for in the food? Is this to check for drugs or are we looking for bacteria spoilage, like salmonella?"

Margaret was made aware all too quickly of how *leaving out non-essential information* is first cousin to lying. She wanted to come up with an answer that was as close to the truth as possible.

"To be honest," she started, and for the first time in the conversation, she really was, "we're not sure what we're looking for. Right now, I just need your help. I can give you more information later."

Evidently Joseph was satisfied. "Well, if the lab isn't too busy, I can put in a word for you and have the results in a couple of hours."

Margaret breathed a sigh of relief. "Thank you, Joseph. You're the best!"

"Well, I'm glad you've finally realized that!"

Normally Margaret would have laughed off a comment like that coming from him. But for some reason, this time was different. He'd agreed to help her without having to know all the details. That spoke volumes about the level of trust and respect he had for her. Then she remembered how she'd felt when she read his card. It was a small gesture, but it had showcased his sincerity and big heart. Her response was from the bottom of hers.

"Maybe I have, Joseph. Maybe I have."

CHAPTER TWENTY-EIGHT

Time had been a tricky thing for Holly since Steven left. It had only been a couple of days, but it felt like longer. Maybe it was because the real Steven hadn't been there in months. Claire's visit, on the other hand, was passing by way too quickly. Thanks to her little sister's support and encouragement, Holly wasn't as nervous now about being alone.

After tending to a few work emails, she made her way downstairs to the kitchen where Claire was preparing lunch, and Olivia was "helping." It was such an endearing scene that Holly quickly found her phone and began taking pictures from the stairwell. Then, when she overheard the conversation ensuing, she switched the camera setting from picture to video.

Olivia was spreading peanut butter on a slice of bread with a spoon. Some of the peanut butter was landing on the bread, but most of it was sticking to her face as she licked the spoon each time before dipping it back into the jar. She was sitting on her knees in a bar chair positioned at the counter next to where Claire was chopping fruit. At first the conversation was about how to properly make a peanut butter sandwich. Olivia's questions were so entertaining that Holly had to suppress a chuckle more than once. Then the conversation took a turn she wasn't expecting.

"Aunt Cwaire, where is my daddy? I miss him."

Claire looked up from slicing an apple. Holly held her breath, wondering how Claire would handle this.

Claire paused for a moment, as if configuring an answer that would satisfy a two-year-old's understanding of an otherwise complicated, grown-up situation. She put the knife down and picked up Olivia. She sat her up on the counter.

"Olivia, your daddy misses you, too. He loves you very much."

"But where is he?" she insisted.

Claire gently pushed Olivia's hair out of her eyes. "Do you remember when your daddy left you in the hot car the other day?"

Holly's heart raced as she quietly moved the camera in a little closer to the kitchen.

Olivia looked down and swung her legs back and forth. "Uh-huh."

"Well, that was a bad thing for Daddy to do. Sometimes when we do bad things, we have to be punished so we can learn not to do those things ever again."

Olivia seemed to be processing what Claire was saying, and then looked up at her. "Like time out?"

Claire smiled. "Yep! Like time out."

Olivia tilted her head to one side. "When will he be back?

"Well, knowing your daddy, I'm sure he already feels very sad about what happened. He will be home soon."

Claire looked intently at Olivia. "Okay?"

Olivia smiled. "Okay!"

"Good! I need you to help me get lunch ready, Miss Peanut Butter Face!"

Oliva giggled as Claire gave her a hug before picking her up and setting her back in the chair. Holly stopped recording and wiped her eyes. Claire had handled the situation with such grace, and it was one less conversation she would have to have with

Olivia. Perhaps it was better those answers came from Claire, as Holly might have let her emotions get the better of her.

Had Holly known the direction the conversation was going to take, she probably wouldn't have recorded it. In fact, why did she? She could have stopped it at any time. Videos of two-year-olds were supposed to display tender moments of childhood innocence. They should capture bare feet splashing through mud puddles and bright eyes spellbound by Fourth of July fireworks. The only memory she'd preserved was one of Olivia's confusion and heartache. It was so unfair for children to have to bear the consequences of circumstances over which they have no control.

Then she wondered about her own actions. *Should I have made Steven leave? Did that make matters worse?* She paused to consider that question. *No,* she decided, *I did the right thing. He needed a wake-up call.*

In fact, perhaps *that's* why she kept recording. Maybe instinctively she'd wanted to have something to show Steven that would further demonstrate how destructive his choices had been. She typed in his cell phone number and hit send.

She wiped her eyes, stood up straight, and joined Claire and Olivia in the kitchen.

Olivia's face lit up, "Mommy, I made a sandwich!"

Holly kissed Olivia on the cheek. "Well done, sweetheart!"

She gave Claire a hug and whispered in her ear, "Well done, Aunt Cwaire."

CHAPTER TWENTY-NINE

Margaret hurried through the hospital parking lot with the paper bag she'd retrieved from the Bennington's mailbox. It made her nervous to think, depending on the results, she could be in possession of evidence that could implicate Wyatt for attempted murder. She wondered if this was how Joseph had felt when he'd been on his way to the lab with that single lock of Horace's hair. Those results had proven Horace was her brother Preston's biological father and had changed all their lives forever.

Once inside the hospital, she navigated through a maze of signs, arrows, and color-coded zones. She finally located the lab and was greeted by a technician who had already been briefed by Joseph. "Hi, I'm Carlton. You must be Margaret."

"Yes," she replied. "It's nice to meet you."

Carlton looked like he'd just stepped off the set of a crime show mystery series. He had thick glasses and equally thick, wiry hair that appeared to have been estranged from a comb or brush for a considerable amount of time.

"Here is a list of what to look for in the samples," Margaret said as she handed him a piece of paper.

Carlton studied the list. "Bacteria, poison, drugs, or alcohol?"

"That's right," Margaret responded.

She could feel her heart racing. *Okay, Mr. Lab Technician, don't start asking too many questions.*

He looked up and smiled. "If nothing else, this will be a departure from what I normally see under the microscope. Perhaps you've just made my day a little more interesting."

Margaret suppressed a chuckle. *Interesting doesn't even come close.*

She heard the door open. Several people entered the room and got in line behind her. Not wanting to stay any longer than she had to anyway, she took this as her cue to leave.

"Well, if that's all you need, I won't take up any more of your time."

"I'm all set," Carlton replied. "I'll call you as soon as I have the results."

As Margaret exited through the lobby, she noticed a tall figure wearing a lab jacket and a hospital employee badge watching her leave. Brushing off the awkward feeling of his stare, she continued out the doors.

* * *

As Margaret faded out of Carlton's peripheral view, a man he'd never seen before stepped up to the side of the long line that had formed. *He must be new,* Carlton thought, observing the man's lab coat and authorization badge. He surely would have remembered someone that tall.

Carlton had stopped working on Margaret's samples to assist the other waiting patients and staff members.

The man smiled at the people in line as he stepped behind the counter and put his hand on Carlton's shoulder. "Why don't you let me take over here so you can work on Mr. Bennington's project?"

Carlton breathed a sigh of relief. "That would be great!"

The man took over the job at the front desk for the next hour or so while Carlton worked steadily in his office. As he was finishing, he heard a light knock at his door.

"Is there anything else I can do for you?"

Carlton spun around in his office chair to find the tall man holding the door open slightly. "Wow, your timing was perfect! I just completed the samples Mr. Bennington authorized. There's no way I could have finished so quickly without your help. Did he send you?"

The man smiled. His voice was kind, yet he spoke with authority. "You could say that." He glanced over his shoulder toward the front desk. "I logged in all of the samples that came in this afternoon, and the blood vials have been stored in the centrifuge. The results are already recorded."

Carlton was shocked and more than a little puzzled. "Wait, I appreciate you cataloguing everything for me, but I can take it from here."

"It was no trouble. I think you'll discover my evaluations to be accurate. You'll never meet anyone who understands the importance of blood more than I do."

The man started to leave and then came back. "Oh, and by the way, Chip, the next time you see Joseph, tell him he should invite you to church sometime."

The office phone rang. Carlton quickly turned and put the caller on hold, but when he turned back around, the man was gone.

Carlton was dumbstruck. The only person who had ever called him Chip was his grandmother, and she'd been gone for years.

Who was that guy?

CHAPTER THIRTY

Margaret turned off the faucet in the shower. She had bathed as quickly as possible since she heard an early evening thunderstorm announcing its arrival. It was the longest she'd allowed herself to be away from her phone since she'd dropped off the lab samples. She towel-dried her hair and put on her bathrobe. Her phone chirped from the nightstand. She rushed barefoot into her bedroom where she picked it up and then, just as quickly, put it back down again. After a moment or so of self-coaching, she typed in her password. Sure enough, there was a text from an unknown number she assumed must be Carlton.

The water contains a highly concentrated form of ethanol. The pastries contain trace amounts of oxycodone. The amount detected is not toxic with moderate ingestion. However, consumption of a single serving of either of these, and especially both together, could cause serious cognitive impairment. I hope this info is helpful.

Margaret felt numb all over as she sat down on the side of her bed. "You bet your boots it's helpful," she said out loud and immediately forwarded the text to Gina, Minnie, and Julia. Their worst suspicions, and fears, had been confirmed.

Gina was the first to text back.

Not surprised, unfortunately. Not exactly murder, thank goodness. But it does sound like he's setting you up for something. I picked up more cinnamon buns from the bakery. I also replaced the water with a fresh pot. Wyatt still thinks the refreshments are spiked. You will need to make him think he has succeeded in making you impaired. I hope you are a good actress!

Margaret laughed wryly. "You have no idea."

Julia responded, *Be careful! I'll have my phone with me all evening. Text me if you need anything. Bill and I can be there at a moment's notice.*

Minnie's response encouraged her the most. *You've been through worse! God is on your side. If He is for you, who can be against you?*

Margaret certainly was no stranger to trouble. She understood that living for Christ didn't mean life would be easy. Storms would still rage from time to time. The difference was now they served to *refine* her rather than *define* her. Still, this situation was affecting her on a deeper level than anything had in years.

She checked the time. She had an hour before she was scheduled to meet with Wyatt. She walked over to her bedroom window. The storm was producing a backdrop of swaying treetops and windblown rain swatting against the side of her house. This was her favorite spot to practice her music. Maybe that's what she needed.

She sat down in the chair and picked up her flute. Ignoring the sheet music displayed on the stand, she took a deep breath.

She began to play a melody. It was a song of worship written measure by measure, note by note. If she could have, she would have played it forever. When she reached the end, she stood up, placed her flute back on the chair and then crumbled to the floor by the side of her bed.

Her shoulders began to shake as she wept. *Lord,* she prayed, *I'm sorry that I'm not stronger right now. I'm tired of my heart getting beat up. I can't believe another Bennington is trying to destroy me. When will it ever end?*

She buried her head on the side of her bed and cried. Then she felt something warm on her back. She turned around slowly and looked out the window.

The rain was still pouring, and the wind was still blowing. But a section of the clouds had parted, allowing the sun to break through.

A familiar voice spoke to her heart saying, *Don't be afraid, beloved. Remember, I prepare a table before you in the presence of your enemies.*

Margaret closed her eyes and basked in the warmth of the sun and her Heavenly Father's love. She knew of nothing more powerful or more life-changing than this love. It was here, in the presence of the One who *is* love, where she could exchange her sorrow for joy. She felt strengthened now, better equipped to complete her mission tonight. Regardless of the cost, she would choose forgiveness instead of self-pity. More importantly, in the face of Wyatt's unbridled hatred, she would choose love.

After allowing herself a few more minutes just to linger, she finished getting dressed and headed for the Bennington estate.

* * *

Joseph had abandoned trying to focus on files and paperwork and decided to take a walk down to the hospital lab. It would serve two purposes: he could check on the progress of Margaret's project and clear his head at the same time. He kept replaying his phone conversation with her in his mind. *Had she really said she realized "he was the best?" Was it just casual banter, or was it more?* Perhaps George had been right, and the greeting card had watered a seed. Either way, there was no *bad* way to interpret it. The whole thing had buoyed his spirits.

When he entered the lab, Carlton seemed eager to speak with him. "Mr. Bennington, I've finished those samples your friend dropped off. There's something you need to see."

Carlton was the newest addition to the hospital lab staff. In the six months since he'd been hired, he'd increased the lab's productivity substantially. Additionally, he'd caught a couple of diagnostic errors missed by more seasoned technicians. Joseph followed him to where he had been working on the samples Margaret dropped off. Carlton quickly sat down in front of a microscope and adjusted the slide underneath the lens. He stepped aside so Joseph could look.

"I've seen numerous types of alcohol under a microscope," Carlton explained.

Joseph raised an eyebrow and looked over at Carlton who smiled sheepishly. "It's something science nerds do in college when they have too much time on their hands."

Joseph laughed and then focused back on the slide. "So, what's so special about this alcohol?"

"Without going into a lot of detail, which fascinates me but would bore you, what you're looking at is something that's really potent. If I had to guess, I'd say it came from a bottle of the infamous Everclear."

Joseph looked up. He didn't know what to say. How odd was this?

"Can you repeat that brand name?"

Carlton quickly obliged, "Everclear. It originated—"

Joseph cut him off. "I know what Everclear is. Strange. Who would still have any of that stuff?"

Carlton raised an eyebrow. "You do know that Everclear is illegal in our state, right? You can't buy it here anymore."

Joseph nodded. "Yes. My dad had a stash, years before it was outlawed. Wyatt made sure he kept a bottle. I've seen it in his liquor cabinet. I'm sure the law enforcement dignitaries he's entertained have seen it, too. Come to think of it, my brother may possibly be the only person in this county who still has any. Or, at the very least, the only person influential enough to get away with it."

"And that's not all," Carlton said, switching the slides. "The Everclear was in the liquid sample. This is what was in the food sample."

"Is that what I think it is?" Joseph asked, squinting into the lens.

"If you're thinking that it's oxycodone, then yes. Which is also illegal without a prescription, I might add."

Joseph's good mood crumbled as he looked back down at the slide. He muttered under his breath, "This doesn't make any sense. This doesn't make any sense at all!"

CHAPTER THIRTY-ONE

Margaret rang Wyatt's doorbell at precisely eight o'clock. She could feel, and hear, her heart pounding. It was so loud she wondered if anyone else would be able to hear it.

This time it was the butler who answered the door. He was a distinguished-looking older man about Gina's age. Margaret wondered if he'd been working for the Benningtons as long as Gina had.

"Good evening, Miss Gates. Please come in."

As Margaret entered the house, Gina was waiting for her. Gina quietly told the butler she would show Margaret to the study. She gestured to the room behind her while she spoke, and glancing in that direction, Margaret could see Wyatt had already taken a seat in the study. He stood up when she and Gina entered the room.

Okay Margaret, she thought, *showtime!*

"Miss Gates, I'm so glad you could come back over this evening!" He shook her hand before she took her seat in the wing-back chair across from him.

Margaret had already determined the way to Wyatt's heart was through his ego. "No, Wyatt, I should be thanking you."

She had a small recorder in an outside pocket of her purse

taping the entire conversation. She didn't know if it would be admissible in court, or if he would even discuss anything with her that would expose his guilt, but she would have it just in case.

Wyatt smiled. It was an evil smile. Margaret's stomach twisted.

She continued, "I can't tell you how much I appreciate you offering to make a donation to the Gates Manor. Hopefully others will follow your example of generosity."

Margaret had expected him to use the compliment as a springboard for more bragging about himself, but he didn't respond. She could tell his focus had shifted.

"I want us to get right down to business. However, I would be a rude host if I didn't offer you a cup of tea and a pastry. Gina, would you please serve Miss Gates some refreshments."

She noted the subtle difference from their previous encounter. Last night he'd merely offered refreshments. Tonight, he hadn't asked; he simply had them served, negating her opportunity to turn them down without seeming rude.

Without a word, Gina stepped forward and poured the tea and placed a cinnamon bun on one of the crystal dessert plates.

She asked Margaret if she needed sugar or cream. Margaret was careful to not make direct eye contact with her as she answered. She blew at the steam before sampling it. She wouldn't have any sort of reaction until after several sips but did make a point to comment on the flavor.

She glanced up at Gina. "Thank you. It's delicious."

Wyatt seemed to be studying her more than looking at her, which made her uncomfortable.

He took the lead in the conversation. "I think the best strategy for my donation is a Charitable Lead Trust. It would benefit me in terms of tax deductions for a designated period of time. During that time, the Manor would receive the interest payments. You know, it's important we all have backup forms of income, especially in the event of an unexpected passing. None of us really know how long we have on this earth."

Margaret wondered if Wyatt was saying this so he could have

bragging rights when she "mysteriously" died. How wise he would appear to have said it just days before her apparent suicide. She could picture him sadly shaking his head and telling everyone that one of the reasons he'd reached out to her was because she'd seemed depressed. Perhaps that's why she had begun drinking again. Ironically, he could emerge as a hero of sorts.

She agreed, "You're absolutely right. Preparation is key." They proceeded to discuss the details of his offer for the next several minutes.

When Margaret estimated that enough time had passed since she'd first started consuming the "spiked" refreshments, she decided it was time for her acting career to begin. She gulped down the rest of the tea. *The next part of this evening might be fun!*

Knowing the conversation was being recorded, Margaret decided not to waste her fifteen seconds of drunken fame. She looked at Wyatt and giggled. "Come again? I'm sorry. I'm having a little trouble following."

Wyatt appeared to be thrilled to go over the details again.

Margaret began to slur her speech. "I think I'll try this yummy cinnamon bun." She raised her teacup in the air, looking at Gina. "Can I get seconds?"

Gina quietly refilled Margaret's teacup while Margaret took an oversized bite of her cinnamon bun. She continued talking, more loudly, with a big wad of cinnamon bun stuffed in her jaw.

"You're so much smarter than I am, Wyatt. I don't understand all of that land and giving and deductions rigmarole." Margaret flopped her hand back and forth while she talked. "Is there any way you can put what you just said in writing?"

Wyatt seemed amused. "I had every intention of doing just that. I wanted your approval first before I had the paperwork drawn up."

Margaret took a loud slurp of her tea. "Well, you certainly have my approval. When can I expect to see that paperwork?"

Wyatt leaned forward in his chair. "How about I touch base

with my attorneys tomorrow? I can't make any promises, but I may be able to pull some strings and have it ready by dinnertime."

"Perfect!" Margaret raised her teacup once more, this time as if toasting to Wyatt's idea.

She figured Wyatt would want to meet again, but she had to make sure that *he* invited *her*. It had to be all him.

"So, if your attorneys get the paperwork finished tomorrow, I can expect it in the mail by," she paused and began counting on her fingers. "Tuesday?"

She looked at Wyatt for a response. For a split second, she thought she detected a flash of fear. He appeared flustered. Evidently, he'd assumed she'd return for a second visit to sign the documents rather than simply having them mailed. Perhaps for the first time that evening, something hadn't gone as he'd expected.

"Why, no!" Wyatt said abruptly. He then took a breath as if he was reeling in his emotions. He proceeded more calmly, "I don't completely trust the mail system. I'd much rather conduct that transaction in person. Plus, we'll want to take pictures for the newspaper."

"Are you absolutely sure? Mailing it would be easier. I don't want to wear out my welcome!"

Pretending to be stubborn, Wyatt clasped his hands behind his head and leaned back in his chair. "I won't take no for an answer!"

Margaret shrugged and conceded. "All right then, if you insist. What time would you like for me to show up?"

"I'm fond of eight o'clock," he replied. "It's worked well so far, don't you think?"

Margaret grinned and slapped her knee. "Eight o'clock it is! Now, do you have a bathroom anywhere in this castle?"

Without shifting his concentrated gaze from Margaret, Wyatt said, "Gina, please show Miss Gates to the ladies' room. And make sure to send her home with a travel cup of the Darjeeling."

Gina politely responded, "Yes, Mr. Bennington."

Margaret intentionally lost her balance and stumbled when she stood up. Gina steadied her and then escorted her out of the study. She pointed down a long hall. "The powder room is the fifth door on the right, Miss Gates."

Margaret pretended to be confused, so Gina escorted her to the bathroom. As she turned on the light for her, she whispered, "Get ready for your Oscar nomination. That was quite a performance."

Before Margaret could respond, Gina stepped back into the hall and closed the bathroom door.

CHAPTER THIRTY-TWO

As soon as Margaret left, Gina quickly disposed of the leftovers. She heard Wyatt on his cell phone in his office, so she tiptoed down the hall and stood just outside his door.

"...Margaret Gates just left my house. I regret having to tell you this, but she had several drinks while we were conducting our business meeting...It surprised me, too...I did offer, but she insisted on getting behind the wheel...a white Hyundai sedan...I don't want her to put someone else's life in danger...about five minutes ago...Thank *you*, officer."

She waited a few seconds and then knocked on Wyatt's office door.

"If you don't need anything else tonight, I'll be retiring, Mr. Bennington."

Wyatt was looking toward the window. His face displayed an expression of sadistic satisfaction. He glanced over at her briefly and responded, "Tonight was a success. I couldn't have done it without you."

"Of course. Good night."

She quickly made her way up to her bedroom where she was prepared to make a phone call to the police and apologize, explaining that Wyatt had been misinformed. Then she reconsidered. What if they pulled Margaret over and found out she was perfectly sober? It would discredit Wyatt, and she could quickly prove her innocence.

Perhaps the best strategy was to just let this play out.

*　*　*

It wasn't until Margaret had driven off the Bennington property that she felt like she could breathe again. About a mile down the road, she pulled over into a church parking lot, turned her car off, and sat quietly. Her heart was still racing. She looked out her window at the church and, more specifically, at its illuminated steeple and upward-stretching cross.

She appreciated the efforts of the architects, but it bothered her that crosses were regularly displayed as showpieces. She reached for her own silver one hanging from her necklace chain. The depiction was far from accurate. What was accomplished by Christ was a beautiful work, but the cross itself represented suffering and humiliation. Far from being smooth and polished, it was jagged and bloodstained timber that tore sinless flesh.

Even though Jesus cancelled sin's debt on the cross, its post-resurrection purpose was to be fulfilled in us. The Christian life was to be characterized by sacrifice and not merely by good deeds and exemplary behavior. Now, in this moment, Margaret realized she had been delivered by the cross so she could have the privilege of carrying it.

Wyatt was an enemy who clearly wanted her dead. He deserved prison. If that's what it took to bring him to Christ, her small sacrifice mattered, even if the price had been her own life. If Wyatt had been worth it for Christ, then how could she offer any less?

Her thoughts were interrupted by a text message from Gina.

Wyatt called the police. It could make matters worse if we intervene. They can't charge you with anything. We need to trust God!

"Okay, Lord," Margaret said, praying out loud, "I embrace my cross, even if it means being falsely accused. Help me to remember that the same thing happened to you."

* * *

The tall man in the police uniform stood up as the dispatcher came back from his break.

"Thanks for your help," he said as he set a bag of fast food and a cardboard drink tray on the desk. "I'd been sitting at that switchboard for six hours!"

"It was no problem," the man replied. "Mr. Bennington, the hospital administrator, is always happy to let his security officers fill in when your office is short-staffed. I have it on good authority that there's going to be a lot of action at this precinct in the next couple of days. You're going to need all the help you can get."

"Yeah? What about tonight?" the dispatcher asked as he opened the wrapper on a cheeseburger. "Any calls while I was gone?"

"Only one. It was a false alarm."

"That's good." He reached down to pick up a napkin that had fallen to the floor. "Hey, so how long have you worked for Mr. Bennington?"

When he looked back up, the room was empty. He stood up and looked around.

"Where the heck did he go?"

CHAPTER THIRTY-THREE

MARGARET'S DRIVE ACROSS TOWN TURNED OUT TO BE COMPLETELY void of blue lights and sirens. As powerful as Wyatt was, she'd expected to have the entire police force tailing her. She was also relieved to find her property wasn't sealed off with crime scene tape when she arrived home. It was as if Wyatt's phone call either wasn't taken seriously or wasn't taken at all. Either way, she was grateful.

She still had tomorrow night ahead of her. She wondered if Wyatt would employ the same method again. Would he try to make her drunk? Or did he have something even more sinister up his sleeve? She was confident Gina would do her best to find out. Assuming they could get access to whatever evidence there might be early enough in the day, she would be making another trip to see Carlton at the lab.

* * *

From where Wyatt sat at his desk, he had a perfect view of his father's portrait. It had hung in the same spot on the dark paneled wall for as long as he could remember. He felt a pang of guilt.

Perhaps he should have visited him more in the nursing home. But, once his father no longer recognized him, what was the point? His relationship with his dad had always been based on mutual benefits. What Wyatt brought to the table had been an understanding of modern technology, his youthful energy, and an extra set of eyes when it came to reviewing business contracts. Horace had provided the connections, his name, and most importantly, his bank account. They had enjoyed a few activities together outside of the business world, such as golf and cigars, but most of their father-son time had revolved around the almighty dollar.

Wyatt shuffled around the office and observed the numerous pictures of his father displayed on bookshelves and end tables. A few were family photos, but most were of Horace posing with this dignitary or the other. The rest were framed newspaper articles heralding his philanthropy. Wyatt stepped over to where the portrait hung. He gingerly touched the brass nameplate affixed to the ornate gold frame and gazed up at his dad.

"I'll never be the businessman you were. Your shoes would be impossible to fill. But I will succeed at the one thing you failed to do," he said, pausing to smirk. "Destroying Margaret Gates."

CHAPTER THIRTY-FOUR

Saturday evening arrived way too quickly for Holly. She and Claire had spent the morning washing and drying what felt like a semester's worth of Claire's laundry. The mercury in the thermometer had conceded a few degrees resulting in an afternoon pleasant enough for them to take Oliva to the park. Afterward, they had returned home and reheated leftover pizza in the oven for dinner. Except for the situation with Steven looming in the back of Holly's mind, it had been a perfect day.

"Okay, I think this is the last of it," Holly said as she hoisted a large pull-string laundry bag into the back of Claire's SUV. She pulled down the hatchback and turned toward her sister. "I don't know what I would have done if you hadn't stopped by when you did."

Claire grinned as she gave her sister a hug. "Probably used a lot less water and laundry detergent."

Holly laughed and hugged her sister even tighter. "Seriously, though. Thank you so much for helping me take my focus off the problem and put it back on the Problem-Solver. I think I can get through this now."

Claire leaned back and swept a stray strand of hair off Holly's forehead and tucked it behind her ear. She winked and replied, "I never doubted that you could."

As Claire was putting on her seat belt, Holly lifted Olivia up to the car window so she could give her one more kiss goodbye.

"Text me when you get home, kiddo!"

Claire shook her head. "You know you sound just like Mom, right?"

Holly's eyes grew wide as she grinned. "Scary, isn't it?"

As soon as Claire's SUV was completely out of sight, Holly felt a pang of loneliness. Claire's visit had been helpful, but neither she, nor anyone else, could fill Steven's shoes. Holly needed her husband, and Olivia needed her father.

Should I contact him, or wait for him to contact me? Lord, show me the right way to handle this. I want Steven to come home, but it can't be like it was before. Please do what it takes for us to be a family again.

* * *

Steven awoke to the sound of a smoke alarm going off. He checked the time. It was a quarter of eight. He'd opted to take a quick nap so he could be sharp and focused for tonight's card game. His cell phone alarm was supposed to wake him in a few minutes, but instead of being roused by a pleasant ringtone, he'd been jolted awake by an ear-splitting screech.

As he approached the stairwell, he was greeted by the smell of what was probably a boxed macaroni dinner gone south. His view of the downstairs was obstructed by waves of thick smoke. The front and back doors were open, and it sounded as though Jake had turned on every available fan in the house.

"So, are you trying to save money on cigarettes? I don't know if you'll get the same buzz from a kitchen fire, but I guess there's no harm in trying."

From where he stood at the sink, Jake shot Steven a look and then focused back on scrubbing a blackened saucepan.

"No, I was actually doing Holly a favor. If you die in a fire, she can collect the life insurance and your financial problems will be solved."

Steven laughed wryly. "Jake, you're all heart. That would work except for the whole *me being dead* part."

Jake rinsed the pan and placed it in the dish drainer. "I got distracted by a phone call. I thought I'd turned the heat down on the stovetop, but, well, you can figure the rest out for yourself."

"You mean the great Jake Dunlop can't cook and talk on his cell phone at the same time?"

"Not this time," Jake replied and appeared to be a little uncomfortable with Steven's question. He gazed out the window over the sink. "I needed to take this call outside."

Steven decided not to press the issue. After all, Jake was doing him a favor by letting him stay at his house and arranging the card game tonight.

"You shouldn't play poker on an empty stomach, though," Jake added as he dried his hands on a dishcloth. "How about I spring for dinner on our way to the Gold Rush?"

"And deprive us of your next culinary masterpiece? That's a tough one," Steven said and then smiled. "Do you want to drive, or should I?"

"I'd better drive tonight," Jake answered. He turned around to face Steven. "Are you ready? I'm not just talking about being ready to leave. Are you ready for the game tonight?"

Steven sighed. "As ready as I'll ever be. All I have to do is watch for your signals, right?"

Jake nodded. "I've arranged with the dealer to use my deck of cards. He's got a stake in tonight being a success, too." Jake made eye contact with Steven and pointed in his direction. "No matter what happens, you stay close to me, understand?"

Steven felt a chill go down his spine. He moved in closer to Jake. "What do you mean *no matter what happens?* Are you anticipating trouble?"

Jake sighed. "You still don't get it, do you? With these guys, there's *always* the possibility of trouble. You need to be more careful who you pick as your friends. People can fool you. They aren't always who you think they are."

As much as Steven hated to admit it, Jake was right. In an odd twist, Jake had become a good friend to him in all of this. He hoped he could repay him one day.

Steven looked down. "I just want tonight to be over."

"That makes two of us," Jake replied. "Let's get out of here."

CHAPTER THIRTY-FIVE

Margaret unscrewed the cap on her water bottle, took a swallow, and then continued pacing. Why was it taking Carlton so long to call her with the lab results? She checked the time. It had been three hours since she'd dropped off the second set of samples. She only had an hour before she needed to leave. She was already dressed, but preparing for this meeting required more than showering and changing clothes. She needed time to prepare mentally for whatever Wyatt had planned.

You're going to wear out the carpet, Margaret. Relax.

Finally, her phone vibrated in her hand. She quickly checked the message. She put her hand to her mouth. Waves of nausea swept over her. She put the phone down, ran to the bathroom, and threw up.

* * *

Joseph tossed his keys on the counter and selected a chicken dinner from the freezer. He punched in the time required to heat it and haphazardly slammed the microwave door. As it hummed to life, he leaned back on the counter and raked his hand through his hair. He'd had to go in today and resolve a patient complaint on top of his already stressful week. Then, budget meetings and staff changes had made for more long hours and short tempers. But all of that came with the territory. What was really bothering him was the situation with Margaret and the samples she had brought to the lab.

He still didn't know what to make of it. Why did Margaret have samples containing ethanol and oxycodone? He kept thinking about Wyatt's stash of Everclear. He couldn't have anything to do with this. Could he? Margaret made it a point to stay as far away from Wyatt as possible. Besides, it was no secret how Wyatt felt about Margaret, so he wouldn't exactly invite her over for cocktails. And if he ever did, surely she would never accept such an invitation. Still, his mind raced with the possible implications.

His thoughts were interrupted as his phone vibrated on the kitchen table. It was a call from the hospital.

"Seriously? Maybe I should put a cot in my office," he said out loud before answering. "Hello, this is Joseph Bennington."

"Mr. Bennington? It's Carlton. I am so sorry to bother you, sir. Your friend brought in more samples today for testing. There's something you need to see."

Joseph checked the time on the microwave. "Look, I agree this is an odd situation," he said to Carlton, "but I really don't know any more about this than you do. I have no idea why my friend has beverage samples of alcohol that could have come from my brother's house. Especially since my brother doesn't like her, and my friend doesn't drink! And as for the drugs, that's an even bigger mystery. What I do know is that I can trust my friend. I've had a long day, and I just got home. So, if it's more slides you want to show me, I think I'll pass on the science lesson tonight."

"Mr. Bennington, I don't know anything about your brother or you friend, but anyone who ingests the refreshments *these* samples were taken from might not survive."

"What are you talking about?"

"These most recent samples contained ethanol and oxycodone, just like the others. The only difference—and this is a big difference—is the *amount* they contained. I'm talking deadly levels. It's none of my business, sir, but you might want to find out what's going on."

Joseph ended the call. He sat down at the kitchen table.

He ignored the sound of the microwave beeping and dialed a number. "Come on," he whispered impatiently. "Pick up!"

An older man's voice answered. "Hello? Mr. Joseph?"

Joseph breathed a sigh of relief. "Yes, Bivens, it's Joseph. Have you got a minute? I need to ask you a couple of questions."

"I'm so glad you called, sir. I have questions for you, as well."

Margaret splashed water on her face and stood at the sink for just a moment. She'd known all along that it was Wyatt's plan to kill her. Now that the event was only a few hours away, she was more afraid than she'd anticipated. Nothing could have prepared her for the crushing sense of sadness and terror that was overtaking her. She'd looked evil in the face when Horace had raped her. But knowing that someone despised her enough to plot her death took it all to a whole new level.

She washed her hands and walked back into the living room. She sat down in a chair and began to focus on her breathing. She rested her elbows on her legs and dropped her head. When she did, her cross necklace dangled in front of her face.

Sitting up, she unfastened the clasp. She held the silver emblem in her hand. Perhaps she was being given a glimpse, in some small way, of how Jesus had felt before going to the cross. Unlike her, He'd been sinless and divine. Like her, He'd been human. He'd tasted the sorrow and the fear. His flesh had been torn by the flogging; but His heart had been torn by the rejection. Love and life incarnate had been made subject to spitting, jeering, and crucifixion at the hands of His own creation.

Then Margaret realized something. *I don't have to do this. I could call Gina and tell her it's more than I can handle. After all, even Christ had a choice. Didn't He pray to the Father in the garden and ask if there was another way?*

But there was no other way. The greatest love had to be demonstrated through the greatest sacrifice. Margaret had been a beneficiary of that love when she'd least deserved it. Now it was her turn to demonstrate it to someone else who was equally unworthy.

If she was going to go through with this, she needed all the support she could get. She dialed Julia's number.

When Julia answered, Margaret forewent the niceties and simply said, "Julia, I'm scared. I'm really scared! The lab results revealed that the samples contained a deadly concentration of ethanol and oxycodone. That's the exact word the lab technician used—deadly."

"Whoa, Gina was right. Wyatt's end game really is murder."

"Do you know how this makes me feel?" Margaret's voice was trembling. "To know this person that I've chosen to forgive and pray for is planning to kill me?"

"But you're not going to die." Julia's tone was firm. "We're a step ahead of Wyatt. I don't know how all of this is going to play out, but God hasn't gotten you this far to let it all fall apart now."

"I need to know that I'm not alone." Margaret sobbed.

"You're *never* alone, and tonight is no exception. Plus, Gina will be there. Even though the rest of us can't physically be present, we'll be with you in prayer."

"I know. I just needed to hear you say it."

"Keep me posted, okay?

Margaret took a deep breath. "Okay."

She ended the call and grabbed her purse, making sure the hand-held recorder was still in there. As she placed the key into the front door lock, she paused. Somehow she knew that after tonight, nothing in her life would ever be the same.

CHAPTER THIRTY-SIX

Joseph missed interacting with Bivens, Gina, and the other members of the estate staff. It was one of the drawbacks of his agreeing to let Wyatt and Delores take up residence there, something they did a few short weeks after Horace's death. Joseph was content continuing to live in his own house, which was conveniently located five minutes from the hospital. Besides, the sheer enormity of the estate, coupled with the air of exclusivity it carried, was more compatible with Wyatt's taste than Joseph's. His only stipulation had been that the current staff be able to keep their jobs. So far, Wyatt had held up his end of the bargain.

After a quick conversation to catch up, Joseph got right to the point.

"Bivens, have you noticed anything suspicious going on at the estate lately? Has Wyatt been acting strangely?"

Bivens paused before answering. "Let me be frank, Mr. Joseph. When your brother and his wife moved in, the staff anticipated it would be similar to working for the senior Mr. Bennington. Wyatt has the same temperament, likes, and dislikes as his father before him. So, I state the obvious when I say that Margaret Gates is perhaps his least-favorite person."

The mention of Margaret's name caused Joseph's heart to skip a beat. "Go on."

"Lately, Wyatt has been quite the emissary of hospitality to Miss Gates. He's had her over for tea the past two evenings to discuss making a large donation to the Gates Manor. Evidently, he didn't want her disclosing this information to you. It was supposed to be a surprise of sorts."

Joseph remembered Margaret turning him down for dinner two nights ago, saying she had plans. She'd been so vague about it, he'd assumed she didn't want to spend time with him. Now he understood. Wyatt had her sworn to secrecy. Margaret would do anything to help the students at the Manor, even sit through meetings with his self-absorbed brother.

"Did anything else look odd to you?" Joseph pressed.

"Last night, Miss Gates seemed a little tipsy after simply sipping on Darjeeling and eating a pastry. I was concerned about her driving home in that condition, but Wyatt opted not to make other transportation arrangements for her. I found it odd, as I know Miss Gates doesn't drink. And Wyatt—*Mr. Bennington*, as he has us address him now—had insisted on preparing the refreshments himself."

Suddenly the pieces fell into place. Wyatt had lured Margaret to the estate under the pretense of donating to the Manor. He'd spiked her tea with the Everclear in the hopes that she'd either die in a car accident, or at the very least, receive a DWI. Once again, her name would appear in the newspaper. This time she had so much more to lose: her Christian witness, her credibility, possibly her job and ministry at the Manor, and maybe even her life.

Joseph had never felt so furious and terrified at the same time.

"Is Margaret scheduled to come back for any other meetings with Wyatt?"

"Why, yes. She's scheduled to come over at eight o'clock this evening."

"Bivens, please don't let Wyatt know we had this conversation."

Bivens lowered his voice. "Is there cause for concern for Miss Gates?"

"Let me put it this way. If something happens to Margaret, the one you'll need to be concerned about is my brother. Call me the minute you see anything suspicious. I'm on my way."

Joseph ended the call and immediately dialed another number. He grabbed the microwave dinner before hurrying out the door.

"911, what's your emergency?"

"This is Joseph Bennington, the hospital administrator. Who is working as the dispatcher tonight?"

"Hello, Mr. Bennington. It's Troy Palter. I'll be here all night."

Joseph sat his meal down in the passenger seat so he could fasten his seatbelt. "Will you do me a favor? I've got a tip that there's going to be a situation at my parents' estate tonight that could require emergency assistance. I'd like to get someone out there stat with no lights or sirens. How soon can you mobilize this? And, Troy, I apologize for springing this on you."

"Actually, that guy who filled in the other night from hospital security said we might want to pull in some extra help for this weekend. I can have an ambulance and a uniform out there in about ten minutes."

"That's great, Troy. Thank you so much."

Joseph was about to end the call when something occurred to him.

"Wait, what guy?" he asked

Troy chuckled. "Funny, I was going to ask you the same thing."

CHAPTER THIRTY-SEVEN

Margaret's walk along the winding sidewalk leading to the Bennington's front door seemed longer this evening. It was as if she could feel the weight of the cross she was carrying. She had to push herself to take each step. She made her way up the front steps and approached the entrance. She hesitated at first, but then reached for the doorbell.

The door unlatched and Bivens greeted her. "Punctual as always! Please come in, Miss Gates."

"Thank you," Margaret responded somewhat formally, still trying to calm her nerves.

Bivens escorted Margaret into the study where, once again, Wyatt was sitting in one of the wingback chairs. The Wyatt from previous evenings had flawlessly channeled a gracious southern gentleman, eager to dispense both his hospitality and his wealth. Tonight, a different Wyatt hosted her. His eyes looked cold and lifeless. Instead of standing when she entered the room, he kept his seat. It was amazing the difference from two nights ago. It reminded her of Jesus entering Jerusalem on Palm Sunday amidst a welcoming crowd shouting, "Hosanna!" Yet one short week later, that same crowd would be angrily shouting, "Crucify him!"

Wyatt's voice was devoid of any emotion as he greeted her. "Hello, Margaret. Please sit down."

Margaret had a quick decision to make. Should she call Wyatt out on his frosty reception, or act as if she hadn't noticed? She decided she would play along as if nothing had changed from their previous meetings.

She politely took her seat.

Gina entered the room and stood by the coffee table. Evidently, Wyatt wasn't as eager to serve the food tonight. In a sick twist, it was as if he were savoring the moment, not wanting to rush the process.

Margaret decided she would break the silence. "Wyatt, I know I've said this before, but the staff and students at the Gates Manor sincerely appreciate your generosity. Do you, by chance, have that paperwork we discussed?"

Wyatt seemed to snap back into business mode and produced a black folder with an expensive-looking law practice logo on the front.

Margaret flipped through the pages of the document. She wasn't an attorney, but it all looked official to her. It did appear she was the only one named as the trustee. How very clever of him. Once she was dead, the document would be null and void. However, it wouldn't be without purpose, and a very important one at that. If Wyatt were questioned as a suspect in her untimely death, this document would be proof that he and Margaret were on exceptionally good terms. Delores couldn't be implicated as she was in Europe at the time. Wyatt had prepared for every possible scenario, except for one.

Margaret wasn't going to die.

CHAPTER THIRTY-EIGHT

The chairs in the back room were arranged in a circle around a marble-top table. A waitress in shorts and a midriff shirt flitted in and out, dropping off full bottles of beer and collecting the empty ones.

It was evident to Steven that the occasional flirtation or catcall was neither new nor offensive to her.

"Hey baby, why can't you be the prize tonight?" Rusty asked as he put his arm around her waist.

"Because you will never be *that* good at poker, Rusty Chambers!"

The room erupted in laughter as she winked and picked up another tray of empty bottles.

This young lady intrigued Steven. She was sharp and seemed very aware of her surroundings, way too polished and professional for a job that required her to be neither. He also noticed that she made eye contact with everyone except the card dealer. Either they didn't know each other, or they were working really hard to give that impression.

Despite there being no indication of trouble or ill will among the players, Steven had to repeatedly wipe his sweaty palms on his jeans. In a card game where even the slightest twitch or blink of an eye could indicate a winning or losing hand, he felt as though he were wearing a neon sign advertising his acute case of nerves.

So far, he had won each of the three hands that had been dealt. Jake skillfully played the dual role of enabler and antagonist. Even though his own trick deck was responsible for Steven's success, he complained and acted annoyed with each of his own losses. With Steven's fourth win Jake angrily threw his cards on the table.

"I don't get it. You're mopping the floor with us tonight!"

This fifth hand would determine whether or not Steven went home with the jackpot. The dealer snapped out the cards to each of the players.

Everything seemed to be going according to plan when the atmosphere in the room suddenly changed. Up until this point, there had been a stream of banter typical of rivals vying for a prize. Then, for no apparent reason, all conversation had stopped. Something didn't feel right. Steven could only attribute it to Jake's warning that with these guys anything could go wrong.

Rusty glanced at Pete and nodded. Pete responded by showing his hand. With everyone's attention on Pete's early fold, the unthinkable happened.

Steven heard the scrape of Rusty's chair across the floor and saw a flash of anger in his eyes. As he stood, he slipped his right hand into his jacket and produced a sleek, black piece of steel. He pointed it squarely at Steven.

Steven instinctively raised his hands. It felt like all the oxygen had been sucked out of the room. He remembered Jake's instructions to stay close to him. He desperately looked over at Jake just in time to hear him yell, "Police! Drop your weapon!"

Jake, the waitress, and the card dealer all had weapons drawn and badges flashing.

"Lower your gun and put your hands where I can see them!" Jake held his own gun steady as he moved in closer to Rusty. "Don't make me shoot you!"

When Rusty's gun hit the table, Steven lowered his arms and was finally able to breathe again.

"Read them their rights," Jake ordered as the waitress and the card dealer began to cuff Rusty, Pete, and Tyrone. Steven sat in shocked silence, as he watched the scene unfold. Jake waited until the others had left the room before he approached Steven.

Steven's mouth was so dry, he could hardly speak. "Jake," he finally managed, "what are you doing? Why didn't you tell me you were a cop?"

"I told you to be careful who you pick as your friends. People aren't always who you think they are."

Steven winced as Jake locked a pair of cuffs on his wrists. "What are you arresting me for? What's the charge?"

"Well, since stupidity isn't a crime, I'm arresting you for disturbing the peace. I have to take you out of here in cuffs or it will raise suspicion. This is for your own good, so play along."

Steven hung his head as Jake pushed him through the noisy crowd of onlookers who'd gathered in the casino. The front of the building was illuminated by a sea of flashing blue lights, and the evening air was punctuated by the sound of police radio chatter. Jake put his hand on Steven's head. Steven complied and crouched into the backseat of the patrol car while Rusty, Pete, and Tyrone looked on. As soon as it was clear that Steven wasn't receiving special treatment, the process was repeated for the others.

As the patrol car began to make its way out of the casino parking lot, Steven silently prayed.

Jesus, thank you for not letting me die in there. Not that I didn't deserve it. Tears streamed down his cheeks. *I'm sorry for trying to fix this my way. Instead of being free, I'm sitting here in handcuffs.*

A roadblock had been set up at the main road, and a policeman with a whistle was directing a line of cars away from the casino entrance. The traffic volume wasn't due to casino traffic as much as it was to a construction detour from Interstate 40. As they waited their turn, a red SUV passed by. For a split second, Steven thought he recognized the driver. Having just looked down the barrel of a gun, he was surprised this would make him anxious. Then he realized what really concerned him.

What if that driver recognized *him*?

* * *

Holly's cell phone rang. She checked the caller ID and saw that it was Claire. How could Claire have arrived home so quickly?

She laughed as she answered the call. "Hey, you little speed demon! Are you home already?"

"Holly, I got rerouted on I-40 because of the road construction. The detour took me by that casino where Steven's been hanging out. I think I saw him."

Holly could feel the anger rising in her. Steven couldn't stay away even for a few days! However, she resolved to not jump to conclusions until she had all the facts. "Did you see his car? Was he driving into the parking lot?"

Claire hesitated. "I'm sorry to have to tell you this, but he was in a police car that was *leaving* the parking lot."

CHAPTER THIRTY-NINE

Margaret set the folder down on the coffee table. When she looked at Wyatt's face, she saw his father. She had to suppress those memories and force herself to focus on what was happening right now.

"It looks as though everything is in order," Margaret said as she took the pen Wyatt offered her and signed her name on the last page.

Wyatt picked up the document and then called for one of his administrative staff members who, evidently, had stayed after hours to help facilitate this transaction.

Wyatt's instructions to the suit-clad young man who'd emerged from down the hall were simple. "Everything is signed. Fax this to my attorney immediately."

After the young man had left the room with the document, Wyatt smiled. "Gina, why don't you serve Miss Gates some refreshments?"

Bivens stood outside the study as Gina crossed the room and placed two finger sandwiches on a china dessert plate. She handed it to Margaret along with a monogramed napkin. She also set a rather large glass of lemonade down on the coffee table. Margaret made eye contact with Gina as she said thank you, but it was more for reassurance than decorum. Gina nodded in her usual professional manner, but it still helped Margaret to not feel so alone. She was also comforted by the fact that Minnie and Julia were praying. Most importantly, she reminded herself, if something went terribly wrong tonight, her eternal fate was secure.

As Gina resumed her post by the door, Wyatt called out, "That will be all for tonight, Gina. You may retire to your quarters."

Margaret forced herself to not react or look at Gina. Neither of them had seen this coming. Gina had always been expected to serve when Wyatt and Delores had guests. Still, Margaret knew Gina had no choice but to yield to Wyatt's wishes. To protest would raise suspicion. But she did make one polite appeal.

"Are you certain, Mr. Bennington? I would be happy to stay in case you or Miss Gates need anything further."

However, Wyatt did not change his mind. "That won't be necessary. Good night, Gina."

As Gina left the room, so did Margaret's feeling of not being alone. She'd come too far to back out now. She took a bite of the sandwich and washed it down with the lemonade.

"This is delicious," she said, taking an even bigger bite. *Might as well get this over with quickly,* she thought. "I hate to be rude, but I haven't had time to eat yet today." She picked up the second sandwich and began to devour it as well.

Wyatt stood up. "Don't be silly," he said. "In fact, I just thought of something I need to take care of. Please enjoy your refreshments, and I'll be right back."

She finished the sandwiches and tried to drink as much of the lemonade as she could. Within a few minutes, Wyatt returned and proceeded to pour himself a scotch.

His back was turned to Margaret as he asked, "So, Margaret, how afraid were you of my father?" He looked over his shoulder at her, his gaze roaming briefly to her empty plate. "I mean, you were young when he started having sex with you. How old were you? Fourteen? Fifteen?" Instead of going back to his seat, he paced slowly back and forth in front of Margaret's chair.

"You must have been terrified," he continued. "You tried more than once to kill yourself. You wanted to die, right?"

Margaret's stomach churned at his crassness and his sinister tone. Her vision swam slightly, and she could feel beads of sweat popping out on her forehead. She hoped it was just her nerves and that something hadn't gone wrong with the plan to switch the refreshments. She put down her glass and struggled to speak. "You're right. I did want to die. But God didn't let me. He had a purpose for my life."

"So, what was this purpose?" Wyatt asked. "Helping a bunch of drug-addicted outcasts? With your parents' wealth and upbringing, I would've thought you'd have pulled yourself up out of that crowd and mingled with people closer to your own pedigree."

Margaret took another long sip of the lemonade. She had to calm down and trust the plan for this to work. "How do you know that I haven't? Maybe that's why we're having this conversation, Wyatt. Just like Jesus didn't look like a Messiah, sometimes lost people don't look…lost."

She could hear the still small voice of the Holy Spirit speak to her heart, *For what does it profit a man to gain the world and yet lose his soul?*

She began to act as if the poison was working. Her case of nerves actually played to her advantage. "Whoa! I don't feel so good."

Wyatt cocked his head to one side. "What's wrong? Is something not agreeing with you?"

Margaret tumbled out of the chair and fell to her knees. "What's happening to me?"

* * *

Joseph's phone rang. It was Bivens.

"Mr. Joseph, can you hear me? I'm calling from the coat closet. I'm trying to be as quiet as possible."

"Yes, I can hear you," Joseph replied. "What's going on?"

"You'd better get here quickly. I think Wyatt has poisoned Miss Gates!"

* * *

Wyatt moved in closer to Margaret. His tone was eerily matter-of-fact. "So, if your God didn't want you to die, then why are you here tonight? Because a high concentration of ethanol and oxycodone in your refreshments tends to do just that—make you die."

He squatted down beside her and lowered his voice, pretending to be secretive. "I originally thought about rodenticide. That would have perfectly represented the pathetic life you've lived, but it's not normally used for suicide. So, I decided to use Everclear combined with a hefty dose of oxycodone. There's more in your car, by the way. After you're dead, the police will conclude that you'd tragically reverted back to your old alcohol and drug addictions.

"You know what Everclear is, right? A very high-proof alcohol that has no taste. It's so potent, in fact, that it's been banned in several states, including ours! It was perfect for you, Margaret. You present yourself as this gifted musician and counselor, when, in reality, you're just a tasteless poison that needs to be eradicated."

He stood and then looked off into the distance. "I can see the newspaper article now." He paused briefly to glance back at her and quipped, "Of course, I'll help them write it. I'll push past my own grief somehow."

He resumed his gaze and used his hands theatrically. "Margaret Gates, known for her work at the Gates Manor, was found dead last night just outside the Bennington estate. According to Wyatt Bennington, Miss Gates had recently approached him requesting money to help finance the work at the Manor. Those attending the spring concert will remember her asking for donations from the community as well. After being pulled over for driving drunk the night before," he paused again and shot her a questioning look. "You did receive a DWI, didn't you?"

Apparently it was a rhetorical question, because he didn't wait for her to respond.

"All in all," he continued, "it's rumored that personal issues, as well as financial problems, could have contributed to the suicide. It wouldn't be the first time that Miss Gates attempted to take her own life. We're all saddened, blah blah blah."

Margaret waited until Wyatt had finished. "What if," she said softly, "I knew that this was going to happen, but I came anyway?"

Wyatt spun around, incredulous. "What are you talking about?"

"What if I *let* you do this because I believed it would eventually lead you to finding life? Not money, power, or status, but *real* life, the kind that can only come from knowing God's love."

Wyatt's face turned red. "Are you mad?"

Margaret grabbed her stomach. After pretending she needed to catch her breath, she responded, "No, I just know how much God loves you. It's His love for you that has empowered me to do this. You don't understand this love yet, but one day you will."

Wyatt leaned in to where his face was only inches from hers. "The only thing I'm going to understand is how good it feels to see you dead, Margaret Gates."

Margaret smiled. "I'm afraid you're going to have to wait a little while for that one, Wyatt."

CHAPTER FORTY

Holly's breath quickened. "What? Why would Steven be in a police car?"

"Well, I don't think they were taking him out for pizza. There were lots of police cars at the casino. If I had to guess, I'd say there's been a raid. See if you can get him on his cell. I'm turning around and coming back to your house. You may need me to watch Olivia tonight."

"Thank you, Claire. I'll see you soon."

Holly ended the call. She slid down the side of the wall until she was sitting on the floor. She began to weep. *Steven, what have you gotten yourself into?*

* * *

Joseph flung the front door open so violently, it slammed against the interior wall. He was followed by two uniformed police officers and a paramedic who were scrambling to keep up.

Wyatt's eyes bugged as he shouted, "What's going on here?!"

Joseph squatted down beside Margaret. He took her face into

149

his hands. "You're going to be okay." He turned to the paramedic. "Take care of her."

He approached Wyatt and answered his previously asked question. "That's exactly what I want to know. What is going on here, Wyatt?"

Wyatt's face was smug as he quipped, "Don't tell me you're here because you *love me too*, Joseph."

Joseph shook his head. "No, Wyatt. I'm here because I love *her*."

Joseph wasn't sure exactly how many punches he landed before the police officers pulled him off. He could hear Margaret assuring the paramedics that she was fine. Maybe he'd gotten there in time after all.

Joseph caught his breath and pointed to the almost empty glass of lemonade. "I think if you test that, you'll find lethal amounts of ethanol and oxycodone." He picked up the empty sandwich plate. "And test these crumbs too!"

Gina spoke up. "No, Mr. Joseph. You won't find anything in that food."

She was holding a jar of liquid and a plastic bag of what appeared to be finger sandwiches. "You'll find it in these. I switched the refreshments so Miss Gates would not be harmed. What you will find in this is consistent with the samples that were sent to the hospital lab earlier today."

Wyatt gasped. "Gina!"

Gina walked over to where Wyatt stood. She took one of the napkins off the table.

"There's a lot you don't know, Wyatt," Gina said as she began wiping the blood from his face. A quiet fell over the room. "I have not betrayed you tonight, as you might believe. I have never left your side, and I won't start now. I will be there for you."

Wyatt jerked away from her. For the first time this evening, or perhaps ever, Joseph thought Wyatt didn't look confident or in control.

"You'll find more incriminating evidence on this," Margaret

said, pulling a small tape recorder from her purse. "I have two witnesses here who can tell you that it's authentic, and that Wyatt wasn't coerced or forced to say anything against his will."

One of the policemen came up behind Wyatt and snapped a pair of handcuffs on his wrists. "Wyatt Bennington, you're under arrest for the attempted murder of Margaret Gates. Anything you say can and will be held against you in a court of law…"

The other officer approached Margaret. "Are you okay, ma'am?"

"Except for my nerves? Yes."

"We're going to need all of you to come down to the station in the morning and make a full statement." He quickly looked around the room and shook his head. "If this all proves true, Mr. Bennington, your new accommodations aren't going to be quite this nice."

As one of the officers walked Wyatt out the front door, Joseph saw several bright flashes of light. Obviously, someone had already alerted the press. He was pretty sure his brother's picture would be on the front page of tomorrow's newspaper.

CHAPTER FORTY-ONE

WHILE JOSEPH FOLLOWED ONE OF THE PARAMEDICS OUTSIDE, Margaret and Gina embraced and wept. The sense of relief was palatable. Sirens blared as the police cars left the estate. Margaret stepped over to the study window and gazed outside until the flashing blue lights were no longer visible.

"Wyatt's arrest is a victory," Gina said as she moved to stand beside Margaret. "But this is far from over."

Margaret put her hand on Gina's shoulder. "As someone told me earlier tonight, God wouldn't take us this far to let everything fall apart now."

Bivens entered the room carrying a bottle of wine and two glasses.

"Gina would you like to join me in a nightcap? I think we've earned this one. Oh, Miss Gates! I didn't realize you were still here."

He set the items down on the coffee table and approached Margaret, taking her hands into his.

"In all my years of working for the Benningtons, I've never seen Mr. Joseph behave as passionately as he did tonight. I want to thank you for being the catalyst for," he paused, "Mr. Joseph walloping his brother!" Abandoning all propriety and repose, he threw his head back and guffawed. "You have no idea how long I've waited to see that!"

His laughter was contagious. First Margaret succumbed and then Gina. Soon all three had tears streaming down their faces. Evidently, a hearty laugh was overdue.

"Well, I hate to leave right when happy hour is starting!" Margaret said as she wiped her eyes. "But I need to catch Joseph before he takes off." She gave them both a hug and then stepped out onto the front porch.

A hot summer breeze stirred the fragrance of Magnolia blossoms from a nearby tree. Margaret breathed in the lemon-scented air. For a moment, that was all she wanted to do—just breathe.

Joseph was standing in the driveway finishing up a conversation with the paramedic. When he saw Margaret, he shook the man's hand and came to join her on the porch.

"Hey, thanks for coming in like the cavalry tonight," Margaret said.

He turned to face her but stared down at his feet. His expression was serious. "I wasn't going to let anything happen to you."

"I don't think you understand," Margaret said. "No man has ever, ever done anything like that for me! Wyatt's words and actions drudged up a lot of painful memories and feelings of rejection. It's strange how, in that moment, I was so sure of how much God valued him, but my own worth came back into question. Then you came in and reminded me that I was loved, too."

She hugged his neck. "I wanted to say thank you."

"Margaret?"

She pulled back and looked into his eyes. "Yeah?"

He threw his hands in the air. "It's true."

"What do you mean?"

"I love you, Margaret." A smile danced on his lips. "I don't just love you; I'm *in* love with you. I'm absolutely crazy about you!" He began to laugh. "I mean, I wake up thinking about you, and I go to sleep thinking about you. Our situation is complicated, and that used to bother me." He inched closer to her. "But I don't care about that anymore. I just want to be with you."

Margaret's heart skittered. Long ago, she'd accepted that because of how she'd spent her past, she'd most likely spend her future alone. She felt like it was what she deserved. After all, for the better part of her life, she'd been told, and treated like, she was damaged goods. She'd always been attracted to Joseph, but had never allowed herself to consider anything beyond friendship. She had been too afraid of being rejected.

Did he say he loves me? Can this really be happening?

Her lip began to quiver. "Joseph, are you sure? Complicated doesn't even *begin* to describe our situation. I mean, this is crazy."

Joseph touched his hand to her cheek. "I'll take complicated *and* crazy as long as it means I get you."

She smiled, but then shrank back. "I need some time."

"How about we start with a first date? As a good friend of mine once suggested, with the flowers, the candy, the whole enchilada?"

Margaret bashfully shrugged. "I've never had a first date."

"Well, in that case, we definitely have to do this right," Joseph said as he got down on one knee. "Margaret Francine Gates, I realize this is a little sudden after, uh, my brother's attempt on your life, but will you go on a date with me?"

Margaret laughed. "I know you understand, if your brother had succeeded, that wouldn't be a possibility. But you're kind of cute. Let me check my calendar!"

CHAPTER FORTY-TWO

HOLLY HEARD HER PHONE RING AGAIN. SHE ASSUMED IT WOULD BE Claire with another update. She looked at the caller ID. It was a number she didn't recognize. She wasn't sure if she should answer, but then realized it could be about Steven.

Her voice cracked as she said, "Hello?"

"Is this Mrs. Holly Sparrow?" a male voice asked on the other end.

Holly panicked. What if something had happened to Steven? As frustrated as she was with him, she still loved him. What if this was *that* call, the one every spouse and every parent never wants to receive?

She quickly stood to her feet. "Yes, this is Holly."

"Mrs. Sparrow, this is Jake Dunlop. I'm an officer with the Raleigh Police Department. I need to talk with you about your husband, Steven Sparrow."

Her heart raced. "Is he okay?"

"Yes ma'am, he's fine. In fact, he's been staying with me for the past several days."

That was the last thing Holly had expected to hear. She thought

Steven would have holed up with one of his gambling buddies, not a police officer. It still didn't explain why he was riding in the back of a patrol car.

"I'm sorry, Officer Dunlop, but I'm a little confused. My husband was seen leaving the casino in a police car. I assumed he was under arrest."

"No ma'am. It was only made to look that way. If you have a few minutes, I'll explain the whole situation."

* * *

By the time the police car arrived at the station, Steven was in a cold sweat. He could hear the officer behind the wheel having a conversation on his phone. When he ended the call, he looked at Steven in the rearview mirror.

"Well, Mr. Sparrow. It sounds like you'll be going home this evening. Officer Dunlop will be arriving momentarily."

Steven breathed a sigh of relief. "Thank you, sir."

As the officer left the car, Steven bowed his head. "Thank you, Lord."

Steven heard footsteps, and the driver's side back door opened. Jake slid into the back seat. He glanced over at Steven and then looked straight ahead.

"I guess I owe you an explanation."

Steven looked down. "You don't owe me anything."

"Yes, I do," Jake said. "I owe you a thank-you."

Steven shook his head. "What could you possibly have to thank *me* for?"

"Let me start by telling you my dad was one of the best cops you'd ever meet. He was the one who inspired me to go into law enforcement."

Steven briefly glanced up at Jake. "You're talking about him in the past tense. Did he die in the line of duty?"

Jake scoffed. "Far from it. He got sucked into the gambling culture and accrued close to twenty thousand in debt. When he couldn't come up with the money, one of his gambling *friends* shot him in the back."

"I'm sorry, Jake. And point taken on the bad friend choices. I guess making bad choices is all I'm good for these days."

"Well, before you beat yourself up too much, I did say I needed to thank you. You see, after what happened to my dad, I wanted to get to the bottom of this local gambling ring. Steven, you weren't losing money because you were unlucky or unskilled. All the games are rigged. They set it up that way so their customers will run up a lot of debt. Then the casino offers to loan them money. The loans are fast and easy, but they're not cheap. That's how they've been making their *big* money. If you can't pay the loan back, they send their thugs after you."

"Thugs like Rusty, Pete, and Tyrone?"

"I'm afraid so. And their methods of debt collection are, shall we say, less than ethical. What you did is help me catch a dangerous group of criminals. I've been praying for God to send me someone who could make that happen. My prayers were answered the night you rang my doorbell."

Steven bit his lip. The last thing he wanted to do was cry in front of Jake, but suddenly he didn't care about appearances. "So, the naïve Steven Sparrow knocks on your door, and you knew you'd found your sucker."

Jake put his hand on Steven's shoulder. "No. The *Christian* Steven Sparrow who was trying to get his life back on track showed up. Look, you're not as weak as you think, and I'm not as tough as you think. I was scared tonight when Rusty pulled that gun on you. And…I don't smoke."

Steven laughed. "Seriously?"

Jake smiled. "What you did tonight took a lot of courage. Plus, I don't think you'll be gambling anymore."

Steven nodded. "Actually, I made a phone call earlier this week to get some help. It's a six-week program. The meetings are at night, so I won't have to miss any work."

Jake patted him on the back. "I think that's a good idea. In my eyes, you're a hero. I told someone else the same thing. She's waiting for you outside."

Steven's mouth dropped open as he realized Jake must be talking about Holly. "Jake, how can I repay you?"

"There is something you can do. After we put these guys away, I'll probably be promoted to detective. I'd be honored if you and Holly would attend the ceremony."

"You've got it. In fact, if you'll unlock these cuffs, we can shake on it."

* * *

Holly was standing in the parking lot by her car. She saw the back door of the squad car open. Steven stepped out with Jake. They shook hands and then Jake pointed over to where she was waiting. She wasn't sure what to do, but Steven made that choice for her. He ran across the parking lot, picked her up, and held her so close she could hardly breathe.

After a moment, he pulled away and looked at her. "Even though I'm giving you my word I'll never gamble again, I want to give you more than that. I've signed up for a program for people with gambling issues. They've requested for you attend a few of the sessions with me. If you don't want to, it's okay. I take full responsibility for this. I think it would help me—*us*—if you did."

She touched his face. "My terms were for you to admit you had a problem and get help. You've done both. I'm just glad you're okay!"

His shoulders began to shake. He collapsed into her arms once again. "Holly, I'm so sorry."

She wasn't sure how long they stood there. Police business was going on in the background, but they were barely aware of it. Holly finally took his hands into hers. "Let's go home," she said.

As they were getting into the car, Holly spotted Jake making his way back to the precinct. Before he went inside, he turned around and waved. Holly waved back. She could've never predicted her prayers for Steven would've been answered in this way. She was sure of one thing.

Tonight was one neither of them would ever forget.

159

CHAPTER FORTY-THREE

PRESTON GATES QUIETLY SLIPPED OUT OF BED SO HE WOULDN'T WAKE Annie. Her pregnancy nausea had been more intense this past week. Normally they would be getting ready for church, but today he felt like she needed to rest. He still couldn't believe he was going to be a father. In a few weeks, they would find out if the baby was a boy or a girl. Margaret had given them a few suggestions for the baby's name and the nursery décor. Once they learned the gender, they could make a final decision on both.

After starting a pot of coffee, Preston stepped out on the front porch. The early morning air was already hot and muggy, a reliable indicator that the day would be a scorcher. He picked up the newspaper, taking it out of the plastic sleeve as he walked back inside the house. The smell of freshly brewed coffee filled the downstairs. He poured himself a cup and sat down at the kitchen table. He'd just taken his first sip when he saw Wyatt Bennington's picture on the front page. He nearly choked as he read the headline:

Wyatt Bennington Arrested for Attempted Murder

Then he read the article.

He slammed his coffee cup down on the table.

"Margaret Gates, you'd better have a good explanation as to why I'm finding out about this from the morning paper!"

* * *

Margaret awoke to the sound of her doorbell ringing. She looked at the time. It was already eight thirty. She rarely slept in this late. She checked her cell phone. She had three missed calls from Julia.

She sat up in bed and sighed. "I can only guess who's at my front door."

She slipped her feet into her bedroom slippers and fastened her robe around her. Without even looking through the peephole, she unlocked the front door.

"Julia, I'm okay, I just forgot to set my alarm."

"It's not Julia," Preston said as he held up a copy of the morning's newspaper. "When were you going to tell me about this?"

Before Margaret could respond, he brushed past her and made his way inside.

She stood at the door and mumbled, "No, really, please come in."

Of all the things she'd anticipated, and dreaded, having to deal with today, Preston hadn't been one of them. She hoped she'd be able to sit down and have a civil conversation with him about what had transpired, and about why she'd kept him out of the loop. The chances of that happening now were slim to none.

"Where do you keep your coffee?" he called from the kitchen.

Margaret reluctantly joined him and produced a bag of coffee from the freezer.

As he proceeded to scoop out enough to make a small pot, he quipped, "I didn't know if you hid your coffee like you do everything else in your life."

His remark partly amused and partly annoyed her. She'd promised to never keep secrets from him again, particularly when it came to the Benningtons. Horace had abused her for years without Preston knowing about it. Of course, he was fifteen years younger than she was, and most of the abuse had occurred before he was even born. It had been more of an effort to protect him than it had been to keep information from him. While this was a different situation, it still wasn't a simple, clear-cut decision. She'd have to help him understand that.

"Look, Preston. It wasn't just my call. We—Julia, Gina, Minnie, and I—decided the fewer people that were in on it, the better. Wyatt has been planning this for a while. We had to let it play out. Knowing you, you would have lost your cool and punched him, like Joseph did last night. Maybe you two *are* related…"

Preston poured himself and Margaret a cup of coffee. "Wait, Joseph decked Wyatt? Sorry I missed that. I knew I liked that guy. Speaking of Joseph, I think he has a thing for you."

Margaret could feel her face turning red.

Preston set his coffee cup down on the table and tilted his head to one side. "Margaret Francine Gates, are you blushing? Is there another Bennington secret you'd like to tell me about?"

Margaret looked down and stirred her coffee. "Ironically, this one wasn't mine to disclose."

Preston grinned and leaned back in his chair. "Go on…"

"Joseph told me he has feelings for me. That's one of the reasons he punched Wyatt. When he found out what was going on and what Wyatt had been planning, he showed up with the police, a paramedic, and a wicked right hook."

"So, with Joseph around, I can retire my brass knuckles?" Preston took a sip of his coffee. "It sounds like he can take care of himself—and you."

"But it's so complicated! You're Joseph's half-brother, and his —*your*—biological father abused me. And, to put the icing on the cake of this weirdest-love-story-ever, last night his brother—a.k.a. your half-brother—tried to kill me."

Preston shook his head. "You don't get the luxury of predictable and status quo, sis. Your calling is to show people there is nothing so messed up that God can't make something beautiful out of it. If you met a guy online on one of those dating sites and he was this regular dude who worked a nine-to-five job and came from a normal family, I would question it. But a guy who is your brother's half-brother and whose father abused you? Yep, that sounds like you."

Margaret reached across the table and took Preston's hand. "What you just said makes me sound like the poster child for dysfunctional relationships. But it does make me feel better."

Preston laughed and squeezed her hand. "Always here to help! Look, I hope you know the real reason I was so upset when I saw that newspaper article. It wasn't just because you had kept something from me. I was scared at the thought of losing you. We've had too many close calls. It brought back a lot of bad memories."

"I understand. And for that, I apologize. So, are we good?"

"We are, but I'll be even better as soon as my state taxes start paying for Wyatt Bennington's room and board. When is he going to be arraigned?"

"Speaking of which—I hate to kick you out—but I need to make some phone calls to see when I'm expected at the police station. I have to submit a statement."

Preston put his empty coffee cup in the sink. "I'll do anything to help put that jerk away for life. Now that I'm up to speed on what's going on, call me if you need anything."

"Will you believe me if I say *I promise*?" Margaret asked as she gave her brother a hug.

"Our family is all about second and third chances, right?" Preston kissed her on the top of her head.

Margaret looked up at him and winked. "I lost count a long time ago!"

CHAPTER FORTY-FOUR

WYATT SPENT THE NIGHT IN A SIX-BY-NINE CELL CONTAINING ONLY A pillow, a blanket, and a sink. His toilet was a large plastic bucket. He had tossed and turned more from anger than from his inability to sleep on the thin, foam rubber pad positioned in a metal frame that was supposed to be a bed. Plus, his face was throbbing from where Joseph had punched him. After being served coffee and a breakfast consisting of a single bagel, packaged cream cheese, and an apple, he was more than ready to make a phone call to his lawyer.

"I don't care if he's still asleep! Wake him up! I don't pay his exorbitant fees to have him dictate to me which hours he can work. Put him on the phone now!"

Wyatt ignored the eye-roll glances the staff at the precinct gave each other. He was unconcerned about any repercussions of his behavior. If he could get his lawyer to show up, everything would be taken care of, and he could go home.

A uniformed officer took him by the arm. "You can wait back here in the interrogation room until your attorney arrives."

Wyatt was indignant and jerked his arm back. "Let go of me! Don't you know who I am?"

The officer remained calm. "Yes, you're a citizen who broke the law. That's it. If you don't want me to put those cuffs back on you, you'll come with me to the interrogation room."

Wyatt grumbled, "I can't wait until Dalton Larkins arrives. You idiots probably don't know who he is either, but it doesn't matter. When he shows up, I'll be out of here before you can perk another pot of that disgusting coffee you drink around here."

Wyatt was led to a small room containing a rectangular table and a few fold-up chairs. There was a two-way mirror, which alerted him that he was being watched. *Let them watch me all they want,* he fumed to himself. *This is only a temporary inconvenience. There's no way it could turn into anything more serious. I'll come out on top. I always do.*

Dalton had informed Wyatt that it would take him at least an hour, if not more, to pull everything together. Wyatt decided that while he was waiting, he would try to sort through everything that had just happened.

First, why wasn't Margaret incarcerated instead of him? She was the one who had driven home drunk the other night. How had she gotten out of that one? And how had Gina known what his plan was? Of all people, he'd thought he could trust her. What was all that drivel from Margaret about God's love? Had she been tossing out religious platitudes to throw him off-balance?

Occasionally, an officer would stop in to offer him coffee or water. The wait seemed to go on forever. Finally, there was a tap on the door.

Wyatt breathed a sigh of relief. "Dalton, what took you so long?"

A few years Wyatt's senior, Dalton Larkins was a tall, handsome man who exuded class and good taste. His rates were much like his Armani suit and shoes: expensive and reserved exclusively for those who could afford them. He gingerly set his briefcase on the table and clicked it open. He produced a document and placed it on the table along with a sleek gold pen bearing his law firm's logo.

"Sign here, Wyatt. You're admitting to reckless endangerment. I pleaded down the original charge of first-degree attempted murder. You'll do six months jail time and one year of probation. It's the best I could do. They have physical evidence, including your voice on tape admitting to wanting Margaret Gates dead. Take the deal. Six months is a gift. If this goes to trial, you could be looking at life."

Wyatt looked up and pushed the document back across the table. "Are you crazy? I'm not doing six *hours* in this place."

Dalton pulled up a chair and sat down across the table. He took off his glasses and rubbed his eyes as if doing so would relieve some of the stress. He took a deep breath and looked Wyatt directly in the eyes. "The district attorney will portray you as a rich, entitled, elitist who thinks he is above the law. A jury will side with Margaret, especially when they learn what your father did to her. Do you really want all of that in the newspapers?"

Wyatt pounded his fist on the table. "I'm already in the newspapers! All they have is some samples of food. Anybody could have tainted it. It's circumstantial."

"Wyatt, you had motive and opportunity."

"I was also going to make a large donation to the Gates Manor. I have that in writing."

"True, but any attorney worth his salt will spin that as entrapment. And, unfortunately, they do have more physical evidence that implicates you."

Wyatt leaned back in his chair. "Such as?"

Dalton sighed. "When Gina and Margaret came in earlier to file their statements, they brought in a bottle of alcohol and a bottle of pills they say were found in Margaret's car."

Wyatt was unnerved but tried not to show it. "So. Doesn't that support our case? Everybody knows she's a junkie, and that proves it!"

Dalton shook his head. "They brought the items in a Ziploc bag. Your prints are all over them. I heard you require your staff to wear gloves from time to time. Didn't it ever occur to you to wear some yourself?

"I can't believe this is happening!" Wyatt stood up in a huff, kicking a chair out of his way.

Either indifferent, or simply accustomed to Wyatt's outbursts, Dalton remained calm. "Have you talked to Delores yet?"

Wyatt leaned against the cold, brick wall. "No," he said flatly.

"You'd better tell her before someone else does. You know, front page coverage and all. Shall I take care of that for you?"

"How many phone calls do I get?"

Dalton stood up and tapped on the mirror. An officer opened the door.

"Can he call his wife before he's transferred?"

The officer nodded reluctantly and shut the door.

Wyatt immediately sat down. "What do you mean *transferred*?"

Dalton took a deep breath. "I'm afraid they're moving you to Central Prison. The district attorney doesn't want it to look like you're receiving preferential treatment. I'm not going to sugarcoat this for you; it's not going to be an easy six months."

For the first time since the police had shown up at his house, Wyatt experienced a spark of fear. Before his pride could step in and extinguish it, he probed. "I have a feeling you're not talking about bad food and a limited wardrobe selection."

"No, I'm talking about your making it out alive. With an attempted murder plea-down, they're throwing you in with some pretty rough characters."

Wyatt wasn't about to let on that he was beginning to feel afraid. "I've dealt with rough characters before. Not everybody in the business world is as honorable as you, Dalton."

"Wyatt, these people aren't from your world. For the next six months, you're going to be living in theirs. The rules are completely different. And you don't get to make any of them."

Wyatt was painfully aware that things had gone wrong—seriously wrong. He wasn't ready just yet to accept the blame for it. He had planned well and executed even better. He couldn't figure out why the results didn't reflect it. Margaret was supposed to be the one in the newspapers and behind bars, not him. None of it made sense. He was desperate and running out of options. He only had one left. It had never failed him before, and he was counting on it not failing him now.

He leaned forward and gave a lopsided grin. "You and I both know how the world works, regardless of whose world it is. How much would it take? I could make a sizeable donation to the state prison system, perhaps outfit them with new exercise equipment. Hell, I could build them a state-of-the-art gymnasium. Of course, I'd want my name on it."

Dalton's expression shifted from one of concern to anger. He lowered his voice and leaned across the table closer to Wyatt. "Obviously, you don't get this, so let me spell it out for you. Going forward, your name will be a mere number stamped across the back of an orange jumpsuit. Your assets will be frozen until your release, and Delores will most likely divorce you the minute she finds out what happened. That black eye you got from your brother is child's play compared to what the other inmates will likely do to you."

He slammed the pen on the table in front of Wyatt. "Sign on the dotted line, Wyatt. I hate to break it to you, but in this situation, your net worth is totally worthless."

Wyatt blankly stared across the table. He was out of options. He was afraid to sign the document, but more afraid not to sign it. He didn't know what the next six months, or his entire future for that matter, held for him now.

This was not what he had planned.

He reluctantly picked up the pen.

CHAPTER FORTY-FIVE

Gina slowly ascended the stairs up to her bedroom. She slipped off her shoes and collapsed onto the bed. She turned over and stared at her dressing table. Her keepsake box was now sitting out in the open. She no longer had to hide its existence or the secrets it contained. At the right time, she would tell Wyatt who his real birth mother was.

She was well aware of the fact that Wyatt's identity had always been the one thing in which he most prided himself. It almost sounded cliché to think anyone would place so much value on their pedigree or possessions. Yet, Gina had witnessed this mindset in the Bennington family for decades. In prison, all of that would be stripped from Wyatt. He would walk in a line like everyone else. He would eat what everyone else ate. He would sleep in a small cell like the other inmates.

But Wyatt wasn't going to be just another inmate. It wouldn't be because of his last name or the balance in his bank account. This time it would be because of something even more powerful and more influential. He was going to have around-the-clock prayer for his soul, and for his God-given destiny to be restored to him.

Gina had already made the phone calls to Julia, Margaret, and

Minnie. They each would be praying and would ask members of their church communities to do the same. She was confident she could count on these ladies, not because Wyatt had earned their devotion, but because they understood forgiveness and redemption. Wyatt was in desperate need of both.

Filing her statement at the police station this morning had left her emotionally exhausted. She was going to allow herself to rest for a little while. Later today, she would stop at the market and then check in on Wyatt. Her mother had taught her years ago, that when your child is sick or in pain, you will do everything you can to alleviate their suffering. You would bear it yourself if you could. Wyatt deserved to go to prison, but Gina still hurt for him. She could only imagine how afraid and alone he was going to feel. She was also keenly aware that, because he was a Bennington, he would have a target on his back. As much as she hated to think about it, there was a chance he wouldn't survive prison at all.

She buried her face in her pillow and cried.

CHAPTER FORTY-SIX

Julia was surprised to discover such a long line at the coffee shop at three o'clock in the afternoon. She was also surprised that, even with the sweltering conditions outside, the customer in front of her was ordering a hot drink. She had decided at the last minute to stop by on her way to pick up Margaret. Last night had been a success with Wyatt's arrest, but it had to have taken a big toll on her. Sometimes little things can go a long way. It was just a Frappuccino, but she hoped it would help to cheer Margaret up.

The plan was to have an early dinner at Minnie's house tonight. It had been a while since either of them had enjoyed one of Minnie's home-cooked meals. After all that had transpired, Julia was looking forward to a little comfort food.

She checked the time as she pulled into Margaret's driveway. Waiting in line had put her a few minutes behind. She was bracing herself for what she anticipated would be a battle-worn Margaret Gates still in her bathrobe and slippers. She hoped it wouldn't take too much coaxing to get her out the door.

She balanced the drink in one hand, shifted her purse onto her shoulder, and rang the doorbell.

Before she could blink, Margaret answered the door. Julia's

mouth dropped open. Not only was she dressed, but she was wearing makeup, too.

"Hi! Oh, yummy, I hope that is for me," she said as she took the drink out of Julia's hand. "Are you ready to go, or would you like to come in for a few minutes?"

"Well, uh, I was going to leave that up to you."

"At least come in until we decide. It feels like an oven out there."

Margaret motioned for her to sit down on the sofa while she took a seat in a chair across from her.

Julia studied her face. "So, how are you doing?"

Margaret took a sip of her drink. "Better than I thought I'd be. Wyatt said some things that were so cruel. But it was like I had a mission to complete, and now I've completed it."

Julia was still trying to wrap her mind around Margaret's unexpected sunny disposition. "So, you're relieved it's over?"

Margaret nodded. "That's an understatement. After serving on the front lines, I'm looking forward to transitioning to more of a behind-the-scenes kind of a role. Speaking of which, did Gina contact you about asking a few church members to pray for Wyatt?"

Julia nodded. "Yes. I got several commitments this morning. Most everyone had already seen the newspapers, so I didn't have to explain *why* he needed prayer."

"That's good. My morning started off with a visit from Preston. Believe it or not, it went really well."

"Wait, you were expecting Preston to be upset."

"He was at first." Margaret rolled her eyes. "You know Preston. After he saw the newspaper article, he was like a bull charging at my front door to get an explanation."

Margaret attempted to catch a stream of whip cream that was escaping down the side of her cup. Her heels clicked on the hardwoods as she walked into the kitchen to get a paper towel. She wiped up a few drips that had leaked onto the counter and then continued, "Once I explained the situation, he calmed down and was supportive. We ended up having a great conversation."

"Okay, can I be honest with you?" Julia asked as she joined Margaret in the kitchen.

"Of course!"

"This is not at all what I expected. I thought I would be scraping you up off the floor, which would have been completely understandable. "Instead, you're smiling, laughing and don't seem rattled at all. You certainly don't look like you're dressed for having a meal with Minnie Morgan and me. You look more like you're—maybe going out on a date!"

Margaret grinned and took a sip of her coffee. "Maybe I *am*."

Julia was confused and incredibly intrigued. "So, how it is that you've been bait for Wyatt for the past week and yet you manage to develop a social—no, a *dating*—life on the side?"

Margaret shrugged her shoulders. "I guess it's not so hard when you keep it all in the family?"

Julia's eyes lit up. "Shut the front door! Joseph?"

Margaret nodded. "Before you even say it, I know it sounds crazy. It's the stuff tabloid covers are made of."

Julia laughed. "If you stop and think about it, most stories God writes are that way. Sarah was Abraham's half-sister and had a baby when she was one hundred years old. Noah built a boat in the middle of the dessert. Overall, I'd say you're in good company!"

Margaret winced. "It gets worse. He told me he loves me."

Julia's mouth dropped open. She walked over and sat down at one of the barstools. "When did all of this happen?"

"Oh, it's hot off the press—just last night. He figured out that Wyatt was trying to poison me. Evidently, that little crackerjack lab technician Carlton clued him in. After that, he spewed out all these feelings that he claims he's had for me for a while."

"How do you feel about him?"

Margaret took a sip of her drink and then set it down on the counter. She pulled out one of the barstools and sat beside Julia. "I wish there was a simple answer to that."

Julia turned to look at her. "What do you mean?"

"I'm definitely physically attracted to him. Do I love him? It's Joseph. What's not to love? I just have this wall up that I don't know how to get down. Honestly, I'm not sure if I'm trying to protect my heart," she looked down, "or his."

"Maybe it's both," Julia said gently.

Margaret shook her head. "My past is so messed up. The abuse did one kind of damage, but then my addiction, along with my bad choices, had a life all of its own. I'm not feeling sorry for myself, although I'm sure it sounds that way. There's a big part of me that really wants this. But, there's another part that's convinced I don't deserve it. Or, even worse…"

Julia put her hand on Margaret's. "That it's him that doesn't deserve you?"

Margaret sighed and hung her head. "Yeah…that he deserves so, so much better."

CHAPTER FORTY-SEVEN

HOLLY TURNED OVER EXPECTING TO SEE STEVEN BESIDE HER, BUT THERE was no sign of him. His side of the bed was straightened as if he hadn't slept there. In her half-awake state, she wondered if last night had happened at all. She pulled herself up onto her elbows and checked the time. She had a few more minutes before Olivia usually woke up. She heard sounds coming from downstairs and smelled coffee brewing. She brushed her hair out of her eyes and reached for her bathrobe at the foot of the bed.

From the top of the stairs, she could hear Olivia laughing. It was that contagious, toddler giggle which exemplified happiness in its purest form. She could also hear pots and pans rattling. She figured Claire must be making breakfast while Steven and Olivia played. She had to get this daddy-daughter reunion on video. She quietly went back to her bedroom to get her cell phone, but it wasn't on her nightstand where she normally kept it. With all that had happened last night, she must have left it downstairs in her purse. She spotted Steven's phone charging on the dresser. She keyed in the password and went to his video setting. His stored videos populated the screen. One caught her eye. It was the one she had sent him of Claire and Olivia talking in the kitchen.

She knew Steven. If he had saved it, he had watched it.

He'd never responded back to her about it. Then again, what would he have said? She had already erased the copy on her phone. Maybe Steven needed the reminder. Maybe that's why deep cuts leave scars. We see those scars and we remember. Remembering can be painful, but not as painful as getting wounded all over again.

She quietly walked downstairs with Steven's phone, recording from the shadows. Olivia squealed when she spotted her and loudly announced, "Mommy, Daddy's home!"

What a sweet depiction of grace. The prodigal had been welcomed back with unconditional love. Holly looked at Steven whose countenance reflected a man for whom, in this moment, only Heaven itself could have brought greater joy.

Holly laughed as pajama-clad Olivia bounded across the room and hugged her around her knees. She could see Claire beaming from the kitchen. She didn't say anything, but she didn't need to. Her sister's prudent instruction to trust God had paid off. He would have been faithful either way, but trusting instead of fretting made for a more peaceful process. Not that she hadn't had her moments.

And she understood that it was far from over.

The next weeks and months would be critical. Steven was going to have to prove himself. She anticipated it would require a lot of work on both of their parts. It was a season she would be glad to put behind her. Steven had made some serious mistakes, but he'd also fallen victim to a scam. The fact that his life had been threatened made her uneasy. If justice was served, those crooks from the Gold Rush would stay behind bars for a long time.

* * *

Jake Dunlop took a seat in the back of the courtroom. Since it was a Sunday, they had to wake up a judge to preside over the arraignment. *Which* judge was always anybody's guess. With it being the middle of the summer, today's choices would be limited to whoever wasn't on vacation.

The district attorney held her head high as she took her seat. Jake had worked with her long enough to know when she was anticipating a win. Her name was Polly Kilbracken, and she was as Irish as her name suggested. With fiery red hair and a penchant for life sentences, she'd put the fear of God into every defendant who'd had the misfortune of sitting across the aisle from her. He didn't recognize the defense attorney. He was young though, which often meant inexperienced. This bail hearing should be a slam dunk.

The bailiff loudly commanded, "All rise."

Everyone in the courtroom stood to their feet. Jake held his breath to see which judge would emerge from chambers. That question was answered, much to his dismay, by the bailiff's next sentence, "The honorable Warren Spencer presiding."

Judge Spencer entered the courtroom looking crumpled and annoyed at having been called in to work. He was an older judge who, according to public opinion, should have already retired. He had a reputation for being crotchety, impatient, and downright rude. Jake could only hope these negative traits worked in their favor today. He was confident Polly could hold her own, but he imagined she wasn't too happy to see Spencer's scowling face take a seat behind the gavel either.

The charges were read, and all three defendants pled not guilty. Jake shook his head. It always amazed him at how criminals caught red-handed would still maintain their innocence.

Polly was poised and professional. "Your Honor, the State requests that no bail be set for these defendants as they each have prior arrests and have demonstrated violent behavior. Other than their jobs at the Gold Rush, which the State intends to prove are not only unethical but criminal, they have no ties to the community and are flight risks."

The defense attorney, who looked so young that Jake wondered if he shaved, stood to his feet.

"Your Honor, these men are full-time employees at the Gold Rush Casino which operates legally under the state's general statutes for businesses licensed for gambling. The Gold Rush's record is clean. It hasn't received a single citation since its inception two years ago. Even the casino's restaurant has an impressive 99.5 sanitation grade."

Jake was watching Judge Spencer closely. Much to his horror, he saw the faintest hint of a smile.

Polly scoffed and shook her head, obviously irritated by this young attorney's attempt at humor. "Your Honor, the Gold Rush is not on trial here, and I fail to see how their sanitation grade affects whether the defendants make bail or not."

Judge Spencer cleared his throat and retorted, "Agreed. Mr. Porter, what is your point?"

The young attorney took of his glasses and looked at Judge Spencer with a self-assurance that seemed unnatural for someone his age. "Your Honor, the State's case against my clients is based on the *presumption* that there is illegal activity going on at the Gold Rush, in which my clients are being accused of participating. The only thing I see that my clients did last night was exercise their Second Amendment right to bear arms. Unless losing at poker has become illegal, I don't see why they can't return to work until the State can provide better evidence to support their incarceration."

Evidently Polly wasn't going to let this novice get the better of her. "The State *has* evidence based on an extensive two-year investigation of the Gold Rush that implicates all three defendants in illegal activity including extortion, racketeering, and violating Federal Trade Commission regulations for interest rates on loans."

"Your Honor," the defense attorney argued, "the Gold Rush isn't a federal lending institution, and, therefore, isn't subject to such regulations. And didn't Miss Kilbracken just say that the Gold Rush wasn't on trial here?"

Jake couldn't believe it. Polly was getting beaten at her own game. He didn't know who this young lawyer was, but he was good.

"Enough," the judge interjected. "Mr. Porter, don't think I am so naïve as to believe that all your clients do at the Gold Rush is count money and make sure the kitchen counters are wiped down. And there is a difference between bearing arms and brandishing one at someone because they happen to be *winning* at poker. While I would like nothing better than to see all three of your clients rot behind bars, I agree with the defense. Until the State can build a stronger case, which I suggest you do, Miss Kilbracken, I am setting bail for each of the defendants at ten thousand dollars."

Jake's jaw dropped. He could see Polly about to object, but the gavel went down, and court was adjourned. When she turned around to look at Jake, her expression was a mixture of shock and regret.

Rusty, on the other hand, didn't seem surprised at all. Apparently, he and his cohorts were accustomed to getting off with a just slap on the wrist. With a good attorney—which they obviously had—they would be back on the streets employing their dirty methods of money collecting in no time. Eventually, someone else would lose a family member, just as Jake had. He had to stop them before that happened.

But how?

As the three men were exiting the courtroom, Rusty stopped abruptly when he spotted Jake. He snaked his way over to where he was standing.

Jake's blood ran cold as Rusty leaned in and spoke in hushed tones. "I trusted you, and you set me up. That was a stupid move. You don't know who you're dealing with."

Jake's stare was resolute. "I know exactly who I'm dealing with. That's why you're going down."

Rusty's eyes flashed with anger. "If I go down, I'm taking a two-faced cop with me."

As the courtroom doors opened and Rusty stepped into the lobby, Jake could see him giving Tyrone and Pete a friendly pat on the back.

Jake shook his head. *I can't believe he threatened me!*

Then he looked off into the distance. *Wait, he threatened me...*

He took out his cell phone and quickly dialed his partner's number. "Dan? Sorry to bother you on a Sunday, but the Gold Rush guys made bail. I've got an idea. Meet me at that coffee shop near the courthouse in fifteen minutes."

After he ended the call, he realized he had another one to make. This one would be more difficult—*much* more difficult. He said a silent prayer and dialed the number.

CHAPTER FORTY-EIGHT

Holly insisted that Claire stop whatever she was doing and be a part of the family video. It was fitting that she was there to celebrate Steven's homecoming.

"Okay, let me finish scrambling these eggs and I'll join you," she called from the kitchen.

An incoming call interrupted the video recording on Steven's phone. Holly immediately gave the phone to Steven. "It's Jake," she said.

Steven, who had been playing a game with Olivia where he was holding her and spinning in circles, shifted the toddler to his hip in order to have a free hand. He took the phone from Holly.

"Hey Jake, is everything okay?"

Claire came out of the kitchen, drying her hands on a dish towel. Holly shot her a look of concern as she watched Steven's expression grow more serious.

He put Olivia down and walked to the other side of the room. Holly followed him while Claire attempted to distract Olivia, who wasn't too happy her dad had chosen talking on the phone over playing with her.

Holly's heart raced as she waited for Steven to finish the conversation.

Anticipating that the news wasn't going to be good, she turned to Claire. "Can you entertain Olivia in her room for a few minutes?"

"Of course!" Claire answered cheerfully for Olivia's benefit. "In fact, I bet I can get there before she does!"

"Nuh-uh!" Olivia yelled as they both took off up the stairs.

"Well?" Holly asked impatiently, noting the paleness of Steven's face.

He lowered his head. "The guys from the Gold Rush made bail, which means they're legally free to do anything except, unfortunately, leave town."

Holly backed up. "I don't understand."

"Jake is concerned they might decide to retaliate by coming after me."

"But you haven't done anything!" she exclaimed.

"Except for cheating against them in poker. They may suspect that I was in on the sting."

"That doesn't make sense! Jake said the police covered their tracks. They made it look like you were arrested and that the charges didn't stick because you had such a clean record."

"Which was the best they could have done. Jake was also protecting me by pretending to be a crook and not a policeman. It went as well as it could have. The cops couldn't have predicted those guys would make bail."

"So, what went wrong?"

"Jake took a risk when he included me on that operation. As much as I hate to use this expression, it really was a gamble. But it wasn't one he left completely to chance. He told me he had committed it to God. So, if these guys got out on bail, it wasn't just bad luck. God allowed it, and we have to trust Him."

"What's the plan?" Holly asked.

Steven pulled back the curtain on the living room window. "Do you see that white sedan across the street? That's Jake and his partner. That's the plan. They'll be tailing me as long as Jake believes I'm in danger. He originally requested I be put into a temporary witness protection program, but the threat wasn't considered that dire since it's only a hunch on his part. Providing around-the-clock surveillance was the best he could do."

He turned to Holly. "I think you and Olivia should stay with your parents for a few days. I can't risk anything happening to you. This situation has hurt you enough already."

She resisted the temptation to yell at Steven again and tell him he had no idea just how much it had hurt them. Besides, she was more worried now than angry due to the possibility of his safety being compromised. And how would this affect Olivia? She'd just gotten her daddy back.

"You just got home. How am I going to explain to Olivia that now she and Mommy have to leave?"

Steven walked over and took her hand. "You won't have to. That's my responsibility."

Holly shook her head. "No, it's not," she said, attempting a reassuring smile. "It's *our* responsibility. We'll tell her together."

* * *

Holly struggled to zip her suitcase.

"Wow. Mom wasn't kidding. You really do overpack," Claire said from her place of observation at the foot of the bed. "You're not moving in with her and Dad, but just staying for a few days, right?"

"Very funny," Holly said. She picked up a pillow and threw it at her. "I'm actually quite proud of myself. I organized mine and Olivia's things in record time. Can you think of anything I might have forgotten?"

"Except that you've already asked me that same question, like, fourteen times? No. And with the way those suitcases are bulging, I think forgetting something should be the last of your worries."

Holly wanted to laugh but her heart was heavy. "I can't believe that, once again, I'm having to choose between my husband and my daughter. I don't like being put in this position."

"It doesn't seem fair," Claire said as she sat beside her. "Under the circumstances, staying with Mom and Dad does sound like the most sensible thing to do."

Holly plopped back on the bed. "Aren't you supposed to tell me to trust God?"

"You already know that part."

Still lying on the bed, Holly grabbed her sister's hand. "You do realize you're stuck with us for a few more days."

Claire laughed. "I'm going to start charging by the hour. Now, let's find a forklift and get these suitcases out to the car!"

As they maneuvered the luggage downstairs, Holly could hear Steven and Olivia playing in the back yard. She wanted him to spend as much time with her as possible before they left. They had explained that she and Mommy were going to visit her grandparents for a few days. Daddy wanted to come, too, but he needed to catch some bad guys. It was Holly's idea to spin it that way. It was important for Olivia to know her daddy was trying to protect her, something he'd failed to do that day he'd left her in the hot car. It had gone as well as it could have, with Olivia being sad about the separation from her dad so soon after he'd come back home.

Steven met Holly and Claire in the driveway. After he'd loaded the suitcases into the trunk of Holly's car and closed the lid, Holly grabbed his hand.

"I want you to know, I'm not angry anymore."

Steven looked away. "You don't have to say that."

Holly attempted to make eye contact. "No, I mean it. We all make mistakes. It's how we handle them that truly shows what we're made of. Right now, you're willing to sacrifice yourself, if that's what it takes, so that your family can be safe. Who knows? If Jake can get these guys put away for life, maybe you're keeping other families safe, too."

Steven put his arm around her as they walked over to the driver's side of the car. "Jake said, with times being financially tough for so many people, gambling is on the rise. Those guys out at the Gold Rush prey on the needs and weaknesses of others. They should be punished. It makes me appreciate people like Jake who put their lives on the line every day. In some ways, it's like God sent him to be my guardian angel."

Holly smiled. "He thinks you're a hero."

Steven raised his eyebrows as he opened the car door for Holly. "I think we both know who the real hero is."

* * *

Steven double-checked Olivia's car seat to make sure it was secure before he gave her a hug and a kiss goodbye. He stood in the driveway and waved until both Claire's and Holly's vehicles were out of sight. Out of the corner of his eye, he could see Jake and his partner parked down the street. He went back inside the house and dialed his number.

Jake answered. "Steven, are you sure you want to go through with this?"

Steven sighed. "I don't see where I have a choice. You said yourself, this whole process could take a while. I can't go through the next several weeks, or maybe even months, looking over my shoulder. Do you have any updates?"

"We received intel that these guys are going to be at the Gold Rush this afternoon. We've got an undercover agent working at the bar. He's going to give the guys a tip that you're being transferred into witness protection tonight. That should draw them out. When they arrive, I'll text you. All you have to do is walk out of your house carrying two suitcases like you're leaving town. When they make a move toward you, we'll get them."

"Is there anything I can be doing in the meantime?"

"No. Stay put and wait for my instructions. And Steven? Thank you."

* * *

"Don't say it," Jake said as he ended the call.

His partner, Dan, shook his head and looked out the window. "You're not going to tell him what's really going on, are you?"

Jake maintained his gaze toward Steven's house. "He doesn't need to know."

"Do you think it would have influenced his decision?"

"No. Plus, it's important he gets to be the hero."

"What about you?" Dan asked. "What are you getting out of this?"

Jake furrowed his brow and answered. "The chance to make sure that what happened to my family doesn't happen to his."

CHAPTER FORTY-NINE

WYATT WAS THE LONE PASSENGER ON THIS TRANSPORT. THE STENCH ON the bus was an olfactory cocktail of diesel, sweat, and stale cigarettes. He wondered who else had sat in his seat. Who had preceded him on this journey? It was a passage from freedom to a world where confinement isn't limited to losing the right to come and go as you please, but where individuality, desires, and emotions are all on lockdown.

If the smell wasn't bad enough, he also had to adjust to looking through steel mesh to catch a glimpse of the world outside. The seats were uncomfortable and several were ripped. The conditions on the bus fostered a feeling of failure, and Wyatt had never experienced real failure before. There had been the occasional bad day on the golf course and a few business deals gone sideways. But nothing had ever delved this far beneath the surface, causing him to feel completely defeated. Losing a third of his father's estate to Preston Gates was the first time he had ever been blindsided, but that had just made him angry. This situation was different. So different, in fact, he still hadn't completely accepted it.

The first thing he'd had to get past had been his conversation with Delores. Of course, one of her society friends had alerted her to the front-page news. Counting on her support, he'd anticipated that she'd see him as a victim of having hired the wrong lawyer. He'd almost looked forward to the "You should have retained my attorney" speech. However, the conversation hadn't gone that way.

"Delores, darling, how are you?"

"I was better before Charlotte Pullmeyer called me. I was enjoying a lovely lunch on the Champs-Élysées. It completely ruined my day!"

"I understand, dear. It's just a big misunderstanding." No response. "Delores, are you still there?"

Delores sniffed. "I called Dalton Larkins. He said that you are going to prison. Prison, Wyatt! How could you do this to me? To us? You have no idea how embarrassing this is. I don't want to know if you intended to kill Margaret or not. Frankly, I don't really care. She's still alive, so what are you being punished for? Being a second-rate assassin? And what is this talk about you giving our money away to that rehab center?"

"The fact that I was making a donation shows I'm innocent. Why would I give money to someone I wanted to kill? It's ridiculous."

"So, you **were** *giving our money away? You should have included me in that decision! What about the drugs they found in the food you were serving her? How do I know you won't try to do the same thing to me?"*

Wyatt knew Delores. The conversation was unraveling, and it was only going to get worse. "How could you say something like that? I would never hurt you!"

Again, there was a silence on the other end. When Delores did respond, she was calm. Too calm. "That's the problem, Wyatt. I'm not sure what I know anymore. More importantly, I'm not sure I know you anymore. I've thought about it and, well, I think we should separate. I don't see how I could ever trust you or feel safe with you again."

The rest of the conversation was a blur except for Delores being devoid of emotion and speaking to him like he was her enemy. What he took away from it was that he'd lost his marriage and, by the time Delores got through with him, more money than he cared to calculate.

The bus lurched to a stop. As the door creaked open, Wyatt was ordered to step off to where a prison official was waiting for him. The activities of the next hour made him feel like he was living someone else's life. First, he was ordered to change into an orange jumpsuit. Time seemed to move in slow motion as he watched the guard stuff his designer clothes into a plastic bag. Then, he was stripped-searched, which was both humiliating and painful. To make matters worse, he sensed an element of the sadistic, almost as if the guard had secretly enjoyed it. He pushed aside this thought as he numbly went through the rest of the check-in process. The music playing inside his head, usually a victory anthem, had now turned into something more of a funeral dirge.

Everything was being taken from him, not the least of which was his possessions. For someone who'd always had everything he wanted, his belongings now consisted of a toothbrush, some toothpaste, and a bar of soap.

As he shuffled down the cellblock with shackles binding his ankles and wrists, the din of heckles and threats made his ears ring. It was clear that they knew who he was. He had never been talked to like that before. These men were vicious and crude. If they carried out their threats, his six months here would be a living hell.

He mostly kept his head down, but inadvertently made eye contact with the man in the cell next to his. For some reason, he caught Wyatt's attention. Perhaps it was the fact that he wasn't participating in Wyatt's less-than-hospitable reception from the other inmates.

The guard removed Wyatt's shackles and ushered him into his cell. The noise outside the cell eventually subsided. Wyatt looked around at his new home. There was a stack of folded sheets on top of his mattress. He'd never made his own bed before, but he was so disoriented right now, at least making his bed would give him something to do. He expected the guard would return in a couple of hours, when it was time for the evening meal.

After he had made his bed, he sat down and looked around at his stark, cold surroundings. Maybe at some point he would be allowed to have photos. But, whose photos would he put up? Delores was leaving him, and his own brother was the one who had turned him in to the police. None of his so-called friends would ever set foot in a correctional facility. Who was left? Wyatt had never felt fear like he'd felt walking down that cellblock. What was taking him even more by surprise was something else he hadn't experienced before, at least not in a way that was so heavy and crushing.

A hopeless sense of being alone.

With nothing else to do, he lay down on his bed. Perhaps he could sleep until dinnertime. He turned over and closed his eyes. They popped back open when he heard another inmate's door being unlocked and the guard informing him he had a visitor. With his eyes open, he saw more than just the water-stained ceiling tiles over his head. For the first time since his arrest, he saw his situation for what it was. He wondered why he hadn't realized it before. Perhaps it was denial, or perhaps it was his pride. The reason didn't really matter. He desperately wanted to look away, as was his custom when situations weren't to his liking. But what he usually did wouldn't work in here. This was prison. Nobody was coming. He was alone. This was his life for the next six months.

For the first time in years, Wyatt Bennington quietly wept.

CHAPTER FIFTY

Julia was glad for the forty-minute drive to Minnie's house because it provided Margaret with something Julia knew she needed after all that had happened: time with her best friend. When they reached Enoburg, the afternoon sky was dark, and the wind had picked up. Rain moving in from the west pelted Julia's windshield as she drove into Minnie's neighborhood. As usual, Julia had left her umbrella in the corner by the back door at home.

She and Margaret had to make a run for it. They were brushing the rain off their clothes when the front screen door creaked open.

"Come in out of that storm!" Minnie called over a loud thunderclap, which sent Margaret and Julia scurrying into the house.

Minnie chuckled. "Julia, did you leave your umbrella at home again?"

Julia laughed as she set her purse on a table by the front door. "You know me all too well, Minnie Morgan!"

Margaret leaned her head back. "Boy, I hope lunch tastes as good as it smells!"

"Well, there's only one way to find out!" Minnie said as she motioned for them to follow her into the kitchen.

The three of them took their seats at the kitchen table and joined hands. Minnie always asked the blessing.

Today that changed.

Margaret and Julia waited a few seconds. Julia opened one eye to see if Minnie was still going to pray, but she was sitting quietly with her eyes closed. Then she spoke. "Julia, why don't you ask the blessing today?"

It wasn't a big change. When Julia thought about it, it really didn't matter who asked the blessing. They were just used to Minnie doing it.

"Sure." She cleared her throat. "Lord, we thank you for all you have done for us in this past week. Thank you for keeping Margaret safe. Thank you for the healing you are bringing to Steven and Holly's marriage. We pray for Wyatt, that you will work in his life to show him your love. Thank you for this food, and please bless Minnie for preparing it for us. We pray this in Jesus's name. Amen."

Minnie squeezed Julia's hand as they all said Amen. She winked as she began to pass the food. "You did that as well as I could have—maybe even better."

Julia grinned and was about to ask Minnie how she had been feeling, when Margaret's phone chirped.

Margaret checked the notification and quickly typed something. Seconds later there was another chirp. She smiled sheepishly as she typed once more. When she realized Julia and Minnie were watching her, she focused an undue amount of attention on spreading a pat of butter across her biscuit.

Julia raised an eyebrow, as she put a helping of mashed potatoes on her plate. "Important messages from someone?" she asked.

Minnie, who never missed anything, looked from Margaret to Julia and then put down her fork. She folded her arms and leaned back in her chair. "Okay, who wants to go first?"

Julia gave Margaret a look she hoped would clearly communicate that this was news Margaret needed to deliver herself.

Margaret, apparently getting the message loud and clear, took a deep breath. "Joseph sort of told me he has feelings for me."

Julia faked a cough.

Margaret quickly corrected herself. "Okay, okay. Joseph told me he loves me."

Minnie paused for just a moment before picking up her knife and fork and slicing a bite-size piece of the baked chicken on her plate.

"Well, it took him long enough," she quipped.

Julia set her iced tea glass down on the table. "So, you saw this coming? I'm her best friend, and I didn't see it!"

Minnie laughed. "I suspected it at that first meeting when he announced the plans he had for the Manor house. I'm sure even *he* didn't see it back then, but I had a feeling it was just a matter of time."

"Why didn't you say something?" Margaret asked. "You know, encourage the situation…or at least warn me?" She laughed as she plunged a fork into her salad.

Minnie paused. "With all you've been through, Margaret, this had to happen in God's timing. I would have gotten in the way. In other words, God didn't need my help."

Minnie slid her plate aside and leaned forward with her elbows on the table. "However, an important question needs to be addressed, and only you can answer it. How do you feel about Joseph? Just because he's in love with you doesn't mean you're in love with him." She sat back in her chair and looked down at her plate as she picked up her biscuit. "Although the way your face lit up when you got that text tells me you don't exactly hate the situation."

Margaret grinned. "Actually, I do have feelings for Joseph. I've just never had a normal dating relationship. Joseph decided we would start out slowly, with a first date. In fact, he's taking me out tonight."

This time it was Minnie who raised an eyebrow. "Well, I knew you weren't wearing those heels for me."

"If nothing else, it will give us a chance to talk about the upcoming Christmas concert," Margaret said in an obvious attempt to downplay the romantic side of things. "Mr. Ortega has an idea for how to better involve the community. He wrote a vocal part for one of the songs and had planned to have an open audition, but then we discovered we have a singing talent right under our noses with one of our new students."

Julia knew exactly who Margaret was referring to.

"You must be talking about Jennifer," she said.

Margaret's eyes grew wide. "Yes, her voice is almost as powerful as her story."

"There have been a lot of powerful testimonies since the Manor opened," Minnie added as she took Julia's empty plate and stacked it on top of hers.

Margaret rearranged a couple of leftover lettuce leaves with her fork. "I guess there are some that pull at your heartstrings more than others."

Julia helped Minnie begin clearing the table. Margaret stood to help but was sternly instructed by Minnie to sit back down.

"You've been through a lot these past few days. You let us take care of this. Besides, we want to hear more about Jennifer."

"Doesn't she have a brother?" Julia asked as she picked up Margaret's plate.

"Yes. They were such good kids growing up. Their mom was a single parent who struggled financially but made sure they were in church every Sunday. When she lost her job several months ago, Jennifer's brother wanted to help. He quickly discovered that flipping burgers a few hours after school wasn't going to keep the lights on. After asking around, he found out he could make a lot of money by being an errand boy for a local gang. It was supposed to be a onetime thing, but it turned into more. They wouldn't pay him until he was officially initiated."

Minnie started slicing the chocolate cake she'd just taken out of the refrigerator. "I'm afraid to ask what that involved."

"Unfortunately, it involved Jennifer. They promised her

brother a big payoff in exchange for his sister," Margaret responded as she held up her hand in refusal of the cake Minnie was offering. "Joseph is taking me out for dessert," she said with a wink.

Julia served them each a fresh cup of coffee before sitting back down. "What happened?" she asked.

"There were three gang members, and the rule was her brother had to watch. After the first one raped Jennifer, though, her brother snapped. He grabbed a gun off one of the guys and shot all three of them."

Minnie shook her head as she took her seat. "And that boy started out just trying to help his mother."

Margaret stirred her coffee. "They all lived, but he's doing time for attempted murder. They did get the one guy for rape. The public defender tried to get her brother's charges reduced to self-defense or a crime of passion, but the district attorney wouldn't go for it."

"I'm not surprised," Minnie said. "I've seen Polly Kilbracken's name in the paper. She has a reputation for being tough as nails."

Julia put her hand on Margaret's shoulder. "I can see why this one pulled at your heart strings. It's a little like your story."

"It's one of the reasons I bonded with her so quickly. I know what it's like to be betrayed by a family member. I saw the same fear and shame in her that I'd lived with for so many years. We're doing everything we can to help her. The first thing she needed was medical care. She received a complete medical exam and was tested for HIV. We're waiting for the results. She's making progress, but it's going to take time. The good news is, since she started getting help at the Manor, her brother is doing better. He was so full of anger and guilt. Jennifer said he's started reading his Bible in prison."

Minnie took a sip of her coffee. "Sounds like the healing is spreading through the whole family. How's the mother?"

"Joseph helped her find a job at the hospital. She's working in the cafeteria. It's temporary until she can get her degree. We're paying for her to take nursing classes at night school so she can become an LPN."

Minnie closed her eyes for just a moment as if reflecting on what she was about to say. "You know, the Lord's work always has a ripple effect. Jennifer's healing is going to show her family that, no matter what you go through, God can always put a new song in your heart. I can't wait to hear her sing at that concert!"

Margaret looked pensive. "I just wish there was a way her brother could hear her perform, too."

Julia thought for a moment. "Why don't we take the concert to him? The band hasn't played at a prison before, but I'm sure Mr. Ortega would be open to the idea."

Margaret's eyes lit up. "That's a great idea! I mean, that's what the Gates Manor Band does! What better place to share hope and the message of Christmas than at a prison?"

Minnie nodded. "In the parable of the sheep and the goats, Jesus was pleased with the sheep because they represented those who fed the hungry and visited those in prison. Jesus charged his followers to go beyond the status quo and love those whom others rejected. It was the kind of love that put Jesus in the company of tax collectors and prostitutes."

"And Margaret Gates," Margaret said.

Minnie reached across the table and took Margaret's hand. "And, believe it or not, Wyatt Bennington. I'm sure, in that prison, status and pedigree make him the most hated man there. As Jesus's disciples, we've all got to be willing to open our hearts to people who are different from us. It's not always kids on the street that we have a difficult time loving and reaching out to. Sometimes it's people like Wyatt."

Margaret's phone chirped.

"Can't that boy let you eat a meal without texting you?" Minnie teased.

Margaret laughed as she retrieved the phone from her purse.

"Well...is it Joseph?" Julia asked.

Margaret put the phone down on the table and put her head in her hands.

Julia couldn't imagine what could be wrong. "Margaret, what is it?"

"You're right; it was Joseph. We just received Jennifer's lab results from the hospital."

Minnie winced. "Don't tell me that Jennifer has an STD."

"No, she doesn't. That's the good news."

Julia was confused. "Then what's the bad news?"

Margaret sighed. "She's pregnant."

CHAPTER FIFTY-ONE

Wyatt could hear the guard walking back down the cellblock. It wasn't time for dinner yet, so he wondered what was going on. He sat up and wiped his tears on his sleeve. When he did, he felt the sting once again of his brother's unerring aim. He stepped over to the sink and splashed a little water on his face. The last thing he needed was for the guard to detect any weakness on his part. He probably wasn't coming to his cell anyway, but Wyatt wasn't willing to take any chances.

Much to his surprise, the guard did stop and unlocked his door.

"Bennington, you have a visitor."

Wyatt was so stunned he couldn't move.

The guard motioned impatiently for him to come forward, and then cuffed him. He led Wyatt to the visitors' area where there were several cubicles the size of voting booths. Partitioned by half-walls, they each had a chair and a phone, with a window separating the booth on this side from an identical booth on the other side of the glass. Wyatt was instructed to sit down and pick up the phone. He couldn't believe who was sitting across from him.

"Hello, Mr. Bennington."

Wyatt was dumbfounded. All he could say was her name. "Gina?"

Gina smiled slightly. "Are you surprised?"

Wyatt, who had managed to compose himself from his earlier show of emotion, steeled himself before speaking. "I'm surprised I have a visitor. And, yes, I'm surprised it's you."

Surprised was an understatement. What was Gina doing here? She had always been around to help take care of him, but that was her job. He was pretty sure coming to visit him in prison was not part of her job description. But, here she was.

"Are you upset with me for turning in the evidence against you?" she asked.

Again, he showed no expression. "If you and Joseph hadn't betrayed me, I wouldn't be in here."

Gina's brows knitted, and she leaned in closer to the glass. "Most likely, you would be, and for much longer. If we hadn't intervened at all, you would be serving a life sentence in a place much worse than this."

Wyatt scoffed and quickly looked around. "What could be worse than this place?"

"A prison you have been in for years."

"What are you talking about, Gina?"

"Iron bars aren't what really imprisons us. You can live in here and be completely free."

Before Wyatt could ask any more questions, he felt the guard's hand on his shoulder.

"Time's up," the guard said.

"Is it okay if I come back tomorrow?" Gina asked, addressing Wyatt.

Wyatt nodded, and he felt his composure slip a little as he whispered a word he'd rarely ever used in a sincere fashion.

"Please."

He hung up the phone but continued to make eye contact with her as the guard led him out. Could she see the fear and dread on his face? He wasn't sure he cared anymore.

Before he lost sight of her, Wyatt saw Gina bow her head, and her lips were moving as if she were speaking. Was she praying for him?

* * *

Joseph put a fresh pod into the Keurig and pushed start. As the machine gurgled to life, he gazed out the kitchen window. He'd made the decision earlier to stay home from church today. With the news of Wyatt's arrest dominating the front page of the morning newspaper, he expected he would be bombarded with questions from members of the community. He still had plenty of his own to contend with. It was the what-ifs that were the most troublesome. *What if Gina hadn't reached out to try to save Margaret? What if she hadn't picked up on the irregularities?* Beyond that, he wondered why, in fact, she had. Her perception went beyond what would have been expected from a staff member, even one as dedicated as she was.

Then there was the other predicament in which he found himself. Imprisonment would cause Wyatt to lose more than just his freedom. It would deal a fatal blow to his social status, popularity, and most of his friendships. Knowing how shallow Delores could be, it would probably cost him his marriage as well. As angry as Joseph was at him, he didn't want Wyatt to have to add his relationship with his brother to the list of casualties.

He and Wyatt had always gotten along well enough but were never the friends their parents had hoped they would be. As far as Joseph could recall, he'd never punched Wyatt before. Perhaps if they had been closer, there would have been more conflict. Their civil behavior had always been viewed as a good thing. In hindsight, maybe it wasn't.

He stirred a little cream into his coffee. Joseph had been afforded the same opportunity as his brother to let the Bennington family's wealth and success go to his head. What he had resisted, Wyatt had embraced.

In view of recent events, Joseph wondered if arrogance and hatred were more closely linked than he realized. Jesus taught that murder is simply hatred all grown up. Wyatt had plotted murder and deserved to go to prison. What he didn't deserve was something that Joseph was commanded in Scripture to offer, and that was forgiveness.

It wouldn't be easy. It would take all the strength and resolve he could muster. Forgiveness always came with a price tag; one that required you to empty your pockets of pride and self-right-eousness. Joseph knew that not doing so would expose his short-sightedness regarding the love and mercy he himself had received. His sins may have been different from his brother's, but apart from Christ, he would have remained just as lost.

Today would be a roller coaster of emotions. There were two appointments on Joseph's calendar. Neither were things he ever thought he would be doing. The first was filing a statement at the police department against his brother. The second was a date with Margaret. He'd hoped the latter would've been under better circumstances. Perhaps what George had said was true; life rarely gets served up in a neat little package. He made a note to purchase flowers and candy before picking up Margaret. He was certain that George would ask.

For now, he would spend some time in prayer before driving over to the police station. He pulled out a chair and set his coffee cup on the kitchen table. He pushed aside the newspaper, which he'd left folded. He didn't need to read the headlines; he'd lived them.

Instead, he opened his Bible to Matthew chapter 18. Peter was asking Jesus how many times he had to forgive his brother. Perhaps this was the best place to start reading today.

CHAPTER FIFTY-TWO

Wyatt endured an encore performance of the jeering as the guard escorted him back to his cell. Halfway down the block, he felt something grip his arm. The guard yelled at the inmate to keep his hands to himself. He backed away, but not before Wyatt heard him hiss, "Rich boy got plenty to give away!"

Once again, the man in the cell next to his didn't participate. Wyatt wanted to know why. He certainly could use an ally, but this man's quiet demeanor didn't necessarily mean he was trustworthy. To the contrary, it could indicate that his hatred for Wyatt, and Wyatt's type, ran deeper than insults and threats could convey. It was a toss of the coin as to whether he ended up being his friend or his worst enemy.

Wyatt sat down on his bed. A drip of sweat stung his eye. He reached a trembling hand up to wipe his brow. He was a man who'd always depended on wealth and status as protection from life's storms; it was amazing how it all had turned on him. His world was crumbling. This was only the first hour. He had days, weeks, and months to deal with more of the same. That is, if he survived to see the end of his sentence.

He leaned over the sink and splashed water on his face once again. Then he heard a voice speak to him from the next cell. It was a low voice, steady and calm.

"Are you Pilate or something?"

Wyatt quickly dried off his face and then sat down on the edge of his bed closest to the door.

"I'm Wyatt," he answered tentatively.

The man snickered. "I know your name. But you keep washing your face, like Pilate washed his hands."

He leaned in toward the wall separating them. "What do you mean?"

"You can wash your face all day long, but it won't make any of this go away. You tried to kill someone—someone who was just doing good for other people."

Wyatt had never thought of Margaret in that way. He had only seen her as a troublemaker.

The man continued, "The only thing that woman ever did was to expose the darkness in your heart, and in your father's heart. Does that remind you of anyone?"

Wyatt didn't have an opportunity to respond. A loud buzzer sounded, and all the cell doors opened. Several guards filed into the area as the inmates were herded into the dining area. Wyatt was terrified after the threats he had received but tried not to show it. He kept his head down while he walked and while he ate.

Afterward, the men were released to an outdoor recreational area. Wyatt positioned himself close to one of the guards. He tried to blend into the shadows as he leaned against the building. The man from the cell next to his stepped over and stood beside him.

"What's your name?" Wyatt asked timidly.

The man replied without making eye contact. "Terrance."

Wyatt was desperate to know if this man was going to be a friend or a foe. He wasn't sure how to go about finding out. For now, he would pick up where their conversation had left off.

"I know who Pilate is."

The man still made no eye contact. "Do you now?"

Wyatt did. Growing up in the Bible belt, he had attended enough funerals and holiday church services to know the basics of the faith. He just didn't believe any of it.

"Pilate was the Roman governor who could have released Jesus but had him crucified instead."

Terrance nodded and looked out over the basketball court where there was a pick-up game underway. "Well, I see you paid attention in Sunday school. You're right. Pilate sentenced an innocent man to death. But that's good news for you. In fact, that's why you're in here."

Wyatt didn't have a clue what Terrance was talking about, but he clung to the words "good news." That certainly was something he could use right now. But he didn't understand how an event that occurred over two thousand years ago could have anything to do with his life today. He looked down as he remembered one Christmas when his parents took him to church. He couldn't have been more than nine years old at the time—

Smack! Wyatt had lifted his head just in time to take the full impact of an airborne basketball hitting his face. He stumbled back against the building. His nose and forehead throbbed, and his vision was blurred. He would have to rely on his other senses until the fog cleared. Terrance said nothing. Wyatt had begun to think perhaps he could trust him. Now he wasn't so sure.

He could hear the guard issue what he considered to be an obligatory admonition to the perpetrator. There were snickers and comments that circulated for a few minutes, but then the sound of a basketball bouncing on the pavement told Wyatt the game had resumed. It was a brief but powerful lesson that delivered a chilling message; he could never relax, and he couldn't trust anyone.

After a few minutes, Terrance leaned over and whispered, "If you want to make it out of here alive, you've got to be alert every second of every day. Even when you're sleeping, you'd better be on guard. You think that hurt? That was nothing compared to what these guys are capable of doing."

As Terrance walked away, Wyatt's heart sank, and the loneliness returned.

Six months suddenly felt like an eternity.

CHAPTER FIFTY-THREE

Steven couldn't do anything, or go anywhere, until he received further instructions. He was confident Jake wouldn't let him do anything too risky. But what if things didn't go according to plan tonight? Rusty and his crew making bail was certainly unexpected. He wouldn't be confined to his house if the arraignment had gone as predicted. He thought about the possible outcomes, as well as the worst-case scenario. What if he didn't make it out alive? Was he satisfied with the last conversation he'd had with Holly? Does Olivia really know how much he loves her? He began to dial Holly's number but changed his mind. He didn't want to worry her. He'd put her through enough already. There was one thing that he *could* do.

He could write her a letter.

He sat down at his laptop. He wasn't sure how to begin. It had to be just right; not too formal, but articulate and well written. He also wanted it to be from his heart without sounding corny. For instance, he wanted to tell Holly how much he loves the way she looks first thing in the morning when the sleep hasn't completely left her eyes. Or how her laugh is both annoying *and* adorable.

Once he started, the words began to flow, and he was surprised at how much he'd typed. What he'd anticipated being a couple of paragraphs ended up being several pages. As the printer hummed to life, he found an envelope in a kitchen drawer and wrote Holly's and Olivia's names on it. As the last page fell into the paper tray, his phone chimed. It was a text from Jake.

In about an hour, my partner will drive up to the curb and wait for you. Come out of your house carrying two large, empty suitcases. I'll be close by, but out of sight. I'll let you know when it's time.

Steven folded the letter, placed it in the envelope, and left it on the kitchen table. He then made his way upstairs and creaked open the attic access. He turned on the light and began searching for the luggage. He and Holly hadn't used the larger pieces since the vacation they took when Olivia was about a year old. That was when it had all started. He would give anything to be able to turn back the clock and never step foot into that casino. Who would have thought it would turn into such a deadly habit? He had never been prone to addictions before. He'd always been able to stop after two glasses of wine and had never had an issue with tobacco. What was it about gambling that held him underwater and wouldn't let him come up for air?

After moving aside some old boxes of college textbooks, he found the suitcases. He brought them downstairs and put them by the front door. His phone chimed again. This time it was Holly letting him know she and Olivia were all settled in at her parent's house.

All that was left for Steven to do was wait. But the waiting was maddening. He'd never felt so restless. He sat on the couch for a few minutes, then stood up and paced. He tried sitting in the chair by the window, but ended up pacing some more.

As the early evening shadows finally began to fall, he became more keenly aware that the clock was ticking. The letter he'd written to Holly and Olivia wasn't enough. He needed to take inventory of his life. It pained him to do so, but it was now or never.

He stood by the den window and looked out into the backyard

at Olivia's play area. As a breeze gently rocked the swings, his mind was filled with regretful memories.

"Daddy! Push me!" A pig-tailed Olivia said as she'd bounced impatiently on the seat of the swing.

"I can't right now, honey. Daddy's busy," he'd said, as he'd worked through emails on his phone. "Mommy will be here in a minute."

It had always been easier to let Holly take the lead. She had the stronger personality and was better at taking care of Olivia. That was never more evident than the day he had left Olivia in the car outside the casino. But his tendency to think that way was what had made him feel like a second-string member of the family. Was his role really all that vital? If something happened to him, how much of a void would even exist? Beyond that, one day in Heaven when the books were opened, would they show that he had done anything noteworthy? Or would it be revealed that he had always chosen to sit back and let others do the heavy lifting?

He had to face the consequences of his choices, and his failures, whether he felt like he could handle it or not. He desperately needed to know if God, as his Father, was pleased with him. He'd never had much of a relationship with his own father, and maybe that was part of the problem. He'd never had a role model to assure him that he had what it took to face life's challenges and difficulties. Perhaps that was what gambling did for him. It made him feel like a winner.

Not knowing what else to do, he got down on his knees and looked up. "God, what's wrong with me? You gave me this beautiful family, and I messed everything up. How can you love someone like me?" He lay face down on the floor and wept. He wasn't sure how long he cried, but afterward he was exhausted. The sound of a man entering the room jolted him to his feet.

He couldn't believe his eyes. There was an older gentleman sitting in the chair across from the sofa. The man had dark, wrinkled skin and looked vaguely familiar.

"Who are you?" Steven asked.

The man smiled. "I didn't think you would remember me, but I remember you."

Steven looked back and forth from the front door to the back door, knowing he'd locked both. "How did you get in here?"

The man leaned forward in his chair. "A year or so before I retired, there was a freshman who came through the band program. He didn't stay in it long, because he and his mom were about to move…again. I wanted to reach out to him, but I never had the opportunity."

Steven all but fell back onto the sofa. He could only whisper the name. "Mr. Morgan?"

The man spoke tenderly. "You never told Holly you had an interest in music because you didn't think it was important. As I recall, though, you wanted to learn how to play the clarinet because it had a softer delivery than, say, the trumpet."

Steven felt the shame coming back. "Yeah, I was such a loser."

The gentleman shook his head. "No, Steven. Every instrument has its place and purpose. It's like the body of Christ. If the whole body was an eye, where would the sense of hearing be? You don't have to be the star of the show for your part to count. Your contribution matters, and *you* matter. Keep surrendering your heart to Jesus. He not only loves you, He's your biggest fan."

A warmth penetrated Steven's heart. Then he heard something chiming.

He opened his eyes, not even realizing he had fallen asleep, and sat up quickly. Jake had texted him.

It was time.

He briefly glanced around before turning off the light. Picking up the two suitcases, he squared his shoulders and opened the front door.

The sound he heard next reminded him of the boom that follows the lighting of a July 4th bottle rocket.

But the pain was unlike anything he had ever experienced. He yelled as, what he could only assume was a bullet, tore through the flesh of his right arm. He lost his grip on the two suitcases and fell onto his knees on the porch, gripping his arm. Then he heard two more shots. To his horror, he saw Jake, who had made it halfway across the front lawn, go down clutching his chest.

"No!" Steven screamed. He struggled to his feet and ran over to where Jake was sprawled out on the grass. Out of the corner of his eye, he could see Jake's partner and two other officers chasing three men across the street on foot. Within seconds, Rusty, Tyrone, and Pete were being thrown to the ground and cuffed.

Steven knelt down and took Jake's hand into his. "Jake, I don't understand! Why didn't you wait on the other side of the street? I thought once I was outside those guys would drive up and try to snatch me. What happened?"

Jake's breathing was labored. "I'm so sorry! I had to shoot you. If I hadn't, you could've gotten caught in the crossfire. They were waiting with their guns out before you'd even opened your front door. I didn't have time to warn you. You had to be down, and fast."

Steven's head was spinning. Blood was gushing from Jake's wounds. Where was everybody? Glancing around, he yelled, "Someone call 911! Help him!" He grimaced as he took off his own shirt. He hurriedly balled it up and applied pressure to Jake's wounds.

"Wait? What do you mean crossfire? Those guys were coming for me, right?"

Jake winced in pain. "No, Steven. They were coming for *me*. You were just the bait to draw them to a public place where I had backup. The other officers followed my partner and me here in an unmarked car. We knew Rusty, Tyrone, and Pete would show up and would make their move as soon as my back was turned. And they would've probably shot you too if I hadn't taken you down first. These guys aren't the type to leave witnesses."

Steven's eyes grew wide. "What?"

"It doesn't matter. We got them." Jake's speech began to break up. "After thirty years. We finally got them."

Steven shook his head. "Jake, this is all my fault."

Jake laughed bitterly. "Do you want me to shoot you again?" He paused to catch his breath. "You listen to me. You put your life on the line tonight. You're a hero."

"I'm no hero," Steven said choking back the tears. "But I'm proud to know someone who is. Those guys are going away for a long time. You finally got justice for your dad."

"That's all I ever wanted," Jake said with a faint smile, his eyes squinting closed. And then his body went limp.

Vaguely aware of sirens and of paramedics running through the yard, Steven dropped his head onto Jake's chest and sobbed.

The paramedics pushed him aside and started performing CPR, but Steven knew it was already too late.

Steven groaned as his gurney was hoisted into the back of the ambulance, jostling his wounded arm against his body. The smell of the antiseptic burned his nose as a paramedic cleaned his wound.

"After what you've been through, this needle shouldn't bother you at all," a pony-tailed female in a white lab coat said as she tapped the end of a syringe. "It'll help with the pain, but it's also going to make you really sleepy."

Steven felt a sting and then the pain subsided. Too bad his grief couldn't be resolved that quickly.

As the medication raced through his veins, his eyes grew heavy. He was alert enough to feel his phone vibrate in his pants pocket. He reached for it, but his hands felt like they belonged to somebody else. After a few clumsy attempts, he finally managed to retrieve it before the caller hung up.

It was Holly. She had already seen the incident on the news and was panicking.

"Thank God you answered!" she said. "Are you okay? What happened?"

Steven knew what he wanted to say, but his mouth wasn't cooperating. "Holllly," he slurred. "I'm fine. But – "

"But what?" she demanded.

His voice cracked. "Jake didn't make it."

Steven would have no recollection later of what Holly had said to him after that. But whatever it was, her voice had comforted him in a way that only she could.

What he did remember was the last thing he said before losing consciousness.

"It's over, Holly. It's finally over."

CHAPTER FIFTY-FOUR

The only sound in the kitchen for the next minute or so was the ticking of Minnie's wall clock. Julia wasn't sure what to say, so she was glad when Margaret finally broke the silence.

"You both know how I feel about abortion," Margaret said, and then threw her arms out wide. "But what do I say to someone who's been raped?"

Minnie's tone was somber in her response. "It has nothing to do with how you feel, Margaret. It has everything to do with what God's word says. It's not that unborn child's fault he was conceived by rape. Someone will want to parent that little one even if Jennifer doesn't. A human being is not property. We don't get to decide if it deserves to live or not. God already made that choice by giving life to this little one. We don't understand it, but we can trust His sovereignty."

Margaret closed her eyes. "Do you know how hard this is going to be for her?"

Julia put her hand on Margaret's arm. As badly as she felt for Jennifer, her heart was breaking for Margaret, too. She spoke softly. "Doing the right thing usually is. She won't be alone, though."

"That's right," Minnie added. "What a testimony to that

unborn child to know his mother understood he had value, regardless of how he was conceived. God wants Jennifer to demonstrate a love that most folks don't even know exists."

Julia watched as Margaret stood and walked over to the kitchen window. With her back to them, she sighed and hung her head. "Maybe it's me who's afraid. I've never had to deal with this. I had unprotected sex numerous times, and I never got pregnant."

"You may not have dealt with this particular situation," Minnie said, "but you know what it's like to be at the end of your rope and see God come through for you in a miraculous way."

Julia could tell that Minnie's words had encouraged Margaret because, when Margaret turned around, her countenance looked a little brighter. She walked back over to where Minnie was sitting and put her arm around her. "Minnie Morgan, what would I do without you?"

"For one, you would be on time for your date," Minnie quipped as she glanced down at Margaret's feet. "You and those heels need to head back to Raleigh."

Julia looked at her watch. "Wow, it's later than I thought! It's always a treat being in your home, Minnie. But, you're right. I think it's time Margaret and I hit the road. Holly and Olivia are probably already at my house."

She looked back over her shoulder as she walked into the foyer to get her purse. "They're staying with us for a few days until the situation with that gambling ring settles down. I'm sure it's only a precaution."

She dug her phone out of her purse. "Oh dear, I have two text messages from Holly… and five missed calls?"

"Is everything okay?" Margaret called from the kitchen.

Julia scrolled down through the texts and gasped. "Oh my God!"

Margaret came running into the foyer. Minnie wasn't far behind.

Julia hands were shaking as she tried to dial the number on her phone. "Steven's been shot!" she exclaimed.

Minnie reached over and grabbed Margaret's hand.

"Come on…answer!" Julia pleaded as she waited for Holly to pick up.

Finally, there was a voice on the other end. Before she could ask for details, Holly began giving her a report on Steven's condition.

"How is he?" Margaret whispered impatiently.

Julia waved her off and continued to listen. After a few seconds, she looked up. "He's okay!"

Minnie and Margaret each breathed a heavy sigh of relief.

"Wait…what did you say? Oh, no…I'm so sorry…Yes, I'll let them know. I love you, too."

"What is it, dear?" Minnie asked.

"There was a sting operation. Steven and Jake, the policeman that was helping him, were both injured." She hung her head. "Jake didn't make it."

Sadness clouded Margaret's features. "I'm sorry to hear that, Julia. I hope that's the last bad news we hear today."

"Bad news is a part of life," Minnie said. "But we have a God who is working all things together for the good of those who love Him. No matter how dark or hopeless a situation may appear, He can make something beautiful out of it. Why don't we take a few minutes and pray for these families?"

Julia smiled ever so slightly. "Well, since I was put in charge of the blessing, I guess I can lead us in prayer for this, too. Can we all join hands?"

Minnie eyes shone with light. "I think that's a great idea!"

CHAPTER FIFTY-FIVE

Joseph's phone chirped. Again.

What flowers did you get her? Please tell me you didn't get carnations. She will think she is going to a funeral instead of on a date. You should get her lilies.

Joseph wanted to write back that it would be *George's* funeral if he didn't quit pestering him.

I've got this. I wasn't exactly raised in the rain forest. I know how to select flowers.

Joseph rolled his eyes as he could see George was writing a response.

Where did you buy the flowers? It's Sunday. The only place open is the grocery store. You don't want to buy her grocery store flowers.

Joseph tapped his foot in frustration, and then he typed back.

You've left me no choice. I don't like dropping names, but I am doing so now, and it's MINE. We have several gardens on the Bennington estate. Bivens put together a beautiful floral arrangement for me.

Confident George would leave him alone now, Joseph reread the fax he'd received regarding Jennifer's test results. His heart was heavy. He knew Margaret would want to schedule a meeting with Jennifer and her mom as soon as possible. As much as he wanted this evening to be as close to a normal date as possible, it was going to be difficult to set aside news like this and gaze romantically at the stars. Then again, nothing about his and Margaret's relationship had ever been, or ever would be, completely normal.

His thoughts were interrupted once more by another text message alert.

Who is Bivens, and what does he know about flowers?

* * *

Minnie waved goodbye to Julia and Margaret from her front porch. As she headed back into the house, the pain in her side she'd felt days earlier had returned. She steadied herself by leaning up against the wall in the foyer. After it had passed, she stepped over to the fireplace mantle and gingerly touched a family picture of her, Caleb, and their two boys. It was the last family portrait taken before their older son Kenneth was diagnosed with leukemia. She walked into the kitchen and took a letter out of a basket of mail on the counter. She read it again, thinking maybe this time it would all sink in. She'd planned to talk to Julia and Margaret about it at lunch, but it hadn't seemed like the right time. She certainly didn't want to upstage Margaret's announcement about Joseph. Beyond that, there had been plenty of other disturbing news to go around for one day.

She folded the letter and placed it back in the basket. She opened the cabinet doors overhead and took out several bottles of pills, dispensing the prescribed dosage from each. After pouring herself a glass of water, she stood staring at the medications.

"And the doctor said this might not even make a difference," she muttered as she began taking them one by one.

CHAPTER FIFTY-SIX

Margaret's doorbell rang at 8:00 p.m. sharp. If she hadn't known better, she would've thought her date was a flower arrangement wearing khakis. She could hardly see Joseph behind the tall bouquet he was holding.

"Wow!" she exclaimed as she took the heavy assortment of lilies and roses. "These are really...*large!*"

Joseph smiled. "Do you like them?"

Margaret eyes were wide. "What's not to like? Let's put them in a vase." Her voice trailed off as she took the flowers into the kitchen. "Or maybe a Christmas tree stand..."

Joseph followed her inside. She rummaged in the cabinet under the sink until she found a vase big enough. After filling it with water, which took a while, she set the arrangement on her dining room table. Once in a vase, the flowers were breathtaking. Their fragrance filled the room, and their color pallet showcased soft pastel petals contrasted against rich, lush greenery.

Margaret turned to Joseph. "They really are lovely. Thank you."

Evidently Joseph wasn't finished. He produced a medium-sized flat box wrapped in thick, embossed wrapping paper. "And this is for you."

Margaret was touched. She wanted to play it cool, but she was curious to see what was inside. She giggled with childlike excitement and sent pieces of wrapping paper flying in all directions.

"How did you know?" she looked up at him in amazement. "I love Turkish Delight! I just never wanted to spend the money on it."

She put the box down and looked up at him sheepishly. "I feel bad."

Joseph looked bewildered. "About what?"

"I didn't get anything for you!"

The look in Joseph's eyes made Margaret's heart flutter. He tenderly stroked her hair. "Sure, you did. You're letting me take you on a date."

Margaret could feel her cheeks get warm. She immediately put her hands on them to conceal the flush of color.

Again, Joseph's eyes displayed something Margaret had never experienced. It was as if she delighted him, not only when she was on top of her game, but also when she was vulnerable and off-balance. She was relieved when he was the next one to speak since, for the moment, she was at a loss for words.

"So, are you ready to go?"

Margaret nodded. "Of course. Let me get my purse."

* * *

Conversation was anything but lacking as they drove to the restaurant. They covered every topic from what was going on at work, to Preston and Annie's pregnancy. Of course, Wyatt was something they discussed at length, and Joseph was sad to hear about Jake. When they arrived at the restaurant, the television in the bar area was broadcasting the story of Jake's shooting. They paused for a moment to watch it before being seated.

A waiter in a tuxedo ushered them to a private table by the window. Their view was a spectacular collection of Raleigh's city lights. They twinkled against a purple summer sky whose sun-kissed hues seemed to resist the onset of nightfall. There was a pink carnation in a crystal vase on the table. Even though the flower was customary, Joseph frowned when he saw it. He was certain George wouldn't approve.

From the wine, to the dessert, to the stroll they took downtown, the evening was nothing short of enchanting. Since the two of them had worked together for over two years, he was spared the awkward formalities typically associated with a first date. Rather than mining a raw piece of carbon, it was more like discovering a new facet to an already flawless diamond.

Joseph had every intention of taking tonight slowly. He wanted Margaret to be comfortable with the pace. Her heart was fragile, and he knew it was important for her to feel she could trust him to treat it with the care it deserved. In fact, he was debating whether or not he should even try to kiss her. They capped off the evening with a cup of hot tea on Margaret's back porch. Everything was going as he'd hoped. Then the conversation took a turn he wasn't expecting.

Margaret had been sitting in the wicker lawn chair across from him. Suddenly, she stood and walked to the edge of the porch. She stared across the back yard.

After a few minutes of silence, Joseph asked, "Are you okay?"

She responded almost as if she hadn't heard his question. "Do you ever regret not having children?"

He took a minute to think about it, and then responded as candidly as possible. "Sometimes. Especially when I see young families in a restaurant or watch grandparents show up with pink and blue flowers at the hospital. It makes me feel kind of empty. Instead of letting it get me down—which I'm often tempted to do —I remind myself that it wasn't my call. I have to trust God."

Margaret continued to stare out into the yard. "I see the kids at the Manor as my children. It fills the void."

Joseph could sense this was a sore topic for Margaret. He joined her on the edge of the porch. "I'm sure the kids see it that way, too."

Margaret turned to face him. He studied her face. She'd never looked more beautiful. The summer breeze gently lifted her silky, blonde hair and swept it back over her shoulders. She tilted her chin as if she was studying him as well.

She shook her head. "By now I should be used to the fact that God is full of surprises. But *you*, by far, are the biggest surprise of all."

Joseph heart began to race. He moved in closer. "I've been called worse!"

"I'm serious. I really didn't expect to feel this way tonight… maybe after several dates, but not after only one."

Joseph thought for a moment. "Maybe we should set aside our plans and let God show us His."

Margaret looked down. "I'm just scared. I don't feel worthy of this—worthy of you."

Joseph pulled her into an embrace. Angry didn't even begin to describe how he felt as he reflected on his how his father's actions, as well as others in his wake, had left Margaret's heart so bludgeoned and broken. As he held her close, he silently prayed for God to let him be the one to show her what love, *real love*, was supposed to look like.

He spoke softly. "I know your heart has had more than its share of pain. I can't undo what's happened to you in the past." He pulled away so he could look into her eyes. He tucked a strand of her hair behind her ear. "But I can be there for what's in your future. I'd like nothing more than to have that honor."

Margaret backed up a few steps. She gasped. "Are you proposing?"

Joseph panicked. This was definitely *not* what he had planned. He couldn't backtrack now though—nor did he want to when he thought about it.

"I guess I am."

He slowly got down on one knee. He stared down at the floor for a moment to catch his breath…and collect his courage. Then he lifted his head. "So, Margaret Francine Gates, I don't have a ring. I don't have a speech prepared. I know this is happening way too fast. But I still want to ask you right here, right now. Will you marry me?"

It felt like an eternity as she looked intently into his eyes. It was as though she was peering into his soul. Indeed, that may have been exactly what she was doing; investigating as far as her gaze and discernment would allow, detecting anything lurking in the shadows that might dissuade her from accepting.

"You're right. It's way too soon. It's our first date." Her mouth curved into a smile. "That's why I can't believe I'm doing this. Yes, Joseph Franklin Bennington, I will marry you!"

Joseph stood to his feet. He cupped Margaret's face with his hands. "I love you. I think I've always loved you."

It was crazy. It didn't make sense. Yet he'd never been more certain of anything in his life.

He leaned down. Their lips met. It was unlike any other kiss he'd ever had. And it was enough. Any more would have taken them beyond what Heaven had blessed for tonight.

He looked at his watch reluctantly. "I guess I should be going. Before I do, I have a confession to make."

"What is it?"

"The flowers and the candy were George's idea."

Margaret looked shocked. "Well, that changes things, doesn't it?"

Joseph wasn't sure if she was kidding or not. "Changes things how?"

Margaret sighed. "I guess I'll have to marry George instead of you."

Joseph looked off into the distance. "You could. But George is a little quirky. And I'm much better looking."

Margaret laughed and took his hand. "I love you. I really, really love you."

It wasn't what Joseph had planned. It was so, so much better.

CHAPTER FIFTY-SEVEN

WYATT LOOKED IN THE MIRROR. BEING HIT BY THE BASKETBALL HAD caused his nose to swell. Coupled with the black eye his brother had given him, his face was one big mess.

He lay back on his bed and considered Terrance's warning to be on guard even when he was sleeping. He couldn't relax. He wished he could. Sleep would afford him a break, albeit a temporary one, from the reality he so desperately wanted to escape.

The loneliness was heavy and oppressive. If he could only find one person—one friend— to help him weather this. He decided to take a risk and talk to Terrance again.

He stood by the door and leaned against the wall adjoining their cells.

"Terrance, are you awake?"

Wyatt waited. Finally, Terrance responded, "Yeah, I'm awake."

"How did everyone know who I was and what I had done?"

"We watch the news," he heard Terrance scoff. "Plus, these guys have connections on the outside."

"What kind of connections?"

Terrance paused. "You don't want to know. What's wrong? You having regrets?"

Wyatt sighed and looked blankly across the hallway. "I just didn't think I'd ever end up in here."

"So, it's the *getting caught* part that's bothering you."

"Maybe. I've always been able to get out of trouble by...other means."

"What you're saying is, your money couldn't buy you a get-out-of–jail-free card this time."

Wyatt nodded even though he knew Terrance couldn't see him. "Yeah, I guess...I didn't like what happened when my father died. This guy came in and took a share of my family's inheritance."

There was a creaking sound as Terrance rolled off his mattress. Wyatt heard his socked feet shuffle across the concrete floor as he approached the door of his cell. "You're talking about your money, right?"

"Well, not *all* of it...I mean..."

"Then that's just greed, man."

Wyatt was curious. "Terrance, if you don't mind my asking, why are you in here?"

There was a long pause. "Somebody took from my family, too."

Wyatt breathed a sigh of relief. "So, we have that in common."

Terrance lowered his voice. "Not even close. My family lost more than yours."

Wyatt wasn't sure what Terrance meant, but he didn't want to push it. "I guess we can talk again later."

No response.

Wyatt felt a little better. He didn't expect Terrance to be all warm and fuzzy; he was simply grateful for the dialogue.

As he crawled under the covers, he couldn't turn off his thoughts. *Do I really feel bad about trying to kill Margaret? Or was Terrance right, and I only regret getting caught? Maybe Preston should've gotten that money. Did Dad ever suspect that Preston could be his son? What other family secrets could there be?*

Then, for some reason, he remembered the box he'd found beneath the floorboards in Gina's closet. *What was she hiding?*

Fatigue was settling in on him. He tried to resist it. He could feel the springs in his mattress pressing against his back. The smell of the prison was one he couldn't quite identify, but it was a far cry from what he was used to. He tossed and turned for what felt like hours. He finally closed his eyes and drifted off to sleep.

* * *

Gina turned down the freshly laundered covers on her bed at the Bennington estate. Bivens had set aside a few of the flowers from Margaret's bouquet and arranged them in a vase for her. From where they sat on her dressing table, their fragrance filled the room.

After reading a passage from her Bible, she turned off her nightstand lamp. She thought she heard the faint rumble of thunder toward the west. There had been a brief shower earlier today, but the grounds could still use a good soaking.

Downstairs, she could hear Bivens rinsing out his wine glass in the sink. The groundskeepers were finishing the last of the mowing by the gardens. Gina was familiar with all the sounds around the estate. The house itself had a musical score that played in the background as life went on from day to day. From the creaking of the hardwood floors to the groaning of the water pipes, she knew it all by heart.

Today was the first day that Wyatt's part was missing. Not that he hadn't ever left the house before, either for a business trip, or so he and Delores could to fly to New York for a day or so, but he'd always returned. Like a rest in musical score, the song eventually resumed. With Wyatt's absence this time, there was a sense of loss. It was as if the song had stopped abruptly or on a chord that didn't provide resolution.

Not that anyone was complaining. Most of the staff didn't like Wyatt, and understandably so. He ran the estate like a tyrant. The only one they disliked more was Delores. Gina assumed she would be swooping in soon to either take charge in Wyatt's absence or to collect her things and move on to the next available trust fund.

The Scripture Gina had just read was the account of the resurrection. It was the greatest triumph in history, following what had appeared to be the greatest defeat. Prison life would deal a death blow to the pride and ego that had defined Wyatt Bennington. What she wanted so desperately to tell him was, that for a heart surrendered to Christ, life always follows death. He was being stripped of only what needed to die so he might understand that.

Gina fluffed her pillow and turned over to face her dressing table. From the faint light filtering through her window blinds, she could make out the silhouette of her keepsake box on her dressing table next to the flowers.

Tomorrow she would take it with her when she visited the prison. It was time Wyatt learned about his true identity.

CHAPTER FIFTY-EIGHT

Julia hung her towel on the rack in the bathroom and slipped into her pajamas. Having just taken them out of the dryer, they felt warm against her skin.

As she stood in the bedroom doorway brushing her teeth, she envied Bill. His steady, rhythmic breathing indicated he was sound asleep. Neither the noises from her getting ready for bed nor the storm outside would interrupt his slumber. Julia, on the other hand, would awake to every thunderclap and surge of rain. She would also hear every time Olivia stirred. She had been that way ever since she first became a mom. Now that she was a grandmother, she feared it would only get worse.

She slid underneath the covers and closed her eyes. The wind was picking up, and the rain was beating down upon the roof. She was almost asleep when her phone vibrated on her nightstand. She bolted upright. Having visited Steven and Holly at the hospital earlier in the evening, she hoped something hadn't changed in Steven's condition.

She typed in her password and saw that it was a text from Margaret.

Sorry to bother you this late, but I have news…

Julia groaned. Why couldn't Margaret simply tell her the news? Why did she have to be so cryptic this late at night?

"Fine, I'll bite," Julia said to herself as she tossed off the covers and sat up on the side of the bed.

What's your news?

It has to do with my date with Joseph (:

Julia was curious but was still annoyed that Margaret wouldn't just tell her what was going on.

Are you two official?

There was a pause.

Then Margaret wrote back.

You could say that.

Julia's heart skipped a beat. "There is no way," she said out loud.

Spit it out, Margaret…

Margaret responded back.

Do you still have that dress you wore to Preston and Annie's wedding?

Julia was confused.

Yes, why?

I want you to wear it to mine.

Julia squealed with delight and jumped to her feet. A sonic boom wouldn't stir Bill, but she didn't want to risk waking Olivia, who was sleeping in the next room. She quickly clapped her hand over her mouth and ran downstairs to the kitchen where she could talk.

After starting a fresh pot of coffee, she dialed Margaret's number.

Margaret was laughing when she answered. "Let me guess. You're making coffee, and you want details."

Julia pulled out a chair and sat down at the kitchen table. "Yes, and yes. Start from the beginning. I've got all night!"

CHAPTER FIFTY-NINE

When Margaret's alarm went off at six o'clock the next morning, she was painfully aware that she and Julia had stayed up talking way too long. Of the two of them, Margaret wasn't sure who had been more excited. By the time the call had ended, they'd all but planned the entire event. Insulted that Margaret thought she would wear a dress she'd already worn to someone else's wedding, Julia had shopped online while they chatted. Margaret eventually pulled the plug around 2:00 a.m.

Aside from being sleepy, Margaret had never been happier. However, the closer she got to the Manor, the guiltier she felt for being on top of the world when someone else's was about to crumble.

She and the doctor waited quietly until Jennifer and her mother, Ruby, arrived. They rushed in fifteen minutes past their appointment time. Ruby immediately apologized as she and Jennifer took seats on the other side of the conference table.

"I'm so sorry we're late. Jennifer was a little sick on her stomach this morning. We're not sure what caused it."

Margaret felt a pain in her own stomach. She knew exactly what had caused it. She was relieved that Dr. Georgia Shane would be the one to convey the test results. Dr. Shane was an older woman with dark-rimmed glasses and bushy gray hair that rested on her shoulders. Having practiced medicine for over thirty years, this surely wasn't the first time she'd had to deliver news that would change someone's life.

The doctor looked across the table at Jennifer and Ruby. "I'm Dr. Shane, and we asked you to meet with us because we have the results from Jennifer's lab work. The good news is that she tested negative for any STDs." Without waiting for a response, she continued, "We also performed a pregnancy test, since her assailant did not use protection during the assault. That test came back positive. Jennifer is pregnant."

There are moments in life that stay etched in your mind forever. This was one of them. Margaret didn't want to look at either Jennifer's or Ruby's reaction, but she forced herself.

Ruby pulled Jennifer close as if trying to protect her from what had been said. Margaret wondered if it was a subconscious attempt to make up for not being able to protect her from being raped in the first place.

Jennifer's jaw dropped. She looked at Margaret as if she wanted her to tell her it wasn't true. She began to cry. "No! This can't be happening!"

Margaret could hardly breathe. She prayed for wisdom. *Dear God, please give me the words!* She stood up and moved to the chair on the other side of Jennifer. She put her arm around her. "You and I have talked about how I understand what it feels like to be raped. Even after being assaulted repeatedly for years, I never got pregnant. I want you to think about that."

"Margaret," Dr. Shane interjected, "did you have a condition that could have prevented you from conceiving?"

"Not that I know of. I had a normal cycle each month. I don't remember ever missing a period."

Ruby was crying. "What are you trying to say? That my daughter was *supposed* to get pregnant? *From being assaulted?*"

Margaret spoke softly, "God certainly didn't want Jennifer to be assaulted. That was an evil act, and God doesn't perpetrate evil. On the contrary, He works on our behalf to bring good from even the most hopeless situations. I wish I had all the answers, but I don't. The only thing I know for sure is that God loves Jennifer, and He loves the child she is carrying."

Dr. Shane folded her hands on the table. "Jennifer, you have a choice whether to abort or carry the pregnancy to term. Before you make that decision, we'd like to perform an ultrasound so you can see what's going on inside of you. Carrying the baby doesn't mean you have to raise him or her. There are hundreds of couples in our area alone who are waiting to adopt an infant. There are Christian couples who have indicated they would adopt a child just like yours."

Margaret looked over at Jennifer's mom. "I know you're still trying to get on your feet financially. The Manor would cover all of Jennifer's prenatal care. We'd make sure every possible resource is made available to her."

Jennifer looked so young and helpless. She put her head on Margaret's chest and wept.

Then, she abruptly looked up with terror in her eyes. "Oh no! What about the guy—the father? Do we have to tell him? Please don't tell him. I don't want anything to do with him!"

Ruby's lip quivered. "I don't want her to ever have to see that monster again!"

"She won't have to," Dr. Shane said calmly. "While the laws vary from state to state, our state favors the rights of the mother. When your assailant was convicted, he forfeited all parental rights."

Ruby paused and looked over toward the window. Her voice shook when she spoke. "I tried to be a good mom. I took my children to church, even when we had to walk to get there. Now my son is in jail and my baby is pregnant by the man that"—she choked on the word—"*raped* her. How did this happen?"

Margaret's eyes welled with tears. She reached over and took Ruby's hand. "None of this is your fault. You can be proud of the values you've instilled in your children. Jennifer is sitting here, wanting to do the right thing for this baby. Most girls her age wouldn't even *entertain* the thought. Your son got into trouble because he was trying to help his family. I know it doesn't seem fair that he's in prison. Maybe there's someone in that prison your son is supposed to reach."

Ruby looked up toward the ceiling. "I pray every day that he's been sent there to help somebody."

Dr. Shane reached around to turn off the pager that had begun beeping in her back pocket. "I'm sorry. I'm needed at the hospital."

She pulled a couple of business cards from her lab coat pocket and set them on the table. "Please call my office to make your next appointment. We're here to help in any way we can."

Ruby nodded and thanked her.

Margaret shook Dr. Shane's hand as she showed her out.

When she returned to her seat, she gently stroked Jennifer's hair. "Why don't we take some time to pray?"

Jennifer wiped her eyes and then looked up at Margaret. "Can we pray for my brother, too?"

Margaret felt her eyes well up again. She'd never met anyone with such a sweet, selfless heart. "I think that's a great idea." She looked over to Ruby. "I feel like I should know his name, but I can't recall if you've ever told me."

Ruby's expression softened. "Terrance. His name is Terrance."

CHAPTER SIXTY

WYATT AWOKE TO THE SOUND OF THE BUZZER AND THE OPENING OF the cell doors. He looked at the clock on the wall across the hall. It was seven o'clock. He had made it through his first night.

He quickly used the urinal and then splashed a little water on his face. A passing glance in the mirror told him he needed to shave.

Breakfast was both unappetizing and uneventful. Still, not having anything thrown at him qualified as a good start to the day. Terrance didn't have much to say this morning but did allow Wyatt to sit with him and a man called Tiny. Wyatt had to smile at the irony, as Tiny was a large man whose size alone would put fear into the heart of any inmate.

After a brief time of exercise, the men were assigned chores. Wyatt's was to clean the showers. There was a dorm-type arrangement at the end of the block that had to be scrubbed and sanitized. The other inmates made it a point to regale Wyatt with details of the activities that had taken place within the tile-clad walls. He wasn't sure which was worse; the vile deeds themselves or the perverse pleasure the men seemed to derive from observing Wyatt's disgust. For a man who had never so much as swabbed his own toilet, he was grateful that he was at least being provided with gloves to wear.

The guard gave Wyatt a mop, bucket, and a plastic caddy containing the cleaning supplies. He opened the door to a room equipped with a long hall of showers on one side and commodes on the other. Closer to the entrance was a row of urinals. Wyatt was required to work until lunchtime, and what he didn't finish today would be waiting for him tomorrow. He had to wonder when, if ever, the room had received a proper cleaning. The stench made him nauseated, but he managed to remain indifferent until after the guard left. Then he ran to one of the commodes and threw up his breakfast.

As he cleaned, the nausea came and went. Nerves could have been a factor. He simply couldn't wrap his mind around the fact that this was his life now.

As he scrubbed at the grime on the shower floors, he heard footsteps. When he turned around, he saw two men had entered the room.

"You don't mind if we use the facility, do you?" one of them asked.

The other one stood over Wyatt as if inspecting his work. "Hey, you missed a spot."

They both laughed and used the urinals, making sure to spill urine all over the floor.

"I bet you have someone else to do this for you at your house, don't you, rich boy?" one of them remarked as he zipped up his pants.

Wyatt didn't respond but continued to clean.

"What? You too good to talk to me?" he asked as he kicked over the bucket of water.

Wyatt knew this was a losing battle whether he said anything or not. He braced himself for what would most likely be a beating that would make yesterday's incident with the basketball look friendly. He'd never felt so alone and afraid.

When he looked into the eyes of these two men, something

happened. It was as if time stood still. He was suddenly aware of how he'd mistreated people over the years. Of course, he would never have beaten up someone in a bathroom. That wasn't his style. He preferred the occasional insult and the constant flaunting of his wealth to make others feel inferior. Why, he'd even convinced himself that it was okay to take someone else's life if he considered that person to be beneath him. He began to see how he'd elevated himself in his mind to a place where he wasn't just above other people; he was above the law. It had all led him to this moment in a prison bathroom where he had nothing and no one. Maybe it was payback. Maybe it was what he deserved. Right now, there was only one thing Wyatt wanted more than not getting broken bones and bruises—or worse.

He wanted a second chance.

He really didn't know any prayers, and this one would have to be quick. He spoke under his breath. "Jesus, I need you. Please help me."

One of the men grabbed him up off the floor by the collar and yelled into his face, "I asked you a question!"

"Leave him alone," said a calm, deep voice from the doorway.

Terrance!

The man let go of Wyatt and turned to Terrance.

"He ain't done nothin' to you," Terrance continued. "Let the man do his work."

The two men looked at each other and smirked. "What do you plan on doing about it, son? Rich boy here don't know how to fight. How you gonna take on both of us?"

Terrance moved closer to the man's face. "I'm not."

The men looked puzzled.

Terrance nodded back over toward the entrance. "He is."

Tiny was standing in the doorway. He pointed over toward the urinals. "You boys make this mess?"

Neither of the men responded.

Tiny walked over to where they were standing. He slammed

one of them up against the wall. Holding the man by his neck, Tiny got in his face.

"I believe *I* asked *you* a question. Did you and your friend make that mess?" Tiny asked.

The man struggled to speak. "We were just breaking in the new guy."

Tiny's face turned red. "You take him on, and you're taking me on. You understand?"

He slung the man down to the floor. The other man started to walk away.

Tiny called out, "Hey, where you think *you're* going?"

The man put up his hands as he took another step backward. "Look, man, I don't want no trouble."

Tiny pushed him down into a puddle of urine. "Too late. Now clean this up."

Tiny and Terrance watched as the other two men quickly cleaned up the urine with paper towels and then followed them out of the room. It was quiet once more. The whole episode ended as quickly as it had begun. Wyatt leaned against the wall. His heart was pounding, and his hands were shaking. He was all too aware of how things could have turned out very differently if Terrance and Tiny hadn't shown up when they did. He was relieved to have been spared what could have been a deadly attack.

But it was more than that.

He was relieved because, deep in his heart, he knew he deserved that beating. Based on how he had treated people over the years, he had it coming. He had no words for what had just happened, except for the two he whispered as he fell to his knees and bowed his head.

"Thank you."

CHAPTER SIXTY-ONE

JOSEPH HAD TO ATTEND A MEETING AT THE HOSPITAL BEFORE HE COULD leave for the Manor. He was having a hard time focusing and kept getting sideways looks from his colleagues.

Of all the things he had on his mind, one in particular was taking center stage.

Margaret's engagement ring.

Wyatt had given Delores their mother's ring, so that wasn't an option. Besides, Margaret wouldn't want to wear anything that was connected to Horace. To say their situation was unique was the understatement of the year. But, then again, God did have a propensity toward the unconventional.

He was still distracted when he arrived at the Manor around lunchtime and headed down the hall to his office. As he turned on the lights, he jumped when he saw George sitting in the chair across from his desk. He put his hand to his chest and tried to catch his breath.

"George! Why on earth are you sitting here in the dark?"

Without making eye contact, Joseph proceeded to unload a coffee cup and a stack of folders he was carrying onto his desk. "You really can be a creepy little man at times, you know that?"

George leaned back in his seat. He was watching Joseph but not saying anything.

Joseph continued to get situated and then sat down in the chair behind his desk. "So, first you scare me to death, and now you're giving me the silent treatment?"

George finally reacted. He pointed his finger at Joseph. "You asked her to marry you, didn't you?"

Joseph was shocked. "How on earth did you figure that out?"

George laughed. "Oh, I have the gift of perception. I can sense things others can't."

Joseph raised an eyebrow.

George sighed. "Ok, I pried it out of Margaret earlier this morning."

Joseph laughed. "Just so you know, proposing was the last thing on my mind last night, especially in light of what had transpired with Wyatt. My plan was to take the whole thing really slow. I don't know what happened."

George shrugged his shoulders. "God's plan happened. It doesn't always make sense at the time. Do you have peace about it?"

Joseph slid the folders on his desk over to one side. "That's the crazy thing. I do. It's like it's what was supposed to happen all along."

"Then it probably was!" George assured him.

"I have to admit, I feel a little guilty for being so happy when others close to us, like Jennifer, are going through such painful trials."

"Jennifer is a special young lady. I am very proud of her for choosing life. I believe God will bless that decision."

Joseph nodded. "He always does. If I heard Margaret correctly, her due date is around the end of December. That being the case, she may not be able to perform at the Christmas concert. I think it might be smart to get a stand-in, just in case."

George frowned. "I agree, but I don't want her to think we are taking the part away from her. She has already started practicing.

If we open the audition up to the community, it might make her feel like it's not really hers anymore."

Joseph tapped a pencil on his desk. "I see what you mean. What if we quietly find someone on our own? I don't think she would have a problem with that. We just won't publicize it."

"I like that idea," George said, nodding.

He shifted in his chair. "Now, back to you and Margaret. Have you gotten her a ring yet? It has to be the perfect ring. You don't want it to be too big or too small…"

Joseph pushed his chair back and went to stand between his desk and George.

"Does she like white gold or yellow gold? That is important. Or perhaps you should get platinum?"

As George continued to talk, Joseph took him by the arm and guided him up out of the chair and across the room. He opened his office door and gently pushed him out into the hall.

"Don't give her the ring at work. Arrange for another special date…" George continued.

Joseph shut his office door and locked it. George was still talking through the glass as Joseph pulled down the shade.

He sat back down at his desk and took a deep breath. "Finally, peace and quiet."

After a few seconds, his phone chirped.

Did you really think you could get rid of me that easily?

CHAPTER SIXTY-TWO

It had been a busy Monday morning at the Bennington estate. A water line had burst overnight, and Gina had decided to stay until the utility company repaired it. She'd originally planned to leave around lunchtime to visit Wyatt, but it was late afternoon before she'd finally gotten away. As the taxi approached the prison entrance, she collected her purse and the keepsake box from the seat beside her. She would need permission from the prison staff to bring it inside. For that reason, she'd also brought along some extra cash.

After going through a metal detector, she was assigned a locker where she was required to leave her personal effects. She turned to the guard who was escorting her to the visitors' area.

"I would really like to take this box in with me." She held it open. "As you can see, it only contains newspaper clippings and a few photos. In fact, I can take everything out and let you inventory it."

The guard shook his head. "I'm sorry ma'am, but you can't take that in there."

She moved the contents aside. "See, no secret compartments.

It's just an old box that my grandmother gave me. If you'd prefer, I can leave the box out here and just take the contents inside. I wouldn't ask if it wasn't important. These keepsakes may help to...well, clear someone's name. Please, officer." Gina put her hand in his, releasing a fifty-dollar bill.

The guard looked at Gina, and then sighed. "Give me the box."

After conducting a thorough search, he handed it back to her.

"You can't tell anyone about this, you understand?"

"Of course."

She was about to walk through the door when she stopped. "Wait!"

The guard turned around. "What now?"

"I really could use a few extra minutes with this inmate."

"I'm sorry ma'am. I'm already bending the rules for you."

"And I thank you." Gina said, as she slipped another bill into his hand.

"Fifteen extra, and not a minute more," he said as he showed her into the visitors' area.

She watched as he spoke in low tones to one of the other guards. Minutes later, a handcuffed Wyatt emerged from his cellblock.

"Looks like you've earned a few extra minutes with your visitor, Bennington," the guard announced. "I'll let you know when it's time to wrap it up."

Wyatt's eyes displayed a questioning look as he sat down across the plate-glass partition from Gina.

Gina had never seen Wyatt look so disheveled. He was unshaven and his face was bruised and swollen. What shocked her most was his demeanor. In twenty-four hours it had completely changed. It was like someone else was sitting on the other side of that glass.

They picked up their phone receivers.

Wyatt spoke first. "Gina, you came back! You have no idea how good it is to see a friendly face."

She smiled. "Of course, I came back. Do not take this the wrong way, but your face looks like it could use a friend!"

Wyatt touched his swollen nose. "Oh…yeah. Someone made sure I was properly introduced to the prison athletic equipment yesterday." Then he scoffed, "But that was nothing compared to what those guys would have done to me earlier today."

"What happened?" Gina asked with concern.

Wyatt looked around and then lowered his voice. "I'm not exactly homecoming king in here. Two guys who simply don't like me for who I am cornered me in the showers. If it hadn't been for Terrance and Tiny, I would probably be in the hospital—or worse."

"Terrance and Tiny?"

Wyatt nodded. "Yeah, they're the only guys I've met so far who don't want to kill me. Terrance has said some things that have made me think about what I've done. Trust me, in prison you have *plenty* of time to think."

"What kind of things?"

"That maybe my anger had nothing to do with Margaret. That perhaps I just needed someone to blame. It wasn't even about the money, although that was part of it. I think I was mostly angry because my family kept a secret from me. I didn't like being blindsided."

Gina could see the clock ticking relentlessly on the wall above where Wyatt was sitting. She didn't have much time. From the looks of Wyatt's bruises after just one day, she wasn't sure he did either.

Her eyes narrowed. "Now you're wondering if there are any other family secrets."

"Well, when you find out you have a brother you didn't know you had, you have to ask what else your family might be hiding. Speaking of which, I ran across something in your closet completely by accident a day or so ago. I had misplaced my liquor cabinet key and thought you might have a spare in the pocket of one of your uniforms. I know it's none of my business. But are you hiding something in a box?"

Gina reached down and put the box onto the ledge where Wyatt could see it.

"You mean this box?"

CHAPTER SIXTY-THREE

MARGARET LEFT WORK A LITTLE EARLY SO SHE COULD START DINNER.
Joseph had just called to let her know he was on his way. So much
had happened in the past several days that it was almost too much
to take in. She couldn't believe she was getting married! This had
to be God's timetable and plan, because it certainly wasn't hers.
Maybe that was why it felt so perfect. She had a schoolgirl kind of
a feeling, complete with old-fashioned butterflies. Her heart leapt
when she heard her doorbell ring.

Once again, Joseph was holding flowers. Not as elaborate as
last night's bouquet, but lovely just the same.

"I'll be able to open a florist shop if you keep this up," she
teased as she took the flowers and gave him a kiss.

He laughed as he made his way into the kitchen and took the
lid off a pot on the stove.

"Man, that smells really good!"

She smiled. "Why, thank you. I hope you brought your
appetite." She gestured toward her kitchen table, which already
had a spread of food on it.

Joseph pulled the chair out for her. When they were seated, he
took her hand and proceeded to ask the blessing. As she sat with

her eyes closed, she was afraid that when she opened them, the scene would disappear. She couldn't believe this was her life now.

Their dinner conversation initially revolved around the trivial: the weather, Joseph needing to get the oil changed in his car, and how Margaret needed to call someone to fix a broken light in her office. Then Joseph transitioned to talking about Wyatt. The topic made Margaret nervous about what she had to tell him.

Joseph stood, walked across the room and picked up an extra napkin from the counter. "You know, I've been reading Scriptures about forgiveness lately. It really hit home with me about how I need to forgive Wyatt. And not just forgive him, but show him love. I've decided to go by the prison later this week."

Margaret heard the words and knew he was waiting for her reaction, but she had something else on her mind, and it must have shown.

"Okay, spill the beans," Joseph said as he sat back down, placing his fresh napkin neatly in his lap.

"Is it that obvious?" Margaret asked tentatively.

Joseph grinned. "To the casual observer? Probably not. But I've been working with you for over two years, young lady. I know when you've got something on your mind."

"Actually, I do. What I have to say is going to be really difficult."

Joseph twirled a string of spaghetti onto his fork. "Okay, shoot."

Margaret hesitated. "I don't want to hurt you. You're the last person I'd *ever* want to hurt. I know you're going to be upset. I hope you won't be mad at me."

Joseph leaned back in his chair and wiped his mouth with his napkin. "Margaret, do you need more time?"

Margaret shook her head. "No, I want to get this over with…tonight!"

Joseph hung his head. "Look, I know everything has happened really fast."

"Exactly! That's why I didn't know when to tell you."

He leaned forward and took her hand. "If you don't want to marry me, I'll understand."

Margaret jerked her hand away. "What are you talking about?"

He wrinkled his nose. "Wait, what are *you* talking about?"

"Clearly not what you *think* I'm talking about. I'm not breaking our engagement!"

Joseph put his elbows on the table and put his head in his hands. "Thank God. You have no idea how scared I was."

"Really?" Margaret reached for his hand once more.

He looked surprised. He leaned in toward her. "Margaret, you're not just someone I met later in life who I happened to fall in love with. You are the love of my life. I'll do whatever it takes to be with you."

"You have no idea what that means to me. You know I feel the same way about you."

"Now, what is it you have to tell me?" Joseph asked as he pulled his hands back and took a bite of his salad.

Margaret winced. "It's about Wyatt."

"Don't tell me he did something else to you," Joseph managed through a mouthful of salad.

"No, it's nothing like that. As soon as we finish eating, maybe we should move into living room where it's comfortable. What I have to tell you might take a while."

CHAPTER SIXTY-FOUR

Wyatt couldn't believe his eyes. "Yes, that's the one! Why did you bring it here? Hold on—how did you get it past the guards?"

Gina smiled proudly. "I am not as unworldly as I may look."

Wyatt grinned. "I guess you're not. So, what's in it?"

Gina's smile faded. "You wanted to know if there were other family secrets. You deserve to know the truth. I have been preparing for this day—this conversation—for years. I have turned it over and over in my mind, hoping to find a way to tell you without hurting you. There is no way."

Wyatt was getting worried and impatient. "Gina, what is it?"

Gina hesitated. "What your father did to Margaret Gates was not an isolated incident. There were others."

Wyatt had always viewed his dad's sexual indiscretions as par for the course for a man of such vast means and opportunity. With business trips all over the world, he suspected it had happened more often than not. When it came to Margaret, he'd held on to the hope—albeit a naïve notion—that, somehow, she had brought it upon herself. The way in which his father had regularly denigrated her had convinced him it had to be so. The look in Gina's eyes told him a different story.

Wyatt tried to stay calm. "Anybody I know?"

Gina's gaze met his. "Me."

Gina told Wyatt the entire story from start to finish. She showed him pictures and newspaper articles. The words and images swirled wildly in his head like leaves tossed in a tempest. He couldn't—or wouldn't—let any of them land and claim ground.

Even though he was despised in prison because of his heritage, it was his last stand. It was the only thing he had left that made him feel like he had value. What Gina had disclosed stripped him down to the core of who he was. For the first time in his life, he didn't know who that was anymore. His pedigree was based on his father, a man whose character he now loathed. Worse, he loathed himself for being so much like him.

The guard came back in and informed them they only had a few more minutes.

Wyatt looked up at Gina, who had tears streaming down her face. He wanted to tell her how sorry he was for all she'd been through. For now, those words would lie dormant beneath layers and layers of his own pain. He hung his head as he hung up the receiver. He knocked on the door, and a guard arrived to take him back to his cell. On the way, he crossed paths with Terrance, who was being escorted to the visitors' area.

When Terrance came back to his own cell a short while later, he appeared to be angry. So angry, in fact, that the guards had put him on suicide watch for the evening. Wyatt owed Terrance his very life. He would have done anything to help ease whatever was causing him to be so upset. But tonight, it was all Wyatt could do to deal with his own hurt. Prison had been swift to teach him that everything he'd gained on the outside profited him nothing in here. His bloodline had been all that remained. Now, even that— the heritage in which he took such pride—had deteriorated into a legacy of shame.

Coupled with the fact that he was a convicted felon, this latest development sealed his fate. Not only would he be alone in prison, but he would also be alone when he was released. None of his friends would want to associate with him. Delores would be halfway across the world before the ink dried on the divorce papers. His black eye strongly suggested he wouldn't be able to count on Joseph either. The only thing worse than everything in his world changing was the fact that he was powerless to stop it.

The sadness was unbearable. Maybe Terrance and Tiny shouldn't have stepped in this morning after all. Maybe they should have let those guys finish the job.

He didn't care who heard him cry. Tonight, he didn't care if he lived or died.

CHAPTER SIXTY-FIVE

At the Bennington estate, Gina was getting ready for bed.
She'd just picked up the Bible from her nightstand when she felt a
strong burden to pray for Wyatt. It was unlike anything she had
ever felt before. She immediately texted several others, requesting
prayer for him. Then she knelt beside her bed and interceded for
her son.

* * *

Joseph had wrestled with what his father had done to Margaret.
Now he had to accept that his father had also done the same thing
to Gina, and likely to others as well. How could his parents go on
with business as usual when they had committed such an atrocity?
For a few minutes, he and Margaret sat on the sofa without talking. Then Margaret received a text from Gina asking for prayer for
Wyatt. Before she could put it away, her cell phone began to ring.

She turned to Joseph. "It's Gina. Should I answer?"

Joseph sighed. "Sure. Put her on speaker."

"Gina? Joseph and I are both at my house. I've got you on
speaker, if that's all right."

"Of course, that is fine," Gina said. "Hello, Joseph."

Joseph's voice cracked. "Hey, Gina. So, how is Wyatt?"

"Joseph, what is wrong?" Gina asked.

Joseph looked to Margaret for support. She put her arm around him.

"Margaret told me the whole ugly story, Gina. I don't know what to say. I'm just so sorry for what my family put you through."

Gina sounded calm. "It wasn't all ugly. I do not regret being Wyatt's mother. I know God put me in that house for a reason. I have been praying for you and Wyatt before either of you were born. God does his best work, paints his greatest masterpieces in the dark seasons!"

Joseph sniffed. "Gina, thank you for being there all those years. I can't imagine how difficult it was for you."

"My faith kept me strong. You have the same faith, but your brother does not. He is suffering in prison. He's been assaulted, and there's been an attempt on his life. He's only found one friend, and, thankfully, he and another inmate took up for Wyatt. Unfortunately, everyone else there is his sworn enemy."

Margaret was curious. "At least he has one friend. Who is he?"

"He's a young man who has been reaching out to Wyatt. From what Wyatt has told me, I think he is a Christian. His name is Terrance."

Margaret cupped her hand to her mouth. She turned to Joseph. "Do you know who that could be? Jennifer's brother's name is Terrance!"

Joseph shook his head in amazement. "Gina, if it's the same Terrance, I think we may be working with his little sister, Jennifer, at the Manor. She's one of our new students."

He paused and looked at Margaret with wide eyes.

"What is it?" she asked.

He leaned in closer to the phone. "Jennifer was raped and found out she's pregnant. I can't think of anyone better equipped than you to encourage someone in that situation. Would you be willing to spend some time with her?"

Margaret gasped. "Why didn't I think of that?"

"Isn't God so good to keep working His plan of redemption in our lives? I would be honored to speak with her. I love Wyatt and do not have any regrets about having him. Now he knows. Tonight, I told him the truth."

Joseph and Margaret exchanged glances. Joseph asked, "How did he take it?"

"Of course, he was shocked, but I think mostly he was hurt. Your brother isn't the same person he was a few days ago. Prison is quickly and decisively breaking down the stronghold of pride in his life. I didn't think it would happen this soon. Then again, I have been praying for him for years. Perhaps God was working behind the scenes all this time to prepare his heart. Plus, transformations don't always have to take weeks and months. If you think about it, the apostle Paul's conversion happened in an instant. When God's presence shows up, anything is possible. Right now, there's a battle going on for Wyatt's soul. It is urgent that we pray for him."

Margaret responded as she squeezed Joseph's hand. "Wyatt has been on our hearts. Joseph is planning to visit him later this week. In the meantime, we'll pray."

"Thank you. Oh, and Margaret? It's been three years, and I've never officially thanked you for something else."

"What's that?" Margaret asked.

"You reached out to Horace, and he is in Heaven as a result. I have never seen anyone love their enemy the way you did. It gave me hope that Wyatt could change, too. I was about to give up, but that helped me to hang on. I've been meaning to thank you for a long time. So here it is. Thank you, from the bottom of my heart."

"You don't need to thank me. There's no way I could have done it without God putting His love for Horace in my heart. He's faithful to give us what we need in those situations."

Joseph stroked Margaret's hair. "She a keeper, isn't she?"

Gina laughed. "Wait, are you trying to tell me something?"

Joseph looked at Margaret and smiled. "Actually, I am!"

* * *

Joseph left Margaret's house around ten. As he drove, he prayed for Wyatt. The more he prayed, the more his heart softened. Had he ever told his brother he loved him? His mind went back to the night of Wyatt's arrest. Unknowingly, Wyatt had asked Joseph an important question then. He wanted to know if Joseph had come to the estate because he loved him. The hard reality was that Joseph should have been there because he loved Margaret *and* Wyatt. Now that he was in prison, did Wyatt wonder if *anyone* loved him? Joseph could only imagine the hatred the other prisoners felt for him. Six months was a long time when your safety and survival hung in the balance every day. Joseph decided to switch around a couple of appointments so he could visit him the next day.

He arrived home and threw his keys onto the counter. He put a fresh coffee pod into the Keurig. Sleep wasn't important. Tonight would be a night of prayer.

CHAPTER SIXTY-SIX

Wyatt awoke with a start. He sat up and looked across the hall at the clock. It was only 1:30 a.m. He could hear two guards talking. He lay back down and pretended to be asleep until he heard them leave. They would be monitoring Terrance every fifteen minutes throughout the night until his suicide watch was lifted.

Wyatt quietly got out of bed and walked over to his cell door. He listened for any sounds coming from Terrance's cell. He didn't want to wake him, but he needed to know if he was still there and, more importantly, if he was okay.

He spoke just above a whisper. "Terrance, are you awake?"

He was surprised when there was a quick response. "Yeah, why?"

"Do you want to talk?"

"Now?"

"Well, we're both awake. I may not be able to help, but I can listen."

He could hear Terrance roll over in his bed. "What good is talking going to do?"

Wyatt didn't know. Perhaps talking wouldn't do any good at all. He just wanted to be there for him.

"You won't know unless you try."

There was a long pause. Wyatt waited. He finally heard Terrance get out of bed. From the sound of it, he sat down on the floor beside his cell door.

"A few months ago, my mom lost her job. She was behind on the bills. I wanted to help out, so I started working for this gang. I didn't steal or nothing, I just ran errands."

Wyatt couldn't relate to being that desperate for money. It made him ashamed for taking his many blessings for granted.

Terrance continued. "They kept putting off giving me my pay. Finally, one night they showed up with a big wad of cash. Said it was mine if they could each have a turn…with my sister. I felt trapped. I only let it happen once. After that, I grabbed a gun off one of the dudes and started shooting. They all lived, but I got convicted for three counts of attempted murder."

"What about the one guy?"

"He's doing time for rape." Terrance's voice started to shake. "My sister still had her innocence, man! She didn't deserve that. I'm not sure who I'm madder at—the guy who did it—or me for letting him."

"It would've been all of them against you, Terrance. Both you and your sister could have been killed."

"It gets worse. She just found out she's pregnant." Terrance began to weep audibly. "Her life is over, man! And the kid is going to grow up knowing he was a rape baby. What good can come out of that?"

Wyatt sat in silence. There were no other sounds except for Terrance sniffing and the occasional snore from one of the other inmates.

Then, it was as if Wyatt's world shifted, like someone had changed the station on the radio.

A presence of joy and holiness entered his cell. Everything suddenly made sense, and what didn't make sense didn't matter.

He slid to the floor and put his head into his hands. He began to weep and then he began to laugh. The despair he'd felt earlier lifted. The lies of rejection and fear began to scatter like roaches when a light switch is flipped on. Sitting on the floor in his prison cell, he knew he had an unseen visitor.

Wyatt wept as he spoke the next words for the first time. "Terrance, I know someone who was conceived from rape."

Terrance sniffed. "Who?"

"Me," he whispered.

Terrance gasped. "You? Are you serious?"

"I didn't know it until today. In fact, the woman that was my visitor? She's my real mother."

Terrance sounded somewhat apologetic. "I guess everyone has problems, even people with money."

"Sometimes money just covers up problems. I'm sitting in prison with no friends, no future, and probably no money when my wife gets through with me, and I've never been more at peace. I never believed in God because I didn't think I needed him. Now that He's all I've got, I realize He's all I need!"

Terrance laughed through his tears. "My mom has been praying that I was put in here to help somebody."

Wyatt wiped his eyes. "Her prayers were answered."

Terrance was quiet for a minute. "If I'm really going to help you, then I need to tell you the best news you'll ever hear. Jesus died for your sins. He loved me—and you—so much that He took the death sentence we deserved. It should have been us dying on that cross. But it doesn't end there. He rose from the grave. Jesus is alive, man!"

Wyatt quietly wept. He could hardly speak. "I know He is, Terrance. He's here in my cell right now."

Terrance moved closer to his door. "Do you want me to pray with you?"

"Yeah, I'd really like that."

"Just repeat after me. 'Lord Jesus, I know I'm a sinner. I've rejected you and gone my own way. I want to come home. I repent of my old ways and give my heart completely to you.'"

Wyatt repeated the prayer, word for word.

Afterward, he felt clean and at peace. His heart was full as he crawled back under the covers a few minutes later. He was about to drift off to sleep when he heard Terrance call his name.

"Wyatt, can I tell you one last thing?"

Wyatt opened his eyes and looked up at the ceiling. "Sure."

"You may think I helped you tonight, but you helped me, too. I needed to see that God had a purpose for me being in here. Your mama must have been praying for you, too."

Wyatt thought about Gina. Then he smiled.

"I'm sure she was."

CHAPTER SIXTY-SEVEN

Before the buzzer sounded signaling breakfast time, Wyatt was already awake. He could hear the snores of inmates catching a few last minutes of sleep. The events of the last three years played in his head like a movie reel. Margaret Gates had shown up out of the blue and disrupted his otherwise "perfect" life. Yet, had it not been for her, last night wouldn't have happened. The person he'd tried to eliminate was the one who could help him the most. Wyatt was certainly no Bible scholar, but he knew enough to know that was what had happened to Jesus. He'd come to do good for others—for the world—and they'd killed him. The story supposedly hadn't ended there. Wyatt used to scoff when he heard the account of the resurrection.

That was before last night.

He'd always viewed Christianity as an old-fashioned set of rules and regulations that told him what to do and how to live. He could make those decisions for himself. He didn't need an invisible God, or a book written thousands of years ago, ordering him around. He was beginning to see that it was so much more than that. Even though he didn't fully understand it all yet, something was different now. *He* was different.

He wanted to pray, but he really didn't know how. Besides Terrance praying with him last night, yesterday's cry for help in the bathroom was the closest thing to a prayer he'd uttered in years. He vaguely remembered Gina tucking him in as a child and praying with him. Maybe that's all he needed right now. Childlike faith. Still, he wasn't sure what to say.

He closed his eyes and whispered, "Are you still here? I'm sorry that our first meeting had to take place in a dirty prison cell instead of my nice home. Although, you *were* born in a stable, so, maybe you don't mind. In fact, you waited until I had lost everything to show me how valuable I am to you. That's what makes all of this so baffling...and beautiful. Thank you. Please help me to change. I know I have a long way to go." He waited a moment and then said, "Amen."

He quietly got up and washed his face. Today he would request a shower and a disposable razor.

He listened for any sounds coming from Terrance's cell. Finally, he heard him stir just as the buzzer sounded.

Perhaps it was the food that was different today, or perhaps it was Wyatt. Either way, breakfast tasted good. Tiny was eating beside Terrance and across the table from Wyatt.

Tiny asked, "Why are you in such a good mood this morning?"

Wyatt looked up from his food. "I guess I'm just glad to be alive. My life was saved twice yesterday."

He smiled at Terrance, and then focused back on his breakfast.

Tiny set his fork down on the table. "Twice? I don't remember but one time."

Wyatt looked up at Tiny. If he had to guess, he would say he was in his late thirties. He had a deep scar on the right side of his neck. He was such a large man, Wyatt shuddered at the thought of who could have overpowered him to cause such a wound.

"You're right." Wyatt said. "You saved my life yesterday morning. Someone else saved it last night."

Tiny looked bewildered. "Who in this joint is going around helping people besides me?"

What happened next was unlike anything Wyatt had ever experienced. It was as if he had been given insight into Tiny's life. Even though he didn't know where it had come from, he was confident it was spot-on. The words came out of his mouth before he had a chance to overthink them.

"Tiny, I really appreciate your help yesterday morning. But I've got to wonder, who helps you?"

Tiny quickly resumed eating. "I don't need nobody's help. I can take care of myself."

Wyatt couldn't believe how bold he was being. "What about that scar on your neck? Who did that to you?"

He could tell he had struck a nerve. Tiny glared at him, his gaze fixed and cold.

"I don't talk about that to nobody."

Wyatt pushed his tray aside. "I didn't think I needed anybody's help either." He hesitated. "Jesus is the one who helped me last night."

Tiny stopped eating. He gazed off into the distance. "Oh, I know who Jesus is. But I also know who Tiny is. A few of these men in here may be innocent, but not me. I deserve to do my time." He looked back down at his food. "Yeah, Tiny's just an old sinner that everybody done gave up on. I just figured Jesus done gave up on him, too."

Wyatt felt genuine compassion for Tiny. This was such a stark contrast from the man he had been just days earlier; someone who considered anybody different from him as not being worth the trouble. He leaned forward on the table. "I deserve to be in here, too. I don't think He loves us because we deserve it. He didn't give up on me, and He hasn't given up on you."

Tiny sat for a moment as if he wasn't sure how to respond. Wyatt noticed his expression change. It was like watching a wilted flower come back to life. A big tear rolled down the side of his cheek. He cleared his throat. "Thanks, man. I needed to hear that."

Terrance gave Wyatt a nod of approval and then slapped Tiny on the back. "You all right, Tiny."

"A lot of dudes in here try to be tough," Tiny said as he picked up his tray. "Most of 'em just need to hear what you told me." He shook his head as he stood up to leave. "But don't nobody ever tell 'em."

As Tiny walked away, Wyatt slowly looked across the room, studying the faces one by one. What if Tiny was right? How many of these men's lives could be transformed if they understood that they are loved by someone who knows all their darkest deeds but accepts them anyway? He didn't know the first thing about the Bible, but Terrance could teach him. They could learn together. It could be dangerous, and not everyone would be open to it. Honestly, he wasn't even sure if he could do it.

But seeing that hope in Tiny's eyes made him determined to try.

After breakfast, Wyatt hurried through what was left of his bathroom cleaning assignment. He was grateful the smell hadn't been as bad as it had been yesterday. Terrance had kitchen duty, so he wouldn't be back until later in the afternoon. Wyatt was looking forward to asking him about the possibility of starting a Bible study.

As he was being escorted back to his cell, a guard stepped out from the visitors' area.

He motioned to the other guard. "Bennington's attorney is here," he said.

Wyatt was led into a different visiting area this time. It was an open room containing two rows of tables. The guards instructed him that no physical contact was allowed as they escorted him to a chair across from Dalton.

He could tell Dalton was taken aback by his appearance. Dalton, on the other hand, was as clean and crisp as ever. Wyatt detected the faint scent of a designer aftershave.

Dalton shook his head. "Wyatt, you look terrible."

Wyatt grinned. "If I had known you were coming, I would have worn my good jumpsuit."

Dalton looked into Wyatt's eyes. "Something's different about you."

"I'm making some changes. It's sad to think it took going to prison to open my eyes to what an egotistical ass I've been most of my life."

Dalton took off his glasses and leaned back in his chair. "I never thought I'd hear those words come from you."

"Yeah, me neither. So, what brings you by?"

Dalton sighed. "Delores's attorney called. She wants to proceed with the separation."

Wyatt looked down. "I see."

"She's flying back from Europe later this week. I suggested to her attorney that she at least stop by for a visit before making a final decision. I'm concerned she's going to take you for as much as she can get her hands on. I assure you, we will fight her every step of the way."

At first Wyatt was tempted to agree with Dalton. After all, Delores had abandoned him when he'd needed her most. The old Wyatt would have stopped at nothing to protect his assets.

But he didn't want to be that Wyatt anymore.

"No, we won't," he responded quietly.

Dalton leaned forward. "What did you say?"

"I'm not spending another minute of my life worrying about money and status and what people think. Give Delores what she wants, then pay yourself."

Dalton's eyes narrowed. "Are you sure you're Wyatt Bennington?"

CHAPTER SIXTY-EIGHT

It was midafternoon before Joseph could finally cut himself loose from work and drive over to the prison. The whole situation still seemed so surreal. After praying late into the night, Joseph felt his heart was more in line with God's for Wyatt. He had already made the decision to forgive him, as forgiveness always boils down to just that—a decision. His emotions could catch up later.

Joseph looked around nervously as he located a parking space. This was his first time at a prison, and there was just something about the place—even walking through the parking lot—that made him jumpy. Dalton Larkins had pushed the paperwork through for him, and a few others, so Wyatt could start receiving visitors immediately. For someone who knew how to curry favor, it was the only string Dalton could manage to pull.

After going through a metal detector, Joseph was instructed to leave any personal belongings in a locker. He obliged by depositing his wallet and his car keys. Then he was ushered into the visitors' area.

It took only three minutes for Wyatt to arrive. Joseph knew this, as there was a clock ticking on the wall across from him. It seemed longer, though. He wondered if that was how prison time worked. Did the minutes drag on like hours? How about the years?

Joseph could not have been more astonished by Wyatt's appearance. He had a scruffy beard, and his nose was swollen and bruised. The punch he had thrown at him just days earlier was evidenced by a black and green circle around his eye. He tried not to show his shock, but he suspected Wyatt picked up on it anyway.

Wyatt seemed just as surprised to see him. The guard removed his handcuffs, and he picked up the receiver.

Joseph picked up his as well, praying he would know how to start this conversation.

"I guess you didn't expect me to be your visitor today."

Wyatt looked sheepish. "I guess I'm safe with the plate glass between us. You throw a mean right hook."

Joseph was taken aback by Wyatt's response. It suggested humility, something as foreign to Wyatt as the prison environment in which he now resided.

Joseph wasn't sure how to respond but decided to stick with the script. "I need to say something to you."

"Can I go first?" Wyatt interrupted.

Joseph sighed and shook his head. "You always did. Go ahead."

Wyatt looked down for a moment. "Something is happening to me in this place. I'm beginning to understand that Wyatt Bennington is not in control. When I first arrived, and the other inmates were threatening me, I was scared I was going to die. Then, by the end of the day, I *wanted* to die. Prison is not something I could just *adjust to* like some of these guys seem to. Maybe that was the plan all along." He paused and then shook his head. "I'm probably not making any sense."

Joseph could feel his heart racing. Had Wyatt really changed? "You're making perfect sense. Go on."

"In some ways, I don't know which end is up. I just found out that Gina is my mother, and that our father was a pedophile. Somehow, I ignored that fact when it came to Margaret. Oh, and did I mention that Delores is going to divorce me? Yet—and this is the strangest part—I feel like I've been set free from the life I thought I wanted, but was actually destroying me."

Joseph wanted to believe all of this was real. "Where did this sense of freedom come from?" he asked.

Wyatt's eyes began to well with tears. "From inside a prison cell."

Neither of them said anything for a moment, as Wyatt appeared to be fighting for his composure. He shrugged his shoulders. "I guess I just came to the end of myself. And someone was waiting for me when I arrived." He wiped his eyes on his sleeve. "I think you know Him."

Joseph could no longer hold back his own tears. "I do know Him. In fact, we talked about you last night."

"So, do you forgive me?"

"Yes, I forgive you." Joseph sniffed. "I need to ask you to forgive me for something."

Wyatt shook his head. "No, I deserved for you to punch me."

Joseph smiled. "It's not something I did; it's something I didn't do."

Wyatt looked puzzled. "Now you're the one who isn't making any sense."

Joseph took a deep breath. "I can't remember ever telling you that I love you. So, I'm telling you now. In spite of the complete, selfish jerk you could be—and what you tried to do to Margaret—I love you. And, as your brother, I'm going to stand by you."

Wyatt shook his head. "I don't deserve it, Joseph."

"You're right," Joseph answered matter-of-factly. "You don't. Then again, none of us do. Aren't you glad God's love is unconditional?"

Wyatt grinned. "So, you're not sorry you punched me?"

"Not in the least," Joseph quickly replied. "You had that coming to you."

They both chuckled, and then Wyatt looked serious again. "You said something when you punched me—that you were doing it not because you loved me, but because you loved Margaret. Are you *in* love with her?"

Joseph wasn't about to approach the topic without knowing if Wyatt was truly sorry for what he did. "Do you still *hate* her?"

Wyatt looked down once more as if he was ashamed that Joseph felt the need to ask the question. He started to answer, and then stopped. He stared down at the floor as if he was trying to collect his thoughts.

"I know this doesn't make up for or excuse what I did. But I think my anger toward Margaret was misplaced. It was easier to take out my frustration on her since Dad had convinced us for years that she was nothing but a problem. I think I was mostly upset that there were things in our family I didn't know about. The Bennington name and money were pretty much all I had. I mean, let's face it, you were the good-looking one."

Joseph had to smile. "No, you're wrong about that. I *am* the good-looking one."

Wyatt laughed. "To answer your question, the only person I've hated since I arrived here is *me*. I've got a long way to go, Joseph. I've got six months in here and then the rest of my life to make up for a lot of mistakes."

Joseph couldn't believe what he was hearing. "Is there any of the old Wyatt still in there?"

Wyatt squinted. "I guess there is. When Dalton came earlier today, I wanted to steal that Armani suit right off him! I took so much for granted before all of this happened. The young man in the cell next to me has been instrumental in helping me, though."

"Are you talking about Terrance?"

Wyatt looked surprised. "How did you know his name?"

"Gina told us. Did you know his sister is a student at the Manor? Margaret has been working with her. Terrance had almost turned his back on God until he saw the progress his sister was making. It gave him hope. That's when he started reading his Bible again."

Wyatt stared blankly down at the table. "So, if Margaret hadn't helped Terrance's sister…"

"*He* couldn't have helped *you*. If you had succeeded in killing Margaret, you would've destroyed your only hope in this place."

Wyatt nervously ran his hand through his hair. "Dear God. He was looking out for both of us."

"To answer your question," Joseph looked intently at Wyatt, "not only am I in love with Margaret, but we're getting married."

Wyatt sat back in his chair. "Wow! I don't know what to say. Should I apologize again before I congratulate you? Or can I just congratulate you?"

Joseph grinned. "You can do better than that."

Wyatt sat on the edge of his seat. "You name it. What can I do?"

"I need my only brother to be my best man."

Wyatt's jaw dropped. "Are you serious? Do you think Margaret would be comfortable with that?"

"We've already talked about it. I don't know anyone who understands forgiveness and the love of God better than she does. She thought it might help you to understand it a little better."

The tears spilled out of Wyatt's eyes. "That's something I don't think I'll ever fully understand."

The guard returned a short while later, and Joseph watched as Wyatt was cuffed and led back through the door leading to his cellblock. He was deep in thought as he exited the lobby area after picking up his keys and wallet and returning his visitor's name badge. Back in his car, he took some time to sit quietly for a few minutes. He watched as a man on a riding mower trimmed the grass along the sides of the parking lot.

Everything in his life was shifting, and at a pace he wasn't sure he could keep up with. For the first time in his life, he had hope that perhaps he and Wyatt could go beyond being brothers and become friends. One thing was for certain; the changes in Wyatt weren't of the self-improvement variety. Sincere humility and brokenness weren't something Wyatt could have manufactured. His redeemed heart could have only come from one source.

The Redeemer.

In terms of Wyatt's safety and survival, he wasn't out of the woods yet. The only thing that had changed was him. His circumstances hadn't changed, and the people around him hadn't changed. Not that they couldn't. After all, God did seem to be on a roll with doing the unexpected.

His thoughts were interrupted as his phone chimed. It was a text from Gina.

I spoke with Margaret, and I will be visiting the Manor around dinnertime to be introduced to Jennifer. Will you be there? Since you were the one who suggested we meet, I thought it would be nice if you could stop by.

Joseph looked at his watch. He really didn't have time, but he would make it work somehow.

Sure. I'll see you at the Manor.

He had two errands to run. One was stopping by the hospital. That could wait.

Picking up Margaret's ring couldn't.

CHAPTER SIXTY-NINE

Margaret grabbed a quick cup of coffee hoping it would help her to get through the last meeting of the day. She had been having trouble sleeping again, but this time she knew why. It was a welcomed change to be awake because of being too excited to sleep.

She could hear Jennifer's flawless voice coming from the band room. Gina was scheduled to meet with Jennifer after the rehearsal, which should've already ended. But Jennifer was obviously determined to go over one of the sections with Mr. Ortega until it was perfect. Margaret hoped Jennifer would be able to perform in the concert. She had put her heart and soul into the song.

Her phone vibrated with a text message from Joseph letting her know he'd be there but had an errand to run that would put him arriving a little later. He also told her a little about his visit with Wyatt. Gina had been right all along. It did take going to prison to produce real change in Wyatt.

Margaret couldn't wait to tell Jennifer and her mom how God was using Terrance. It was like Minnie said; "God's work always has a ripple effect!"

She heard a tap on her office door. It was Gina. She quickly rose from her seat and greeted Gina with a hug.

Gina stood back and looked at Margaret. "You look so much happier than you did the last time I saw you!"

"I definitely am! Thank you so much for coming to talk with Jennifer. She's looking forward to meeting you. I told her that—"

"Wait." Gina put her index finger to her lips. "Who is that singing?" she asked.

Before Margaret could answer, Gina followed the sound of Jennifer's voice into the band room. As they tiptoed over and stood by the wall, Jennifer hit a high note with such precision, it gave Margaret goosebumps.

Gina broke into applause. "Young lady, that was quite impressive!"

Of course, Jennifer was surprised by Gina's comment. Someone else was also surprised.

For the first time that Margaret could ever remember, George Ortega was at a loss for words.

* * *

Joseph patted the small box in his pocket once more for good measure. He'd put a lot of thought into where he wanted to present Margaret with her engagement ring. He was confident he'd selected the perfect place. He assumed Margaret was still in the middle of her meeting with Gina and Jennifer. He decided he'd just stick his head in, wave, and then retreat to his office until she was ready to leave for the day.

When he opened the band room door, instead of finding Jennifer and Gina becoming better acquainted, it was George and Gina who were chatting like old friends. Margaret and Jennifer looked more like spectators. Joseph was about to step in and politely evict George when he stopped. He had never seen Gina smile like that. George, while being George, was demonstrating a genteel demeanor Joseph hadn't witnessed before. Joseph made eye contact with Margaret, who just grinned and shrugged her shoulders. Joseph tilted his head to one side as he observed the two of them and then quietly closed the door.

* * *

George finally excused himself, but not without getting all of Gina's contact information. He was headed toward the front drive when he heard Joseph calling after him.

"George, wait up!"

George spun around and stood with his arms crossed.

"What's wrong?" Joseph asked. "It looked like you and Gina were hitting it off in there!"

George began thrashing his arms. "What is wrong with you, Joseph Bennington? You had this angel working in your home all this time, and you didn't introduce us?"

Joseph backed up. "Whoa, I'm sorry! I didn't think about it. But now that I see the two of you together, it makes sense."

"Of course, it makes sense. What else are you hiding from me?"

Joseph paused. "Did she tell you that she sings?"

"Yes, she did. In fact, she has agreed to be Jennifer's backup in case the baby arrives early."

"So, will you two be spending more time together?" Joseph asked, tongue in cheek.

"We have to make up for *lost time*," George quipped. He shook his finger at Joseph. "You should have introduced us sooner!"

"Is there a thank-you in there somewhere?"

George rolled his eyes and then looked away. "Fine…thank you."

"She does have an amazing testimony, George. She is a strong woman of faith."

George's expression softened. "I could tell. I am looking forward to getting to know her better."

"Does she know that you dance with music stands?" Joseph asked playfully. "Perhaps I should fill her in on that one."

George felt a slight panic. "You wouldn't!"

* * *

Margaret stepped out onto the sidewalk looking for Joseph. She jumped back when she saw George chasing him toward the Manor. When George spotted Margaret, he gave up the chase, and headed toward his car instead, shaking his head.

"What was that all about?" she asked as Joseph came jogging up to her.

Joseph laughed while he leaned over and caught his breath. "Just a little friendly blackmail between colleagues."

Margaret raised one eyebrow. "Okay, if you say so."

He put his arm around her. "Are Gina and Jennifer still talking?"

"No, they finished up a few minutes ago. Jennifer was tired after the rehearsal. Do you want to grab a bite to eat somewhere?"

"I'd love to, but can we stop by the band room first?"

Margaret agreed, and they made their way back inside.

Margaret turned on the lights. Joseph took her hand and pulled her over to the other side of the room.

She giggled. "Where are we going?"

"Right here ought to do it."

"Do what?" she asked.

Joseph looked up behind them. Margaret followed his eyes to her plaque hanging on the wall.

"My old band award?"

Joseph took her hands into his. "As talented as you were—and are—you should have a trophy case full of those."

Margaret was trying to figure out where Joseph was going with this. "These kids that I help every day are my reward. I'd rather see progress in their lives than have a million plaques hanging on the wall."

Joseph looked into her eyes. "What I'm trying to say is, your true value as an artist and as a woman was hidden for many years. God made sure it didn't *stay* hidden. As your soon-to-be husband, I want you to know that I cannot wait to have the honor of showing you off as my wife. I wanted to make sure your engagement ring reflected that."

Margaret was amazed at how being in Joseph's presence made her heart melt. She still felt so unworthy of this new life. How could she tell him she didn't need a ring? Her cup was full. She needed nothing more.

"I realize I've already asked you to marry me. But last time I didn't have a ring. So, if you don't mind marriage proposal part two…" Joseph got down on one knee. "Margaret Francine Gates, will you marry me?"

Margaret gasped as Joseph took a velvet box out of his pocket and opened it to reveal one of the most beautiful—not to mention largest—diamond rings she'd ever seen.

She burst into tears. "Oh, my gosh! Joseph, I don't deserve this."

Joseph took the ring out of the box and slipped it onto her finger. "That's where you're wrong. Look, a perfect fit." He kissed her hand. "In more ways than one."

Margaret was overwhelmed by the ring but couldn't take her eyes off Joseph.

She sniffed and then shook her head. "I don't know what to say!"

Joseph grinned. "How about *yes*?"

CHAPTER SEVENTY

THE NEXT MORNING DAWNED COOLER AND WITH AN OVERCAST SKY. BY the time Holly and Steven reached the cemetery, a light drizzle had begun. They had to descend a hill in order to reach the graveside service, and the black umbrellas below looked like ink blots against the green, manicured lawn.

In addition to a sizeable number of family and friends in attendance, the entire police force had shown up in full dress uniform. A reverent silence fell over the crowd as William Jacob Dunlop's flag-draped casket was lifted out of the back of the hearse. The officers' white gloves swung in unison as they transported Jake to his final resting place, right next to his father.

Jake's pastor delivered the eulogy. Afterward, the police commissioner made his way to the front. His words were some that Steven would not soon forget.

"Today we have before us two fallen officers," the commissioner began. "Jake's father, also a dedicated policeman, took a bullet over ten years ago; Jake, just last week. Jake's father became aligned with the very thing he'd been commissioned to fight against. It happens. These men and women you see in uniform before you today are not perfect. They know that. Their oath to serve and protect requires them to be exposed to the darkest and most evil forces that threaten our society. Most will remember where the lines are drawn and fulfill their oath without incident. A few may not. But *all* put their lives on the line every single day.

"They need our prayers. They deserve our support. Jake made it his mission to dismantle the gambling ring that took his father from him. I am proud to say he succeeded in that endeavor, and our city is better off because of it. It cost him his life, which he gave bravely. Not all of us will be required to make that ultimate sacrifice. But what we are required to do, let us do it wholeheartedly and, like Jake, with honor."

Steven swallowed hard as the bugler played taps for the folding of the flag. White gloves snapped to foreheads as a twenty-one-gun salute was executed. Steven's arm hurt underneath the sling he was wearing. The doctor said the wound would leave a scar. Steven didn't regret that it would. It would be a reminder.

Some experiences warrant a lifetime of remembering.

CHAPTER SEVENTY-ONE

MINNIE PUT DOWN THE MAGAZINE SHE'D BEEN THUMBING THROUGH IN the waiting room and located her cell phone in her purse. Margaret had sent pictures of her engagement ring. Minnie scrolled through the images. She hoped Margaret and Joseph wouldn't wait too long before getting married. This was one wedding she didn't want to miss.

She also had a message from her son, Lee, assuring her that he and Amanda would handle the bakery orders for today. She wasn't sure how much longer she would be able to keep up with the work. She didn't have the stamina she used to have.

A nurse with a chart in her hand appeared at the door leading to the examining rooms.

"Minnie Morgan?"

Minnie picked up her purse along with a large Ziploc bag containing her medications. After being weighed and having her vitals taken, she was shown to a room. She'd just gotten situated on the examination table when the doctor stepped in. After a brief greeting, he wasted no time in getting right to the point.

"Minnie, your latest test results show that your heart is getting weaker. With this particular valve issue, unless you get the valve repaired, it's not only going to affect your heart, but your liver as well."

Minnie put her hand on her upper right side. "Maybe that's why I keep having pain right here."

The doctor adjusted his glasses. "It's very likely. At your age, there are more risks for any type of surgery. The sooner we can perform it, the better. I'll have my nurse follow up with you in a couple of weeks. I don't want you to put this off. In the meantime, keep taking your medication and call the office if any of your symptoms change or worsen."

Minnie forced a smile. "I will."

Before he left, the doctor listened to Minnie's heart and lungs and then helped her off the table.

Alone again, Minnie collected her things and walked back through the lobby. As she headed for the exit, she stepped aside so that a young man could push an elderly woman in a wheelchair out the automatic doors. She watched as the woman sat helplessly while her son picked her up and put her into the car.

Minnie's heart sank. She had always been so independent. She was more comfortable in the role of caregiver than care *receiver*. She was certain that Lee would want her to have the surgery. But it wasn't without risks. What if she died on the table? Which option would give her more time?

"Okay, Lord," she whispered under her breath. "You have all of my days numbered. Please show me your plan."

CHAPTER SEVENTY-TWO

MARGARET WAS AMAZED AT HOW QUICKLY THE NEXT WEEKS AND months passed leading up to the Christmas concert. The summer heat displayed a defiant disregard to the calendar as daytime temperatures held steady in the eighties through mid-October. Band rehearsals abounded, as did ultrasound results. Preston and Annie announced they would be having a girl. Jennifer found out her baby was a boy.

By the time November arrived, Margaret found herself sitting at Julia's house with a crown of gift bows gracing her head at her bridal shower. She and Joseph had decided to keep the wedding details a secret. Information was only disclosed on a need-to-know basis. Family and guests were just told to make sure they attended the upcoming Christmas concert at the Manor.

Joseph's visits with Wyatt had become a weekly event. No longer something he did out of obligation, Joseph looked forward to spending time with his brother. Terrance and Wyatt had been studying the Scriptures together, and Wyatt always had something new he wanted to discuss with Joseph.

The prison Bible study had grown to twenty attendees, not including staff members who would sit in occasionally. Even though he remained behind bars and had recently forfeited half of his assets to Delores, Joseph said that Wyatt had never seemed happier or more fulfilled.

The positive effect Wyatt was having in prison was not going unnoticed by the other inmates. Most of the feedback had been positive, but not all. There continued to be threats made on his life. These were no longer due to his pedigree, but because of his bold outreach for Christ. He only had a few weeks left on his sentence but planned to continue the studies even after his release.

To everyone's delight, George and Gina had become much more than friends. No engagement plans had been announced yet, but Margaret guessed that it was only a matter of time.

Something that was a growing concern for Margaret and Julia was Minnie. Her phone calls had become less frequent and she often opted out of business meetings for the Manor. Margaret and Julia had plans to leave church early and drop in on her with lunch in hand. They each had prepared "Minnie Morgan" type dishes. The idea was for them to serve her for a change—that is, if she would let them.

Margaret took a sip of her coffee and gazed outside at the milky-gray sky. The thermometer on her back porch displayed a chilly forty-two degrees. She enjoyed these moments of solitude, but it was time to start transferring the lunch items from the refrigerator to the cooler and leave for church. As she loaded the cooler into the back of her car, she realized that her sweater wasn't sufficient against the wind, which had picked up. She darted back into her bedroom and grabbed a coat from her closet. Before leaving, she stopped for a moment to look at, probably for the hundredth time, her wedding dress hanging on the back of her door.

She just couldn't wipe the smile off her face.

* * *

Wyatt was grateful the guards were letting him and Terrance use the outdoor recreational area as the location for their Bible study.

After noticing improvement in the men's behavior, and in the overall atmosphere on the cellblock, the prison staff had been more than accommodating. This morning Wyatt could tell, with the mercury beginning to drop, the study would soon have to move inside.

Leading the study had helped Wyatt learn more about the Bible, and even more about himself. Over time, he began to understand that making his initial commitment to Christ was only the beginning. As he immersed himself in the Scriptures, the mirror of God's word exposed areas of his life that needed to change. The day-to-day prison environment served as the perfect backdrop for teaching him humility, something that would prove to be his greatest challenge. Dealing with the unbelief and rebellion in the other inmates was easy compared to facing his own need for cleansing from old attitudes and thought patterns. One discipline that had become an effective tool was confession. He maintained a posture of transparency with the other inmates, which made him more relatable. After all, he may be leading the study, along with Terrance, but he himself was also a student, and a new one at that.

He was usually glad to see new faces, but there was something about the three men who had shown up that morning that made him uncomfortable. The inmates who regularly attended were sincere, and their changed lives motivated Wyatt and Terrance to continue in their efforts. The group always welcomed those who were seeking. However, every now and then, one or two would show up for the sole purpose of giving the others a hard time. Over the past several months, Wyatt's discernment had sharpened to where he could tell if someone was genuine or not. This morning, the three new men were saying all the right things, but there was something in Wyatt's heart that told him they were less than trustworthy.

After the study had concluded and the other men had dispersed, Wyatt's suspicions were confirmed. The three newcomers cornered him and Terrance. Tiny had kitchen duty and wasn't there to help. That's most likely why they'd picked this day.

The biggest of the three pushed Wyatt against the wall. It was rumored that the security cameras didn't work in this area. Wyatt wasn't sure whether or not that was true, but figured it was why they'd chosen this location.

"You're cutting into my profits," the man said, getting in Wyatt's face. "We still have deals coming in and business slacked up because you're pushing all of this religious stuff on my men."

Terrance stepped in between the two. "Look, man. Leave him alone."

The man shoved Terrance aside. His nostrils flared. "Everything was fine until rich boy here showed up."

Wyatt remained calm. He'd known this day was coming. He'd heard the whispers and the rumors. Persecution was a possibility for all Christians. For those in prison, it was not a matter of *if*, but *when*.

"We aren't making anybody do anything. You're the one forcing and threatening these men. We're offering them a choice for freedom and life. They can leave the study anytime they want. Do they have a choice with you, or do you call all the shots?"

The man moved in closer. Wyatt could feel his breath on his face. He cursed at him and then said, "Don't be trying to tell me how to operate my business. Just stay the hell out of it."

Wyatt looked into the man's eyes. "I'm only interested in my Savior's business. Whether you believe it or not, He must be interested in you, or you wouldn't be here."

For a split second, Wyatt could see something stir inside the man. It was as if he desperately wanted a way out of the life he was living. But that second passed, and he growled, "I ain't gonna tell you again. Now, you stopping these meetings or not?"

Wyatt could feel the point of a knife against his body. His heart was racing.

"No. Not while there are guys like you who need to hear that God loves them."

Terrance pushed the man out of the way, but not before the knife had penetrated Wyatt's abdomen. The man fell backward, dropping the weapon. Terrance was able to grab the knife from the ground before the man jumped back up and rushed at him. The knife sliced into the man's thigh and the two exchanged several punches before the guards came rushing out through the doors.

Wyatt held on long enough to make sure Terrance had made it out alive.

The last thing he remembered was Terrance telling him he was going to be okay. Then Wyatt slipped out of consciousness.

CHAPTER SEVENTY-THREE

For the better part of their drive to Enoburg, Julia and Margaret discussed the upcoming concert and wedding. However, as they got closer to Minnie's neighborhood, the conversation shifted to their concern for Minnie and her health.

Pulling into her driveway, Julia noticed something peculiar. She pointed to the front porch.

"Is that Minnie's newspaper?"

Margaret craned her neck as Julia brought the car to a stop. "Sure looks like it."

Julia shook her head. "That's not normal. She gets that newspaper at the crack of dawn every morning."

Something didn't feel right. Julia grabbed her purse as she and Margaret exited the vehicle. They quickly made their way up the front porch steps. In addition to the newspaper resting undisturbed, there was a church bulletin stuck in the front door, as if Minnie had missed the morning's service.

Julia knocked on the door several times. She tried the knob. It was unlocked. She looked at Margaret, who nodded in approval. They stepped inside.

"Minnie?" Julia called. "It's Julia and Margaret. Your door was open."

Margaret walked into the kitchen. "Minnie? Are you here?"

Julia cracked open the door to Minnie's bedroom. She gasped. "Margaret, hurry!"

Margaret rushed into the bedroom. Julia had already grabbed her phone from her purse. She tossed it at Margaret.

"Call 911!"

* * *

Julia followed the ambulance to the hospital while Margaret stayed behind to keep an eye on the house and catch any phone calls. It took a few minutes to reach Lee. He'd turned his ringer off for church and had forgotten to turn it back on. He assured them he and Amanda would get to the hospital as quickly as possible.

After parking her car, Julia ran into the emergency room. She had collected Minnie's driver's license and medical insurance cards before leaving for the hospital. After getting her registered at the front desk, she got permission to stay with her until Lee arrived.

She pulled back the curtain in the cubical that served as Minnie's temporary hospital room. She was surprised at how small Minnie looked; the bed seemed to swallow her. Julia was outraged to learn that her surgery had been delayed so that a group of criminals could receive treatment. Of course, the doctors had stabilized her, and she was being closely monitored. But her heart condition wasn't considered life threatening compared to a punctured spleen and a severed femoral artery. Julia considered how, in a case like this, it was unfortunate that doctors weren't allowed to choose who deserved treatment and who didn't.

She moved the lone, metal visitor's chair close to Minnie's bed. She took her hand. "Minnie? Can you hear me?"

Minnie opened her eyes and turned toward Julia. "Yes, dear."

Her hand felt cold. "Are you warm enough?" Julia asked.

Minnie said nothing and closed her eyes once more.

Julia stood up and unfolded the blanket that was stretched across Minnie's feet. She spread it over her legs and loosely tucked it around the sides of her bed.

"I'm going to wait with you until the surgeon arrives. Lee texted me and said that he and Amanda are only a few minutes way. It won't be much longer now."

Minnie opened her eyes and gazed up at the ceiling. "Julia, I'm going home tonight."

Julia sat back down. "That's ambitious, even for you. I'm afraid this hospital is going to be your home for the next several days. If all goes well with your surgery, you'll be released by the end of next week."

Minnie turned her head toward Julia. Her eyes, usually bright and full of life, looked tired. "I'm talking about my heavenly home," she whispered. "You're going to have to run the rest of your race without me."

Julia couldn't believe what she was hearing. The possibility of Minnie not making it out of the hospital hadn't occurred to her. While she didn't know the full extent of Minnie's heart condition, she did know Minnie's heart. She was a fighter. But lying in that hospital bed, she didn't look much like a fighter anymore. She looked like a frail, elderly woman whose heart had given for a lifetime, and was now giving out.

She put her hand on top of Minnie's. She wanted to make it warm again. She wanted to turn back the clock to when Minnie was bustling in her kitchen serving home-cooked meals. She wanted to rewind to two years ago when Minnie had first opened her bakery and the two of them had been delivering orders of banana pudding all over Enoburg. Those days had been some of the happiest of Julia's life.

"This is unfair, Minnie! Those criminals are probably going to make a full recovery. You deserve to be in that operating room right now, not them!"

"Did Jesus deserve to go to the cross?" Minnie asked.

Julia grabbed a tissue from the bedside table and wiped her eyes. "No, of course not."

"Did Barabbas deserve to go free?"

The whole situation suddenly made sense. She hung her head. "No."

"I'm ready to go, Julia. Those men aren't. Think about what their eternal fate would have been if I had been in that operating room instead of them."

Minnie drew a ragged breath. "God is going to use Wyatt to reach those men, and more like them. He's just beginning his race. I've run mine. What better way for me to finish than carrying my cross?" She shook her head. "Julia, this is an *honor* for me. Don't you be sad, you hear?"

This was all happening too fast. Then Julia thought about Lee. She dialed his number again, but there was no answer. *I'll bet he's somewhere in the hospital where there's no cell phone reception.*

Julia wasn't ready to let Minnie go. Not yet.

"Listen, you're going to have one of the best heart surgeons in the country. You can do this, Minnie! You have to keep fighting."

"There's a time to fight, but this isn't that time."

Julia wouldn't hear of it. "Isn't that giving up?"

Minnie opened her eyes. They looked cloudier than they had earlier. Her breathing was becoming shallower.

"Surrendering to the will of God is a different kind of surrender, Julia...doesn't mean accepting defeat...can be your greatest victory."

Julia could feel Minnie's hand gently squeezing hers. Minnie smiled faintly and continued by whispering, "...and your finest hour."

Julia's eyes welled with tears. "I love you, Minnie Morgan."

Minnie mouthed the words, "I love you, too," and then closed her eyes.

What happened next was something Julia couldn't explain. A light breeze suddenly swept through the room, carrying with it the scent of fresh flowers much like those that bloomed around

Minnie's front porch in the summertime. Julia looked around to see where it could have come from.

That moment was interrupted by the alarm on the heart monitor.

Julia looked back at Minnie.

She was gone.

Julia buried her head in Minnie's pillow and wept.

* * *

Wyatt opened his eyes. The hospital room was blurry. He could make out the image of a nurse taking his blood pressure. He heard Joseph's voice.

"Wyatt, how do you feel?"

His mouth was dry. He managed to croak out, "Sore."

As the fog began to clear, he vaguely remembered what had happened.

"Is Terrance okay?"

"Terrance is fine. He only had a few minor cuts and bruises."

Wyatt attempted to sit up but winced at the pain and put his head back down on the pillow. "What about the other guys?"

"They're both in recovery. They're going to make it."

Wyatt closed his eyes as the anesthesia tried to reassert control. "So, everybody is okay?" he whispered.

Joseph took Wyatt's hand. "Not everybody."

CHAPTER SEVENTY-FOUR

Julia was deeply touched at Wyatt's generosity. Not only did he pay for Minnie's funeral, but he also offered to take care of any medical expenses her insurance didn't cover. At first Lee refused, but Wyatt wouldn't take no for an answer. Meanwhile, Dalton appealed to a judge to consider Wyatt's hospital stay and recovery as time served. Based on his exemplary behavior in prison—save the current episode which was not his fault—the appeal was approved. Dalton also went to bat for Terrance and was successful in getting his sentence reduced as well.

Watching Joseph push Wyatt in a wheelchair at the memorial service gave Julia a lump in her throat. Even though he was still recovering from surgery, he had insisted on attending. It was his first outing as a free man.

The service consisted of a moving eulogy by Minnie's pastor followed by a time for friends and family to share stories about how Minnie had made a difference in their lives. It was a fitting tribute to a woman who truly lived out the faith she professed.

Wyatt and Joseph left immediately after the service concluded, while Julia, Bill, and Margaret lingered a few minutes at the graveside. Wyatt had made sure that no expense was spared. A breathtaking spread of red roses, lilies, and baby's breath covered a powder blue casket with silver trim. Julia and Margaret quietly stepped over to it, each with a long-stem white rose. Margaret gently set hers down and then walked back over to speak with Joseph and Bill.

Julia stood statuesque, her mind going back to the first time she met Minnie. As usual, she hadn't had her umbrella with her and was soaking wet when Minnie had creaked open the front screen door. She remembered how it felt to be in the Morgan's home. She didn't ever want to forget how Minnie had looked, how she'd smiled, and how her eyes had twinkled behind her glasses. As a bitter December wind blew against the flowers surrounding Minnie's grave, Julia pulled her coat collar up around her ears. She crossed her arms for warmth and looked heavenward.

"Minnie Morgan," she whispered. "I know you can hear me. I'll bet you're having the best time catching up with Kenneth and Mr. Morgan. I don't know if they eat banana pudding in Heaven—but if they do—I bet they'll start using your recipe." Her chest heaved as she began to cry. "I'm going to miss you so much!"

She wiped her eyes with an overused tissue, which she then stuffed back into her coat pocket. She kissed the rose she was holding and laid it beside Margaret's.

As they began buckling their seat belts back in the car, Margaret said, "I haven't attended a funeral since Horace's. I know money isn't as important to Wyatt as it used to be, but it's not right that Delores got so much of it. She didn't even give him a chance. He's not the same person he used to be."

Julia looked over her shoulder at Margaret in the back seat. "I don't think Delores would like the new Wyatt. It makes you wonder if she was only in the marriage for the money."

Margaret gasped. "Wait a minute! When Wyatt was trying to convince me he wanted to make a donation to the Manor, he had his attorney draw up the paperwork for a million-dollar Charitable Lead Trust. I only went through with it to make him think I was buying his story."

Bill turned to Margaret. "Do you know how long the term was?"

Margaret nodded. "Yes. It was for a year. The Manor has been receiving the payments. We have six left."

Bill scratched his chin. "The trust will expire just after Wyatt and Delores's divorce is final."

"What happens to the principle after that?" Julia asked.

"Well, since it was sheltered, it goes back to the name on the trust."

Margaret's eyes grew wide. "So, what you're saying is…"

Bill smiled. "That million dollars goes right back to Wyatt. Delores won't see a dime of it."

CHAPTER SEVENTY-FIVE

It was nearly impossible to put the pain of losing Minnie aside and focus on the concert and the wedding, but Margaret was sure that's exactly what Minnie would've wanted. The only people privy to the wedding details were family, close friends, and the Gates Manor Band.

The local weather forecasters were predicting snow flurries for tomorrow night's concert. With lots of activity beginning early in the morning, Margaret decided she would spend the night at the Manor. She especially wanted to keep an eye on Jennifer. Even though her doctor had assured her that she hadn't dilated yet, Margaret didn't want to take any chances.

Just before bedtime, she heard a timid knock on her door.

"Margaret?" Jennifer called.

Margaret had been writing a letter to Joseph for him to read on their wedding day. She set her laptop aside and opened the door.

"Can I talk to you for a minute?" Jennifer asked.

"Sure, come in."

Margaret pulled out a chair for Jennifer. "Are you nervous about tomorrow night?"

Jennifer fiddled with the armchair covers for a moment and

then responded, "A little. I really hope I don't have to miss that concert."

Margaret studied Jennifer's face. "I understand what it's like to miss an important concert because of something someone else did to you. I also know what it's like to see God do amazing things because of it."

Jennifer's expression didn't change.

Margaret leaned forward in her chair. "Jennifer, is there something else you want to talk about?"

Jennifer nervously looked down at the floor. "I need to ask you a favor, a really big favor."

Margaret didn't know what Jennifer could be talking about. She'd already agreed to be with her during labor.

"As long as you don't need me to sing, I'll do anything."

Jennifer's jaw tightened. "Margaret, this is serious."

Margaret got a funny feeling in the pit of her stomach. "What is it?"

"As much as I hate the fact that I was raped, I've chosen to forgive my rapist. And I understand that it's not the baby's fault."

"That's what we've been working toward in our counseling sessions. So, what's bothering you?"

"This baby is coming soon. I finally realized that it's not just *a* baby or *his* baby. It's *my* baby. I'm the one who's carried him these nine months. I've grown to love him. I don't want just *anybody* raising him."

Margaret smiled and patted Jennifer on the knee. "We all want what's best for your son. The adoption agency is supposed to make its final decision in the next day or so. There are two wonderful couples they are considering."

Jennifer shook her head. "I don't want some wonderful couple. I want the right couple. I want to pick who adopts my son."

Margaret was feeling more and more uneasy about this conversation. "Jennifer, I don't understand. I thought we agreed that—"

Jennifer put her hand up. "I haven't changed my mind about

the adoption. It's just that I already know a couple who would be the perfect parents."

"Who is this couple?"

"This is really important to me," Jennifer pleaded.

"Of course, it's important. The well-being of your child is at stake here."

Jennifer swallowed hard. "I want you and Joseph to adopt my son."

CHAPTER SEVENTY-SIX

JOSEPH THREW ON A SWEATSHIRT AND JEANS AND HEADED OVER TO THE Manor. He couldn't imagine what Margaret could want to talk to him about that couldn't wait until morning. After assuring him she wasn't having cold feet about the wedding, the only thing she would tell him was that it was time-sensitive.

It was after midnight when he arrived. She was waiting for him outside the door at the front entrance. As soon as he walked up, she pulled him into a hug.

After holding her for a moment without saying anything, he stepped back and looked at her. "Are you going to tell me what this is about?"

She took his hand and led him inside the Manor to a sofa in a room just off to the side of the foyer.

"I didn't mean to scare you. I just couldn't talk about this over the phone. I needed to see your face. It's a decision we need to make together, and we don't have a lot of time."

Joseph took her hand as they sat down. "Okay, I'm listening."

"Jennifer came to my room tonight to talk. The reality that the baby is not just a result of unprotected sex, but actually her child, has made her rethink the adoption process."

Joseph was trying to process why this would be an emergency. "So, she's decided to raise the baby herself?"

Margaret shook her head. "No, she still believes adoption is what's best for her son. She just wants a say in who adopts him."

"What does this have to do with us?" Joseph asked.

Margaret took a deep breath. "She wants *us* to adopt him."

Joseph let go of Margaret's hand and sat back on the sofa. He ran his hands through his hair.

Margaret got up from her seat and started to pace.

"I always wanted to be a mom, but my lifestyle hasn't exactly lent itself toward motherhood. The students at the Manor have been my kids, and I've been content with that. This opportunity is not something I was looking for. *It* found *me*. I feel like I'm being given a second chance. It would be such an honor to raise a child—who otherwise could grow up thinking he wasn't planned or wanted—and let him know he was created to be my second chance. I...*we* could teach him about redemption. Joseph, are we too old? Would you even be open to this? I know this is a lot to spring on you..."

Joseph's head was spinning, but his heart knew the answer. "Yes."

Margaret stopped pacing. "What did you say?"

Joseph looked up at her. "I said yes. I don't fully understand it, but I have complete peace that this is what we're supposed to do—that God created this child for us."

Margaret gasped and cupped her hand to her mouth. "Are you sure? I know it's a huge decision to have to make so quickly. I wouldn't have planned it this way."

Joseph smiled. "None of this is how we would have planned it. But it isn't really *our* plan, now is it?"

Margaret squealed and jumped into his lap. She wrapped her arms around his neck.

"I can't believe this is my life. I think we should go tell Jennifer together."

Joseph pointed at her. "But then I have to go home." He

winked. "I need my beauty rest. After all, I'm getting married today!"

CHAPTER SEVENTY-SEVEN

Julia showed up midafternoon at the Manor to find the caterers and the florist making preparations for the big night. It was like a beehive of activity. She excused herself past a crew of decorators hanging Christmas ornaments in the foyer. A large, live tree had been erected and there were two workers atop ladders stringing lights.

The noise and commotion tapered off as she approached Margaret's old bedroom. She gently tapped on the door. She could hear heels on the hardwood and the rustle of a dress.

When Margaret answered the door, Julia gasped.

Margaret's eyes twinkled as she curtsied and smiled.

Jennifer looked at her watch. Again.

Okay, Jennifer, she thought. *It's only been thirty seconds since the last time you checked.*

However, with it now being 6:45, she only had fifteen minutes left to finish warming up her voice. She needed to do something else equally as important.

Calm her nerves.

She'd started practicing a few scales when she heard the doors leading from the lobby to the auditorium being unlocked and pushed open. She stopped singing and pulled the stage curtain back just enough to where she could see the concert attendees filing in. She smiled as she observed them gazing wide-eyed around the room and commenting about how it had been transformed into a winter wonderland.

With the florist working steadily that afternoon, it had only taken a few hours to do just that. Fresh cedar wreaths with red and white bows graced the ends of every aisle. The front of the stage was draped with garland tied up in sections by white bows. Strings of tiny lights hung from the ceiling over the stage like glistening snowflakes.

After the parents and other guests took their seats, Jennifer watched as the band members quietly walked onto the stage. They each wore matching dark-washed jeans and long-sleeved white shirts. The concert opened with a bright and lively medley of old Christmas favorites such as "Jingle Bells" and "Jolly Old St. Nicholas." The next set included an impressive arrangement of "Carole of the Bells." That was followed by two more numbers, and then it was time for Jennifer's solo.

Jennifer said a quick prayer, took a deep breath and made her way onto the stage. She wore a gold, full-length dress that sparkled under the lights. As she took the microphone, she asked if she could say a few words. Mr. Ortega nodded.

She looked out over the audience. "This Christmas, I understand a little better how Mary must have felt some two thousand years ago. She was young like me. Her life had been interrupted. I bet she was scared. My situation and Mary's are different"—she took a deep breath and looked down—"because I was raped. But God asked both of us to do the same thing—*trust Him*. When this first happened to me, I couldn't see any good that could come out of it. Earlier this morning, I found out that my baby is somebody else's miracle. Only God could do that." She paused and smiled.

"And only God could make sure I didn't go into labor today so I could sing for you tonight."

The audience applauded.

When the music started, Jennifer closed her eyes for a moment and pictured herself practicing with Mr. Ortega. Any nervousness she'd felt earlier left, and she gave a flawless performance. When the song concluded, the audience jumped to its feet in a roar of applause. Jennifer's mother, Ruby, was beaming from the front row and wiping her eyes.

When the applause subsided, Jennifer spoke once more. "Thank you. Now, ladies and gentlemen, we aren't quite finished, so please keep your seats."

* * *

Margaret was sitting at the vanity in what used to be her old bedroom. She'd just put the finishing touches on her makeup when she heard a tap on the door. Julia entered the room.

"Are you ready to do this?" Julia asked as she approached Margaret and squatted down beside her.

Margaret could see both of their reflections in the mirror. She smiled confidently. "I don't think I've ever been *more* ready for anything in my life."

Julia made sure everything was just so with Margaret's dress, and then the two of them walked down the hall to join the others in the lobby. As the doors at the back of the auditorium were opened, Margaret could hear the band playing Canon in D. She watched as Julia walked in first, wearing a floor-length forest green dress and carrying a bouquet of red and white roses. Much to the delight of the audience, Olivia followed her, tossing red and white rose pedals. Margaret could hear Mr. Ortega asking the audience to stand.

This was her moment. She looked over at Preston. He winked at her and then offered his arm.

With Preston as her escort, she began taking steps into the auditorium. She wore a stunning white gown with detailed beading and a cathedral-length veil. Her hair was pulled up into a French twist and her makeup and accessories were just as she'd always dreamed they'd be on her wedding day. The gasps of awe from the audience were audible.

And then something happened that rarely happens at weddings. Someone began clapping, and it caught on like wildfire.

Margaret had to force herself not cry. Not only was she touched by the audience's overwhelming support, but also by the look of pure joy on Joseph's face. She wasn't sure which was the bigger miracle; seeing Joseph standing there beaming, or seeing Wyatt proudly standing next to him.

The rest of the evening was nothing short of a fairy tale. At one point, Margaret glanced over at Julia who shook her head in amazement. Even though no words were exchanged, Margaret knew what Julia was thinking. A little over three years ago, Margaret would have never dreamed this would be her life. Tonight, her life felt like a dream.

One from which she never wanted to awaken.

CHAPTER SEVENTY-EIGHT

THE WEATHER FORECAST FOR FLURRIES THE NIGHT OF THE CHRISTMAS concert had proven to be a conservative one. The entire area ending up receiving several inches of snow and ice. As a result, the Gates Manor Band's trip to Central Prison had been delayed until the roads were passable. It would be their last performance before the start of their winter break.

Jennifer still hadn't gone into labor and was able to accompany the band for this concert. Once again, she gave a moving performance; one that received a standing ovation from the inmates in attendance. Wyatt noticed that several of the men, not the least of which was Terrance, had tears in their eyes. When the concert concluded, Wyatt made his way up to the front.

He looked out at the inmates and staff members who were present He cleared his throat and said, "Many of you may recognize me. I was an inmate here for nearly six months. I'll never forget my first day in lockup. I felt like one of the most hated men who had ever walked down that cellblock. Do you know why? Because I was rich. It's funny how we all have our prejudices. I used to look down on poor people and basically anybody who was different from me. That was wrong. It's just as wrong to hate someone because they happened to be born into privilege.

"A wise person once said that lost people don't always look lost. I was probably the most lost person in here. I'm happy to report, I'm not lost anymore. It has nothing to do with money or status, or even whether I'm in prison or not. In fact, my moment of freedom came while I was still behind bars.

"What changed is—I finally understood that I was loved. Not because I *deserved* to be loved, but because there is a God who *is* love. He came to this earth, lived a sinless life, and took the punishment for my sins and your sins. He's my friend who will never leave me, even if everybody else does. And trust me, most everybody else did. But that's okay. God has brought new people into my life—all of you. I want to offer you the best Christmas present ever given—God's son.

"We don't have an official altar, but that doesn't matter. I received Christ on the floor of my cell. If you want to receive him today, then come forward."

Wyatt stepped back and waited. A few of the men tentatively got up out of their seats. Then a few more. And then a few more. The man who'd stabbed Wyatt was the last to make his way to the front of the room.

He knelt to pray with each of them. He could see the chains breaking, the light penetrating the darkness.

Wyatt choked back the tears. He knew what was happening.

Prisoners were being set free.

When Wyatt arrived back home that afternoon, he paused on the front steps and gazed heavenward. There were only a few passing clouds against an otherwise brilliant, cornflower-blue, winter sky. He took a deep breath. The clean, crisp air reminded him of the fresh start he'd been given. Secret plans and secret sins were now things of the past. For the first time in his life, he was experiencing abundant life; the kind that can only come through surrendering to the Savior.

And it was a sweet surrender indeed.

ABOUT THE AUTHOR

Jan is a native North Carolinian who is proud of her small town heritage. She has enjoyed writing since elementary school and claims that her earliest work came fresh off a mimeograph machine. (This was, of course, back when her red highlights were natural!) The goal of her writing is to bring the truth of God's love to everyday life through messages that are fresh and relevant. Her first novel, The Gates Manor Band, was released in January of 2016. Her collection of devotionals, Burnt Toast: Devotions for Imperfect People, released on February 20, 2018. Jan has over eleven thousand followers on her Facebook author page where she posts inspirational blogs. She currently lives in Clayton, North Carolina with her husband, Billy. They have two grown daughters, Hope and Cara, and two grand-puppies, Gatsby and Daisy.